Copyright © 2008 by Ronae McGuire

All rights reserved. No part of this book may be reproduced or transmitted in any form or by any means electronically or mechanical without permission in writing from the publisher.

Disclaimer: This is a work of fiction. Names, characters, places, and incidents are, either the product of the author's imagination or are used fictitiously, and any resemblance to actual persons, living or dead, business, companies, events or locales is entirely coincidental.

ISBN: 978-0-9767558-0-7
Library of Congress Control Number: 2005923661

Printed in the United States of America
Second Edition

Edited by: Lynn King
Cover Design by: Alpha World Press
www.AlphaWorldPress.com

Porte Des Morts

A Novel by Ronae McGuire

Alpha World Press, LLC
Green Bay, WI
www.AlphaWorldPress.com

The Death's Door Legend

For an area that provides so much relaxation, easy living, and natural beauty, this is indeed a foreboding name.

There are stories of Native American war parties being drowned here in this three mile-wide channel that connects Lake Michigan to Green Bay.

The narrow passage has turbulent currents at times. Add to this the strong sudden Great Lakes' winds, and it is plain why this could be dangerous for fragile Indian craft.

Thus, the Indians called it the "Door of Death"; which the early French explorers translated into Porte des Morts, our Death's Door of today.

Before today's modern navigational aids many ships foundered here. In the fall of 1872 over 100 large vessels were stranded or damaged sailing through "Porte des Morts".

Porte des Morts

"Go to hell," muttered Carly McCray. From shore she watched the running lights on her thirty-five-foot aft cabin motor yacht. The departing craft fought the choppy waters and cool unpredictable winds of the late September evening as it fled like a thief into the night.

Sinking her hands into the front pockets of her skirt, she strolled along the shoreline in darkness and gazed up at her gray stone mansion with a feeling of nostalgia, recalling happier times from her childhood when her home abounded with laughter and love.

Carly turned to look at her yacht. It was just outside the harbor now, heading north toward Washington Island where they were to have spent the weekend together. Apparently, Susan had other plans and left without her. She didn't even bother to answer Carly's calls.

The chaos of Lake Michigan drowned the quiet engine hum. Still attacking the fierce waves at full speed, it diminished into the dark distance.

It happened just as Carly reached the driveway at the top of the slope from the beach. It was a huge explosion. So loud and powerful, in fact, that it nearly sent her to her knees. The weather and the late hour made it almost impossible to make out anything but a smoldering mass where the luxury yacht once was. But from the fire-lit scene, she saw the huge black plumes of smoke rising up from the wreckage and being carried off by the wind in diffusing shades of black and gray.

* * * *

"I love your freckles," Abby crooned while playing connect-the-dots on the back of Jesse's shoulder with her tongue. Abby moved Jesse's t-shirt off her shoulder. Her mouth left a blazing trail of moist heat as she turned Jesse to face her and made her way up Jesse's chest. "And I love your piercing emerald eyes," she murmured, kissing each closed lid. "And I love your wild curls," she breathed, nibbling now on Jesse's earlobe.

Jesse opened her eyes. Abby smiled at her. They both knew where this was going. Taking her hand, Jesse let her lead the way to the bedroom.

In their seven years together it wasn't as if they'd never done this before, but something was different today. All the way down the hall Jesse had the strangest sensation that they were floating. Even when Abby did away with their clothes and lowered Jesse to the bed, Jesse was perplexed by the fact that she couldn't feel the mattress below her.

In the distance a machine groaned to a screeching stop. There was a knock on the door, and someone said Jesse's name. *Not now!* Jesse screamed. *Go Away!* But there it was again, that voice. Who could it possibly be? They weren't expecting company.

2

"Ms. Ferren!"

"Honey, wait," Abby whispered. She lifted her head, giving Jesse better access to her neck. "Someone's at the door."

"Ignore it." Her skin muffled Jesse's voice, and Jesse moaned when Abby's fingers skimmed along the inside of her thigh.

"Sweetheart, you've got to answer it."

"Ms. Ferren?"

"Dammit!" Jesse jumped to her feet, wide awake now, angry at having been taken away from her dream. It took her a moment to come around - and even longer for her to figure out just where she was. Still in California? No. How about Atlanta? No, no, left there six months ago and started driving. So where am I? She wondered.

She took a quick look out the window, hoping that would give her a clue. The sky was a pale gray; the small storefronts across the street were all decked out in black and orange for Halloween. Several of them also posted election signs for various political candidates.

And then she remembered: While hanging out in Chicago with her brother Scott, trying to figure out what to do with the rest of her life, she agreed to go with him to his friends' resort on Washington Island off the Northern tip of Wisconsin's peninsula. It seemed that just about everyone from Chicago escaped to Door County for the summer.

Door County is a quaint little tourist community in Wisconsin, located about an hour Northeast of Green Bay and consisting of several small towns where everybody knows everybody. Jesse's brother explained, using his hand as a prop, that the Door Peninsula was the thumb, with the Bay of Green Bay on its West side and Lake Michigan on its East. Washington Island was just off the tip of his thumb.

Having grown up in California, Jesse had always wondered what would draw anyone to the Midwest, especially Wisconsin, the beer-drinking, cheese-eating capital of America. It certainly couldn't be the weather, which Jesse had heard can be absolutely wicked with the excessive snow and cold in the winter and the heat and humidity in the summer.

Scott's friends claimed it was the hospitality of its people that made them buy a small resort on tiny little Washington Island.

Since Jesse had nothing better to do, she spent a week with her brother and his friends, taking in the sights of Door County, which, in late July, was a huge mistake because the tourist season was in full bloom. Nonetheless, they did manage to do a little wine and cheese tasting at the local vineyards--and a lot of beer drinking.

They had taken separate cars; Scott in his new Audi, Jesse in her ancient Fiat. Her plan was to leave here and head east. To Maine, maybe. But her car had other plans. It broke down just two miles from town, stranding her in Bailey's Harbor, on the Lake Michigan side of the Peninsula.

Because she was running short of funds and needed to re-evaluate things, she decided to spend more time here to save up some money. Luckily, her brother's friends were kind enough to rent her a small cabin at their resort. They gave her a deal she could not refuse, which included the use of the resort's boat to ferry her to and from the island.

That was nearly four months ago. Her car's still unpredictable, but she had found some odd jobs to keep herself occupied. And now that the tourists have left, she was looking forward to living in peace with the Island's 700 other full-time residents.

The woman in the blue suit brought Jesse back to the present. "Jesse, this is Carly McCray," she said, introducing the woman to her left.

Jesse found herself standing toe-to-toe with a woman whose imposing presence seemed to fill the entire room. Her eye level was a good five or six inches above Jesse's, and the woman stared at her with equal shock, her gaze taking in the detective's beige trousers, her black cowboy boots with the silver tips on the points, and her athletic t-shirt, finally coming to rest on the two identical thin, plain gold wedding bands on Jesse's left ring finger.

This meeting had been arranged by Beth Cox, Attorney at Law. Jesse had gotten there early and was immediately shown to a private conference room. The only thing she knew about her potential new client was what she had read in the newspaper. She could feel the woman's eyes examining her and willed herself not to blush.

Her features were delicate, although she'd always felt that her ears were a little too big for her head. They weren't freakishly big, but she'd always kept her sand-colored curls long to hide them, kind

5

of an early Sheryl Crow look, where they have no particular order to them.

At five-four, one hundred and eighteen pounds, she wasn't exactly a commanding presence.

The woman before her was obviously pleased and surprised by Jesse's appearance. She smiled and extended her hand. "It's nice to meet you," she said warmly in a deep, smooth voice, gripping Jesse's small hand firmly. "I'm sorry to have kept you waiting." She turned to the receptionist and nodded, excusing her. "Thank you, Kristen."

"I should tell you right now," Jesse said in her quiet alto rasp, wiping the sleep from her eyes as the receptionist shut the door, "that I'm not licensed here."

Carly wondered if the woman's voice always sounded like that or if it was that way because she had just woken up. She took the chair across the table from her. "I know. Beth told me. She says that you've done some work for her and that you were a detective in Atlanta and in California?"

Jesse nodded. "I was," she said, emphasizing the past tense.

"I suspect you know why I had Beth arrange this meeting?"

Jesse nodded again. With a flick of her glance, she directed Carly's attention to the week-old Gazette on the conference table; a candid photo of her with her arm around a woman was on the front page under the headline: "Death of McCray's Lover Ruled Accidental." The picture, while not unflattering, did not do this woman justice.

Jesse studied this majestic creature. Wearing a perfectly tailored black pinstripe business ensemble, she was minimally accessorized with a thin gold necklace, matching earrings, and an elegant gold watch. Her make-up was also understated and refined. A chic kind of European sophistication emanated from her, and she appeared to be larger than life when in reality she was probably only a little more than average height. Her posture was perfect, and a mane of thick, free-flowing ebony curls framed her flawless complexion.

Jesse lifted her gaze to Carly's intelligent eyes, which, surrounded by naturally long and full black lashes, were the exact color of the slate water bordering the town. "You're richer than God, aren't you?"

Carly surprised her with a nervous chuckle and dipped her head in modesty as she reached beside her into her briefcase to retrieve a folder. "No, I don't think so."

"I'm sorry about your loss," Jesse said, motioning toward the paper.

McCray simply nodded. "Beth told me that you might be able to help me."

"Uh huh."

Any time something big like this happens, rumors fly. And in a tiny community like Bailey's Harbor, where the very rich live side-by-side with the very poor, everyone seemed to have a unique perspective of the tragedy. In the weeks since the explosion, Jesse had heard them all: The explosion was not meant to kill McCray's

7

lover, Susan Stevens, at all. McCray's womanizing nephew was the real target; Susan had emotional problems and killed herself. While Jesse was checking out at the grocery store, one woman even speculated that McCray killed Susan because they'd never really gotten along and she knew she could get away with it because of her social standing. Everyone had an opinion.

"I don't know exactly what you want me to do," Jesse said. She pulled out a cigarette and lit it despite the sudden look of disapproval from McCray. "Like I said, I'm not licensed here, and I don't really do this kind of work anymore."

McCray released a deep breath and lowered her gaze to her loosely clasped hands in her lap. "I...I really hope I can convince you to change your mind. I'm not entirely certain that the explosion was an accident," she confessed vaguely.

Jesse took a long drag on her cigarette and waited, staring. She'd always found that her stare makes people uncomfortable. She used it a lot because she had come to realize that people hate silence. For some reason they think they have to fill it with the sound of their voice. And when they do that, they usually say something that they didn't necessarily intend to say.

Apparently, however, Jesse's stare had no effect on this woman. "You think Susan was murdered," she prompted while exhaling. The smoke cloud traveled over to McCray and wreathed her head like a halo. "So why come to me? Why not tell the cops and have them re-open the case?" Jesse followed her gaze to the Gazette, and the answer became apparent to her.

McCray toyed with her hands. "The simple fact of the matter is that neither I nor my company can afford any kind of adverse publicity. I need you to do this discreetly. My company...Have you heard of my company?"

"Something to do with computers," Jesse told her, nodding.

Her lips pursed into an impetuous grin. "McCray Technology develops computer systems and software, most especially encryption software to secure sensitive data and preserve privacy in the personal and commercial sectors." She looked hard at Jesse. "Right now we're working on some very lucrative contracts and I don't want the media or the authorities involved unless it's absolutely necessary. Do you understand?" She asked as she slid the manila folder across the table to her.

Jesse shrugged and reached for it, but McCray didn't let go immediately.

"I mean it." She waited to lock eyes with the detective. *"Nobody* can know about this."

Jesse shrugged again and tugged it from under McCray's hand.

"That's a copy of the case file," she told Jesse. "Everything is there. Copies of the police report, the report from the Fire Inspector, the Coast Guard report, photos, and the, um, Coroner's report."

"They did an autopsy?" Surprised, Jesse picked up the newspaper. She found it hard to believe, with the waves as high as they were, and then with the storm, that a body could have been recovered.

A grim line of tension thinned McCray's lips. "There…there wasn't much left of…of her, not…not much of…just body parts they fished out of the water. The, uh, explosion was so intense and happened so suddenly, they concluded that she was piloting from the lower helm station and never had a chance."

The room turned ungodly quiet while Jesse turned through the pages and looked over the photos.

Watching her, McCray waved her hand in front of her face to clear the smoky air.

"Faulty gas valve," Jesse muttered. Keeping her eyes on the report, she flipped open the leather cover to her notepad and made a note. "I'm not an explosives expert, but I guess there's a chance that it could have been tampered with. Had it ever given you a problem before?"

"No!" McCray exclaimed with such vigor that it startled Jesse into lifting her head to look at her. She seemed insulted that Jesse had even asked such a question. "I've had that boat for years and it's never given me any problems."

After a few moments more of reading through the documents, Jesse scratched her head with her pen, adding even less order to her hair. "If I was going to kill someone, I wouldn't do it that way. I'd go out on the boat with them a good distance from shore, get them good and drunk and then toss 'em overboard. No witnesses, nothing to prove they'd been murdered. No case for the D.A."

Jesse loved doing that. She loved to see people's reactions when she told them how she'd kill someone. It scares people and they usually look at her the same way this woman was looking at her right now. She was no doubt wondering if Jesse was merely thinking out loud or if she was actually plotting a crime.

A ringing came from McCray's briefcase, and Jesse listened to Carly's end of the conversation while she went through the rest of the file.

"Yes, Doug…What time are you leaving? Is Stephanie going with you?…Oh, wonderful…You'll be back Monday, right?. . .Mmm-Hmm….And Jerry gave you everything you'll need?…Okay, have a nice time. No, I'm fine….I will….Good bye, dear."

Jesse waited for her to close the phone and replace it in her briefcase. She let a long stretch of silence pass to see if she was going to talk. She wasn't. "I just skimmed some of the reports and from the looks of them, it doesn't seem to me that anyone did anything very thoroughly. Even though it looked like an accident, and even though they don't have a lot of the resources that bigger cities have for investigating these things, the cops should have treated this as a murder investigation from the start. What's this about a candle?"

"Where?" McCray leaned forward to get a better look, made an unreadable face, and then sat back. "Susan loved to burn candles."

"Hmmm." Jesse was a little baffled that this wasn't investigated. Everyone knows that a candle is the most common ignition device in arson. "They weren't complete at all. Look at the death certificate. It doesn't even include her parents' names."

"They asked me for that information, but Susan never spoke of her family," she said. "As I understood it, they'd been estranged for years. I had my nephew try to find them, but..." She threw up her hands.

Jesse made a note before going back to the file. "Look at this Coroner's report...." She paged back through the documents, scowling. "Granted, he didn't have much of her body to work with, but he didn't even do a Medical-legal autopsy, just a cursory exam and made a ruling based on the circumstances. He didn't x-ray her skull for trauma or check for traces of carbon or water in her lungs. For all he knows, Susan could have been long dead before the explosion. Hell, she could have been dead before she even got on the boat." Setting the report aside, Jesse turned the page in her notepad and put her cigarette out in the empty Pepsi can in front of her. "I'll start with the most obvious question: Who would have had the most to gain from Susan's death; either financially or emotionally?"

"I really don't know. She didn't seem to have any enemies."

"How long were you with her?"

"Seven months," she replied stiffly.

Boy, Jesse thought; this is one cold fish. Seven months with Susan and she knew absolutely nothing about her. And instead of grieving over her loss, she sits here unemotional and unattached, as if she's going over a profit-and-loss statement with her accountant.

She ran a weary hand across the length of her forehead and

brushed the hair from her eyes, realizing at that moment that she needed a trim. "I want you to know right now that without any physical evidence, something tangible, it'll be next to impossible for me to prove that the explosion was intentional. If you'd have come to me right after it happened, maybe I would have been able to do more. At the very least I would have insisted that the cops do their job. And the Coroner, too. If someone really did kill Susan, the Coroner blew it by rushing through his exam, not performing the proper tests. Any tests."

"Dr. Kendall was a friend of my father's and I think he thought he was doing me a favor by expediting his part of the investigation," McCray said.

"Some favor. Maybe, if we need to, you could pull a few strings with the county authorities and we can have the body exhumed and…"

"Susan was cremated," McCray stated quite matter-of-factly. She seemed to be growing impatient. "Look, right now I'm not concerned with a criminal trial, Ms. Ferren. I'm asking you to find out what happened. That's all. We'll let the authorities deal with the rest later." With a sort of forced nonchalance, she pulled her soft-sided leather briefcase onto her lap. "I'm afraid I'm going to have to cut this interview short. I've got another appointment in ten minutes. You will take the case, won't you?"

Jesse hesitated. "You know," she said, "Like I told you, I'm not licensed here. I don't…There are firms in Green Bay that are much better equipped to handle something like this. I'm not saying that I'm not qualified, it's just, well, I've been here for only a few months and don't really have a working knowledge of the region and culture here. I don't have any contacts or..."

"I came to you because you're *not* with a firm, because Beth told me that you have experience with this sort of thing." Her gaze seemed to be sending Jesse a subliminal message - something just below the level of consciousness that she understood, but couldn't quite grasp. "Like I said, the fewer people who know about this, the better. Beth told me that you'd worked with her on a case last month and that you were extremely competent. I...I have complete faith in you. Please, won't you help me?"

The petition was more of a demand than a request for help. Jesse really had little choice in the matter. "Okay," she said finally, watching as McCray quietly let out the breath she'd been holding. "For starters, I want a list of all of Susan's acquaintances. Give me the names of anyone who had access to your boat, anyone who might have something to gain by her death."

McCray was searching through her briefcase for something. "I believe I've still got her address book on my computer. Or maybe it's on her laptop. I'll look for it and fax a copy to you," she said, distracted. "Or, do you have an e-mail address?"

"Nope," Jesse told her as she pulled out another cigarette from the pack. "No computer, no fax machine."

"Oh," McCray frowned and checked her watch again, no doubt

wondering how anyone can get along these days without a computer. She returned to the search of the insides of her briefcase. "My house is rather difficult to find if you've never been there. My appointment should only last an hour. I'll meet you at the corner of Elm and Third at three. You can follow me home and I'll get you Susan's contacts." Closing her briefcase, she looked across the table, and, blushing, said, "I don't seem to have my checkbook with me. My housekeeper must have taken it this morning. Is it okay with you if I pay you later?"

Jesse almost laughed out loud. Here was one of the wealthiest people in the state asking her, Jesse Ferren, for credit. Jesse nodded, and in one fluid motion, McCray smoothed her slacks as she stood and slung the strap from her briefcase over her shoulder.

"Good. I'll see you in an hour then."

"I have two rules for all of my clients," Jesse said, and McCray, who was already at the door, turned back. "Well, three, actually. The first is that you have to be totally honest with me no matter what I ask you. No evading questions, no intentional understatements or exaggerations, no 'oops, I forgot to tell you...' When I ask a question, I ask it for a reason, and if I find out that you've deceived me by omission or in any other way, I'll withdraw from the case right then and there. No second chances. Get it?"

McCray nodded, and Jesse continued, leaning back in her chair, "Next, any time I tell you something, initial findings, the direction the investigation is taking, it stays between us. You're not to talk to anyone else about this."

"And the third rule?" she asked, opening the office door.

"The third rule is that you follow my advice."

"What if I don't agree with it?"

She's challenging me, Jesse thought, both amused and annoyed. She exhaled a puff of smoke and leaned forward in her chair. Her laser-beam gaze cut through the smoke to find McCray's gray eyes staring back at her. "Then tell me. I'll explain my reasoning and if you still have a problem you'll have to hire someone else. I do this my way or I don't do it at all."

Jesse knew that McCray was thinking that she was a control freak, so she said, "I know it sounds like I'm a control freak." She watched McCray's skeptical frown lift to a beam of amazement and added in a foreboding voice: "But in my line of work, I've found that if I don't have complete control over a case there's a good chance someone'll end up getting hurt."

McCray swallowed hard, nodded solemnly, and backed out of the office, carefully closing the door as she left. Jesse heard the groaning old freight elevator bring McCray back to the first floor and got up to look out the window.

Jesse watched her look left, then right, then stop near the rear of an older model sleek black Mercedes sedan. As she bent to set her briefcase into the trunk, she appeared to be looking under the car for something. At first Jesse thought maybe she was a bit paranoid, but when she saw her slip into the Mercedes and pretend to check her make-up while making a careful inspection of her surroundings, she knew that it was more than that.

"Shit," she muttered to herself on the way to the door. Could it be that she has reason to believe that the explosion was meant for her, not Susan? Was she supposed to have been on the boat that night? Damn! Why didn't I think of this while she was still here? I should have - at the very least - asked her what she expected me to find. Usually people don't retain Private Investigators unless they have some idea of the investigation's outcome. They just want us to confirm or refute it for them.

The more she thought about it, the more it made sense. For one thing, it was McCray's boat that exploded, not Susan's. Susan just happened to be on it at the time. And the woman was too business-like. Jesse didn't believe for a moment that she cared enough about Susan to be so driven to find out exactly how and why she died.

Jesse was starting to get a little pissed off. If her theory was correct, and she truly believed that it was, why hadn't McCray told her? Normally Jesse didn't stand for clients withholding that kind of information, but for some inexplicable reason, she tried to rationalize it rather than dwell on it.

Was she afraid? That must be it. It's got to be pretty unnerving to think that something so violent was meant for you, and that whoever did it is still out there.

Jesse didn't believe that the circumstances that brought her here were random at all. She was sent here for a reason. Sure, her car's old and was bound to break down sooner or later, but she was certain there's a reason it broke down when and where it did. There's a reason the boat exploded. There's a reason Beth sent her to me, rather than a Green Bay firm. She could have gone to any one of them. But she chose to come to me. Why? Did the fates send me here? Is this my Mitzvah? My Divine Commandment? A good deed that I need to perform?

Eleven years ago, before she met Abby Cohen, this would have sounded absurd to her. She never would have had such thoughts. And if someone had spoken to her about these things back then, she would have dismissed them immediately. Well, first she would have mercilessly ridiculed them. Then she would have dismissed them. But her relationship with Abby changed her. True love does that. It changes your whole being, your outlook on life. It makes you think about your spirituality. At least it did Jesse.

Abby was a Reformed Jew, born and raised. She was very observant - never worked on the Sabbath, kept Kosher, prayed every morning, afternoon, evening, attended services regularly. She'd taken Jesse with her to services a few times when they first started dating. At first Jesse thought it was strange, people chanting in Hebrew, standing and facing East during one of the prayers. But the more she went, the more she wanted to go.

She would never forget the day, eight years ago, when she converted. It wasn't a big leap in terms of her beliefs; she was raised Catholic, but never truly believed in it. And because the religious right had given God such a bad name, she had drifted further and further not just from any form of organized religion, but also from her spiritual self. She never completely understood or believed in the trinity, or original sin, or in the premise that you needed to go through someone else to talk to the divine. Nor did she need a Pope - or anyone else - to interpret God's word for her or tell her right from wrong.

In contrast, Judaism, most especially Reformed Judaism, was a much better match for her. She liked its laws, its emphasis on justice, truth and charity, the discipline. She liked the concept of personal responsibility, a concept that Christians ignore completely. It all made perfect sense to her. Not only did it make sense to her, but it mattered to her, and after secretly completing a year of classes with Rabbi Glickman, she surprised Abby by telling her that she was ready to convert.

Abby was thrilled. She cried when Jesse asked her to be a witness at her *Micvah*. And Jesse will never forget the pride in Abby's eyes when she heard her recite the Shema in Hebrew. It was one of those life-changing moments, like having a baby, a moment that you never forget. By the time Jesse stepped out of the ritual bath, they were both in tears.

Ever since, Jesse has had an entirely different perspective on life. And so she knew that she was not sent here by accident. Abby used to tell her that coincidence was God's way of remaining invisible. She's right, Jesse thought.

Tossing the empty Pepsi can in the trash, she slung the strap to her backpack over her shoulder and headed out the door. "Shit," she muttered.

* * * *

Under the dimming light of the frigid pewter sky, Jesse found the black wrought-iron gates opened at the end of the McCray driveway just before four. The drive was about a quarter of a mile long with a wooden bridge that crossed a deep and wide ravine. As it turns out, her house is closer to Moonlight Bay, the small community just north of Bailey's Harbor. The directions she received from a nearby gas station weren't very complete - or accurate. It had taken her three passes before she finally found the hidden entrance, and her Fiat hissed angrily after having been subjected to the rolling farm hills along the way.

The estate's drive, lined with evergreens, maples, and mature oaks, went on forever. And the vine-covered gray brick Victorian mansion that loomed over her as she parked behind the Mercedes screamed *old wealth* with its impressive stone columns leading down to a porch that wrapped all the way around to the back.

Its five gables were covered with gray ceramic roofing tiles. A set of French doors on the second floor led to a balcony that overlooked the front of the estate, and the imposing spire that topped off the architectural masterpiece looked something like a lighthouse because of all its windows and the way it towered over the house.

The barometer had been falling steadily all week, and the brisk mid-October wind pierced Jesse's wool blazer. That's one thing she'd not quite learned yet about this area: if you don't like the weather, stick around. It'll change. Fast. The high yesterday was in the mid-seventies. Today the mercury barely approached forty.

Wishing she'd had enough sense to have worn something more appropriate for the weather, she started for the front door. On the way there, she took in the vast expanse of land on which the mansion was situated. Forming a crescent moon that conformed to the contours of the cove, the estate seemed to have no end. The leaves on the old trees of the grounds had long since turned their vibrant shades of yellow, orange, and red and dropped from their branches, but there wasn't one to be found on the front lawn, which was as meticulously landscaped as the grounds of an exclusive country club.

Over the sound of the waves racing to the shore behind the house, Jesse heard whinnying from the stable a hundred yards from the driveway. She stopped, glanced at the front door, and then looked again at the stable. Her curiosity got the better of her.

As she neared the huge red building, she came upon a tall burly dark-haired man with a weathered face stacking bales of hay on a wooden cart just inside the stable's door. He looked up, they acknowledged each other with a nod, and Jesse felt his uneasy stare on her back when she passed.

The stable was brightly lit and gave off a surprisingly pleasant aroma of horse and oats. Directly to her left, behind the inside row of stalls, was an enormous indoor riding arena from which emanated the sound of hooves pounding the ground with a drummer's cadence. Rounding the corner, she saw her new client.

Seated on the back of one of the most magnificent horses Jesse had ever seen was a completely transformed McCray. No longer was she wearing the black business suit that she had on earlier. Instead she was wearing well-worn tapered jeans and a dark purple and forest green nylon jacket over a white polo shirt. Jesse couldn't get over how drastically this woman's appearance had changed. The last time Jesse saw her, she was the paragon of a successful businesswoman. Now, dressed casually with her hair tied back loosely, she looked like a model of good clean country living.

Leaning slightly forward and moving up and down with the horse's canter, she seemed perfectly relaxed and calm and in complete control of the huge animal. She sat erect on the thin black saddle, shoulders back, the small of her back arched forward a bit. Her hands were held low in front of the saddle so that the reins and her arms formed straight lines from the bit to her elbows.

She didn't seem to notice Jesse standing there, so Jesse went into the glass-enclosed office near the inside railing of the arena. From there, through a huge pane window, she watched her new client command the lustrous black horse with grace and ease using voice commands, a tap of the foot, or a subtle adjustment of the reins.

Taking the chair behind the desk, Jesse browsed through what appeared to be the horses' training journal. The entries since Susan's death three weeks ago were excessive, all in McCray's handwriting, that precise and elaborate scrawling that looks like calligraphy. Her strong Puritan work ethic, which Jesse recently discovered is common in this region, apparently applied to her horses as well. Susan's entries weren't nearly as detailed. And her handwriting looked more like Jesse's - a not so precise, not-so-elaborate scrawling.

Jesse closed the book and turned her attention to the wall behind her.

A trophy case took up the long wall opposite the arena. The wall adjoining it was plastered with a collection of colorful ribbons, plaques, and photos. One photo in particular arrested her attention. It was of McCray when she was maybe six or seven, dressed in formal riding attire. She was standing beside a chestnut-colored horse, holding a trophy. From the tip of her velveteen helmet all the way down to the black wool riding coat, the perfectly knotted tie, the gray rider breeches, and her shiny black boots, she looked incredibly regal, confident, and proud. Even at that young age her poise and charisma seemed to radiate from her like the glow of a candle's flame.

The photo beside it was of an adult McCray in a similar pose with similar attire. She wore a bright smile in this photo as well, but as Jesse took a step closer to get a better look, she detected a certain detachment below the surface of that beautiful smile, a detachment that didn't exist in the younger McCray.

"I'm not accustomed to being stood up, Ms. Ferren," a voice scolded from the doorway. Jesse spun just in time to see McCray turn away from the office door and lead her horse to the cross-ties half-way down the aisle. She wasn't perspiring, but the color of her face was heightened as a result of her strenuous routine. "I waited for you for fifteen minutes. You didn't show. It is now past four o'clock. You're over an hour late." To control the horse for his rub-down, she secured a line to the halter and patted his neck. "Good boy."

"Sorry," Jesse said, unconcerned. She stepped down from the office to watch her remove the black leather saddle from the horse and was about to tell McCray that her car was acting up again, but she was never given the chance.

"From now on," McCray continued, "when we agree to meet, I expect you to be there. On time." She turned from the horse and without so much as a second glance at Jesse, walked into the tack room to retrieve her supplies. "Most days I run on a very tight schedule." Returning to the horse she very deliberately, very briskly sponged him down. "I cannot afford to sit around and wait for you. I'm paying you well for your services; the least you can do is keep our appointments."

Jesse had always made a conscious effort to remain civil, no matter what the circumstance, but this woman really grated on her. If this was the hospitality that the Wisconsinites are known for, they've gotten a very generous reputation. "Wouldn't it be great," Jesse sniped under her breath, "if the world revolved around that silver spoon you've got lodged up your ass?"

"Pardon me?" McCray stopped abruptly and turned to stare at her. "Did you say something?"

Jesse just returned the glare. Sure, her comment went beyond the boundary of professionalism and well into rudeness. But she couldn't help herself.

To cool off, she walked down the red-bricked aisle and stood on her tip-toes to peek into each of the stalls. In the end one, there was this tiny horse. The nameplate on the stall door said, "Mr. Billy." He wasn't a pony; nor did he look like a foal. Jesse didn't know much about horses, but she did know that much. This was a full-grown horse. What she wanted to know was what kind of accident of nature produced this little guy. He wasn't that much bigger than her German shepherd.

She was going to comment about him when her client asked, "Did you at least manage to read through everything I gave you?"

This is going to be pleasant, Jesse thought. Picking up the sarcasm in her voice, she pivoted on her foot and replied in the same snotty manner, "Not yet. Not everything."

When she returned from her self-guided tour, McCray graced her with a faint but insincere smile as she ducked under the horse's neck to get his other side. "Hand me that currycomb, will you?" She gestured toward the wooden box at Jesse's feet.

"The what?" she asked. Apparently, she need not say "please".

"The currycomb. It's right there," she told Jesse, waving her finger impatiently. "The blue rubber thing."

Keeping a safe distance from the horse, Jesse grabbed it and held it out to her.

"Thank you." It was during the exchange that she noticed the oil on Jesse's hands. She worked on her horse a little while longer and then, as if reaching an abrupt decision, said in the sweetest, most conciliatory tone, "I've invited friends for dinner tonight. Will you join us?"

The invitation took Jesse by complete surprise, but she managed to hide her shock by averting her glance. "Uh, no thanks."

"Perhaps some other time." Stroking the horse in small deliberate circles, she peeked up at Jesse. "Do you have any idea how long this investigation will take?"

"It's way too early to tell. It depends on how quickly things unfold. It could take days, weeks, maybe months. Like I said earlier, I can't guarantee that I'll find anything."

She watched her move down to comb out the horse's tail. He didn't seem to care for that and nodded and shook his huge head irritably, neighing loudly and stomping his front feet on the bricks. Embarrassing herself, Jesse jumped back, well away from them, until her client brought him under control. She knocked over a pitchfork that was leaning against one of the stall doors. It clanged loudly to the floor, which, of course, agitated the horse even more.

"He's a little skittish," McCray told her, noting her anxiety. "Do you ride?"

Jesse laughed to herself. "Uh, no."

"Father started training me when I was two and I was competing by the time I was four. I don't know what I'd do without my horses.

Sometimes I think they're the only things that keep me sane." Leaning to pick the horse's foot, she looked up. "Do you need more information from me?"

"Not yet," Jesse told her. "When I'm through with Susan's contacts and reviewing the reports and everything, I'm sure I'll have a better idea of what to ask you. There is something..." McCray looked up again, and Jesse said, "My retainer."

"Oh, yes. That's right," she said distractedly, holding the horse's hind leg between hers, picking the dirt from its hoof. "Remind me before you leave to give you a check, will you?"

"Normally I prefer cash, but I suppose I'll make an exception in your case," Jesse told her dryly.

McCray looked over the horse's back with a small smile. Taking this break in the ice as her chance to do a little fishing, she asked, "How long have you been a Private Detective?"

"Eight years."

"And what did you do before that?"

"I worked at an insurance company."

"Doing what?"

"Special investigations in the Fraud Unit. I did that for three years, put myself through school, and quit once I got my degree."

"What did you study?"

"I, uh, got my Bachelor's degree in the humanities."

McCray nodded, taking it all in. "Beth told me that you're originally from Santa Barbara. What made you decide to move all the way up here?"

That seemingly innocuous inquiry brought a deluge of chaotic images to Jesse's mind - the moment she first saw Abby at the company picnic, their first kiss three weeks later, the look on Abby's face when she read the card that accompanied the flowers Jesse sent on their last anniversary together, the unforgettably sweet sound of her laughter, the private, mysterious smile in her eyes when she peered at Jesse over her coffee cup every morning.

It must have taken Jesse a bit too long to respond because McCray had been unchaining the horse from its tie-down and attaching a lead to the halter and stopped what she was doing to glance over at her. But Jesse was too deflated to answer. Not only that, but she wasn't about to share something so deeply personal with someone she'd just met a few hours earlier. It was none of her business. If she had questions about her qualifications, fine. That's one thing. But her personal life - especially if it had to do with Abby – was hers and hers alone. It was off limits.

McCray looked like she was about to repeat her question when she was interrupted by the sound of a car door slamming and a voice calling to her. "I'm in here, Chris." Her questioning gaze remained on Jesse a moment longer before checking her watch and smiling down the long aisle to her friend, who came in through the rear stable door. "You're early."

Jesse rolled her eyes, grousing about this woman's hang-up on punctuality. Funny how that hang-up only went one way, though.

She had waited for nearly forty-five minutes for McCray to make it to the appointment at the attorney's office. Had Jesse not fallen asleep, she would have walked out long before this woman finally decided to show.

The woman walking toward them easily topped six feet. She was attractive in a wholesome, tom-boy sort of way with closely shorn sorrel hair that highlighted her deeply-set brown eyes. Her tight Levis and jean jacket revealed a very athletic form with a narrow waist, but strong, wide shoulders. While giving McCray a quick hug, she glanced in Jesse's direction.

"Chelsea called," McCray told her friend. "She said she hadn't been able to reach you all day. And I stopped to see you earlier, but Deena told me that you'd taken the day off. I was beginning to wonder if you were going to make it tonight."

"Oh...I, um, I must have been catching up on housework or running errands or something. Guess I forgot my cell phone." The woman choked out a nervous laugh and adjusted her elliptical silver-framed glasses. That's when Jesse noticed how large her hands were. They were the big, sturdy kind that Jesse's grandmother called peasant hands because they were so well-suited for manual labor.

McCray was too preoccupied with her horse to have noticed Chris' unease. But Jesse noticed. There wasn't much else to do but watch their exchange from the sideline, so she took in their every word - spoken and unspoken.

"Did Chelsea say why she called?" Chris looked a little irritated.

29

"I told her before she left this morning that I'd just meet her here tonight."

"Well she's not going to make it," McCray said. "She's been asked to work a double shift again."

"Oh." Chris' face turned dark red. An angry look briefly crossed her face, but she quickly recovered with a forced smile. "Do you mind if I take Hoosier out?"

"Of course not," McCray replied. "If you'll wait a few minutes, I'll join you. I was looking forward to taking Murphy on the trail tonight. I'm just finishing up here and then I've got a few things to take care of in the house." As she turned to walk the horse back to his stall she noticed that Chris was staring at Jesse. "I'm sorry. Where are my manners? Jesse Ferren, this is my friend Chris Masters. Chris is a pilot. She and her brothers own their own charter airline, Peninsula Air."

"Ha!" Chris laughed. She grinned a humble, confident smile. "Some airline. We've got a helicopter, a few planes for flying lessons, getting the tourists up here from Chicago, and bringing the supplies to Washington Island in the winter."

"Oh, Chris. Don't be so modest. She's got a small but growing fleet of corporate jets and, what, five Gulfstreams?" McCray smiled at her friend. "She's also my personal pilot."

Chris laughed again. She traded a private glance with McCray that told Jesse just how close those two were. "Oh, *am* I?" She asked, still sporting a wide grin. "I thought you fired me last month after

30

that storm over Detroit." She looked at Jesse. "You should have seen her when we hit the bad stuff. She was bouncing around, white as a ghost. The whole time, she's screaming, '*Don't let me die in Detroit! Don't let me die in Detroit!*'"

McCray looked only mildly amused. For her friend's sake, she added, "Jesse's a private detective."

"A private detective?" Chris seemed deeply confused. But only for a moment. Her friendly disposition changed immediately to concern and disappointment. "Carly, you've got to let it go. *It was an accident.*"

"Let it go," McCray repeated bitterly. She waved a hand. "How can I just let it go?" she asked, her voice ascending as she spoke. "You weren't there, Chris, in the morgue! You didn't have to identify what was left of her! That image will be indelibly engraved in my mind - a few charred and broken bones. I've never seen...." She blinked hard a couple times, apparently fighting back the image - or maybe tears, Jesse couldn't be sure. "There was nothing left of her, Chris! Nothing!" The color had again drained from her face, and her hand trembled just a little as she tightened her grip on Damien's lead and walked away with him.

"I checked on Hoosier's tendon earlier," she called to Chris from Damien's stall in a much calmer voice. Chris responded with a nod. After a quick glance at Jesse, she started off toward Carly, who was still broadcasting from Damien's stall. "Make sure you use the tack wrap on that ankle before you take him out. I don't like crossing the bridge in the dark so we'll take the short trail tonight. I don't know if he'd be able to manage the long one anyway. I'll have Victor treat the ankle when we get back."

Chris stepped into the stall with McCray and the horse, leaving Jesse a good twenty feet away. She was pretty sure they didn't know that she could hear them.

"Carly, are you sure she's a private detective?" she asked in a quiet but excited voice as she gestured to Jesse. "I...she's the one...the bass player in that band that I've been telling you about, the one Chelsea and I have been bugging you to see."

Carly glanced in Jesse's direction, then back at her friend. She, too, seemed confused. She shook her head. "No. No. She's a private detective. Beth put me in touch with her."

"Hmmm," Chris commented at the mystery. She watched McCray fill Damien's water and changed the subject. "You still haven't gotten a decent night's sleep, have you?" McCray ignored her, and Chris said, "I'll take that as a 'no'." With her hand on McCray's shoulder, she studied her friend closely, and McCray, holding the end of the hose, stood perfectly still, staring at the stream of water as it flowed into the tub. "Did you at least call Dr. Taylor?"

"I don't need a psychologist," McCray whispered angrily. She shut off the water and lifted her gaze to her friend. "I need to know what happened."

Chris frowned. "Sweetie, you already know what happened. You've read all the reports. Why'd you hire this detective?"

"Because something's wrong, Chris. I...I can't explain it. Even before the accident, something's been *off.* I've felt it. I can still feel it."

"What you're feeling is a bad case of the guilts. That's all it is, Carly. Please call Dr. Taylor. He'll help you work through it so you can get some closure. Or at least get some sleep. Hiring this detective is just going to prolong things. She's not going to find anything."

"You don't know that."

Chris' frown deepened. "Carly."

"What if it wasn't an accident? What if my procrastination cost her her life?"

"You made the right decision. You know you did."

"How can you say that? If...." She hesitated, glanced Jesse's way, and lowered her voice, moving closer to Chris.

Jesse looked away as if bored and made herself appear distracted by examining the pattern of the brick floor at her feet.

Carly whispered, "If I had broken up with her when I intended to, she'd at least be alive right now."

"Carly, you did the right thing. It wouldn't have been right to break up with her when she was that sick. And besides, you don't know that she'd still be alive. Who knows? She might have been so torn up over losing you that she would have driven her car off a cliff or something."

McCray frowned dubiously while her friend chuckled.

Chris quieted her whisper, and Jesse really had to strain to hear her. "So what's with this detective? Where'd you find her?"

Jesse couldn't hear all of her client's response, just that she'd heard from her attorney, that she was from California and, more recently, Atlanta, and that Jesse had just moved here.

"Well I don't like her," Chris muttered. McCray gave her a *don't start* look, but that didn't stop her. "I mean it, Carly. When I...God, I could swear she's the bass player in that band, but I....I guess I was wrong. It can't be the same woman. The drummer was hot. This detective....she looks like a cranky little troll. Doesn't she blink?" She looked over in Jesse's direction. "Doesn't she speak?"

Carly joined her friends' gaze in checking Jesse out. Jesse, however, was now focused on the thick pine rafters above, looking bored, but keeping them at the very edge of her senses.

McCray reached for the latch on the stall door. It didn't release. She tried again, jiggling harder this time, but it still wouldn't give.

"What's wrong?" Chris asked.

"This wretched latch is stuck again." McCray caught Jesse's eye. "Will you...."

Before Jesse could get to them, Chris thrust her long arm through the bars and reached for the outside handle. "I'll get it."

"You can't reach it from the inside, Chris," McCray insisted, stepping out of her way. "Why don't you let...?"

Jesse was so entertained by Chris' stubborn need to come to her friend's rescue, she watched her work on it for a good minute, reaching and thrashing and cursing and reaching some more. Her fingertips came close a few times, but Jesse's restraint was wearing thin. So with the tiniest of satisfied grins, she reached out and opened the latch.

"Thank you." McCray brushed her hands on her jeans. "Let me get those addresses for you." On their way out of the stable, she moved a large space heater from the area near the doorway where the dark-haired man had been stacking hay. "You'll have to excuse Chris. She means well, but at times she has a tendency to be a bit overprotective of me. We've been friends since we were in Kindergarten. Father wanted to send me to a private school in Vermont, but I couldn't bear to leave him - or her. He traveled quite a bit when I was young, and any time he couldn't take me with him, I always insisted upon staying with Chris and her family. She has nine siblings, so there was never a dull moment. We kind of adopted each other."

They had reached the corral, and McCray excused herself momentarily to speak with the man Jesse had nodded at earlier. They spoke only in Spanish, and even though Jesse was far from fluent in the language, she understood from McCray's elaborate hand gestures precisely how she wanted him to treat Hoosier's tendon.

"Muchas gracias, Victor." McCray smiled, starting for the house again. Jesse fell into step beside her. "Nine years ago," her client said, picking up where she had left off, "after my father died, Chris was my salvation. Father and I were very close. And when he died,

I…I was…I don't know what I would have done without her." She looked sidelong at Jesse, and Jesse couldn't help but wonder what had compelled her to spill out what must have been her most painful memory to a total stranger.

Was this important to the investigation? Jesse wondered. Probably not. So why, then, was it so important for McCray to disclose this private and obviously still intense grief? Did she share this information with everyone she met? Did she want sympathy? Was this her way of seeking some sort of immediate familiarity?

Whatever the case, Jesse didn't stop her.

"Chris took care of everything for me: The funeral arrangements, the media, the lawyers, you name it." McCray turned to her with a brave smile. "I have hundreds - perhaps thousands of acquaintances, but very few close friends. Chris has always been the closest. There's nothing we wouldn't do for one another."

They finally reached the front door, and McCray stomped her feet on the mat before entering. In the foyer, she closed the door behind them and gestured toward a wooden bench. "Have a seat. I'm not sure where I last saw her laptop, so this might take a while."

Jesse watched her ascend the grand staircase with its shiny hardwood steps. The rich, detailed design in the banister and the balcony above suggested that it was all hand-carved. The living room off to her right contained that same ornate style in its trim.

Jesse had never seen anything like it. The room was quite large and, like its owner, had an understated elegance to it. The polished black grand piano sat in simple harmonious silence on a beautiful rug in the far corner. Among the precious heirlooms, sculptures, and pieces of classical art, the formal conversation area, done in rich dark shades, had a strong warm and welcoming aura about it. But almost equally as strong was its chilling sense of emptiness.

McCray loped down the stairs empty-handed. "It's not in her room. My nephew has already begun to pack her things, but I know I've seen it recently."

At her beckoning, Jesse followed her, taking everything in as they traveled down a long, wide corridor. "Do you use your security system?"

McCray shook her head. "Rarely. Usually when I go out of town, I'll click it on. I've never liked the idea of having to punch in a code just to get into my own home. It's so restrictive. I don't even like the fence, to tell you the truth. Father had it put up to keep hunters off the property." She stepped into her library, which was so huge it spanned the entire north side of her house. "You'll have to pardon the mess."

Jesse tried to figure out what she meant by that. Everything appeared to be in perfect order.

"We've got the Ford people coming a week from Tuesday, and we've got some pharmaceutical reps coming in on Friday that week." She looked up at Jesse as she cleared some of the papers from her shiny mahogany desktop. "Those are a couple of the contracts I told you about earlier. So as you can see, the next few weeks are going to be very busy. That's why I wanted to get you to work right away because I'm not going to have time to sit down with you to answer questions and things." She momentarily glanced at the screen on her notebook computer and leaned over to begin rummaging through the drawers. "Now, let's find her laptop."

All Jesse could think of, standing in that enormous room, was how much it must cost to heat in the winter. Sure, there was the floor-to-ceiling field rock fireplace on one wall, but it's not like you'd light a fire every night. And even if you did, she thought, you'd have to spend a fortune on the wood. But then, that wouldn't bother someone like McCray, would it?

Jesse wondered if she has ever even actually seen a utility bill. She probably has an accountant or someone who takes care of all that stuff for her. From the looks of things, Jesse guessed that she'd never struggled a day in her life; never suffered the misery of bouncing a check or wondering how she was going to pay the phone bill or put gas in that Mercedes of hers.

In the far corner on the front and north wall, a spiral staircase vaulted to the landing on the second floor, then proceeded all the way up to the spire above. Because the spire was mostly glass, and despite the overcast sky, light shown down that staircase as though it was lit from heaven above. The view from this room wasn't half bad; a wooden deck, then a small back yard that fell into Lake Michigan. Jesse bet that the three-hundred-and-sixty-degree vista that the spire above had to offer was even more spectacular.

To her left, a pair of matching black leather sectional sofas formed three sides of a square around a massive coffee table that matched the desk. The sofas rested on a thick, expensive -looking rug and faced the fireplace. One of the other walls was completely covered with glass-cased shelves, which housed countless volumes of leather-bound books. The remaining wall contained a state-of-the-art media center.

As if that wasn't enough, there was still plenty of space in the middle of the room for a giant conference table, which was flanked by high-back leather office chairs. The table, of course, was mahogany to match the other furniture in the room.

"Here it is," McCray proclaimed. "Let me get the file printed up for you." She took a seat behind her desk, and within seconds, her fingers were dancing across the keys of the laptop. Moments later, the printer behind the desk whirred to life and began spitting out pages. "That reminds me - Susan never mentioned her parents, and I don't know how to track them down to let them know that she….that she passed. I was wondering if you'd be able to find them for me. They're not listed in here, and I'd like to send her personal effects to them; you know, her jewelry, photos, trophies. I think those things should stay in her family, don't you?"

"I can find 'em. If you know her birth date and where she was born I can track 'em down."

"Her birthday was May twenty-eighth, and I know she grew up in Indiana. Other than that…" McCray waved her hand as if she couldn't be bothered with such details. "She really didn't talk about her family."

"Did she leave a will?"

"Yes. For some reason, she left everything to me. As I've said, my nephew has already begun to pack up her room. Aside from the things that I want to ship to her parents, I'm donating everything to charity."

"How about insurance?"

"Two hundred and fifty thousand, and, yes, I was named the sole beneficiary." Jesse raised an eyebrow, and McCray added, "I plan to send that to her family as well."

"When did she take out the policy?"

"Six and a half months ago as part of her employment package. I didn't even know that I was named the beneficiary until this past week. My nephew had been going through her things and found the policy."

Behind the desk, between the two bay windows which overlooked the cove, hung an oil painting of a handsome couple. The woman was seated; the man was behind her with his hand resting on her shoulder. They looked as though they were in their late forties when they posed for the painting, and Jesse guessed by their stoic expressions that they were McCray's parents. Despite the fact that they appeared very uptight, Jesse got the sense that they were warm and caring people. It had to have been something about the way the woman's head was cocked slightly toward the man, the position of his hand on her shoulder, something in their facial casts.

McCray was an exact duplicate of the woman with her thick jet-black hair, her high cheek bones, the fine and serious line of her mouth. But she had her father's eyes; those pale, pale eyes.

The printer gasped out its final page, and McCray slid the papers across the desk to Jesse, noting that she was staring at the painting. She turned to face it. "Mother and Father," she said. "You can't tell, but Mother was pregnant with me at the time they had this done. She died of complications two days after she had me."

"I'm sorry," Jesse said lamely. As she went to take the papers off the desk, her hand bumped one of the many photos lined up on it. This particular photo was turned away from Jesse, facing McCray. Jesse picked it up. "This was Susan?"

She looked different than she did in the newspaper. Her hair was much longer in this photo, styled differently.

"That was taken six months ago, just after she moved in with me," McCray said.

She was a very pretty woman, but there was also something unusual about her. Jesse thought she looked like a collie. Her face was exceptionally narrow; her hazel eyes were set right on her long slim nose. Even her blonde hair, the way it was layered back from her face, made her look like Lassie. And she had a wide mouth. So wide, in fact, that Jesse could see every filling in it. "She was a lot younger than you," Jesse noticed out loud, emphasizing the word "lot".

McCray seemed hurt by Jesse's candor. "She was twenty-two; eight years my junior."

Who talks like that? Jesse wondered. *Eight years my junior. Pretentious snob.* Jesse studied her again and determined that she looked her age, but maybe with a good night's sleep, she'd look a little younger than thirty. "How'd you meet her?"

"We met at a horse show in Milwaukee over a year ago. She was a trainer for the Moriartys from Crystal Lake, Illinois at the time. She gave me a tip just before my class, and Damien ended up taking first because of it. We'd met a few times after that, during the summer circuit, and when she came to visit me in March, well, she stayed on to help me train my horses." As if in a trance, she gazed at the photo with a solemn, reminiscent smile. Her rich low voice dropped a decibel. "She was truly gifted. I loved watching her. When she rode, the way she made her horse perform. It was beautiful, magical."

"Hmmm," Jesse commented, returning the photo to the desk and preparing to leave.

"When can I expect to hear from you?" McCray asked, following her to the door.

"I'll call you as soon as I've had a chance to go through everything. I'll work on it over the weekend."

Apparently satisfied, McCray handed Jesse one of her business cards. She stopped at a small table in the foyer to jot something on the back. "This is my private cell number," she told Jesse, handing her the card.

"I'll call you," Jesse promised as she snapped the card out of her hand and made her way out to her Fiat.

Unfortunately, she was forced to return to the house a few minutes later. A small woman in her mid-to-late seventies answered Jesse's knock. She wore a typical maid's outfit complete with a crisply starched white apron. The only thing missing was the tiny white cap. Her dark and gray hair was drawn back to form a perfect bun, and a perennial frown was forged into her wrinkled face.

"I need to talk to Ms. McCray."

The maid gave her a harsh look. "Is she expecting you?"

"No," Jesse said with an impatient gesture, "but I was just here a few minutes ago."

"Let me see if she's available." Turning almost pleasant, she opened the door further. "Please come in."

While waiting in the entrance hall, Jesse overheard McCray's unmistakable voice from the library. "He what? Is he okay? Oh, for heaven's sake, Jacey, don't worry about that. I'll take care of it…No, really; it's fine. I've been thinking about getting away for a little while anyway…Doug? No, I can't send him to something like this. Don't worry…No, of course I don't mind. You just take care of Isaac, will you? Tell him I hope he feels better."

There were a few moments of silence, and McCray suddenly appeared in front of Jesse. "Yes?" Her deep voice echoed in the foyer, reverberating the warm tone and timber of that single word over and over.

Jesse had been sitting on the bench in Rodin's *The Thinker* pose. She jumped to her feet. "My car stalled again and I can't get it started. Do you have some tools I can borrow?"

"Let me get Victor. He knows all there is to know about cars."

"No!" Jesse exclaimed, annoyed that this woman assumed that she'd need a man's help. "I can fix it. I just need some tools. I don't like anyone touching my car. It's kinda temperamental."

"Oh. I see." McCray smiled indulgently at that. "Well, I don't know what you'll need, but you're more than welcome to use any tools I have. I'll have Victor show you where they are." She noticed the detective's anxious glance toward the grandfather clock in the living room and sensed her urgency. "Would you like to borrow one of my cars?"

Naturally, Jesse balked at the idea, but McCray added, "It's no trouble. I insist," with a disarming smile and in a voice that invited no opposition. "I'll send Karen with the keys to the Lexus," she called over her shoulder as she walked away.

In the next moment, Jesse heard her on the phone again. "Charlene, Jacey's not going to make it to the summit next week. Her son Isaac had an accident at school and broke his leg, so I'm going instead....No, no. I'll take care of it. I'm having dinner with her tomorrow night so I'll pick up a gift for him and get the details from her. All I ask of you is that you call....Right, have them change the credentials from Jacey's name...No, no. Cancel the airline tickets. Chris will fly me out there...right..."

Jesse perked up when she saw the maid coming toward her, but relaxed again when the old woman veered off into a different room. McCray was silent now, and Jesse guessed that Charlene was on another line, making the arrangements.

When she did speak again, her tone was warm and light, but still quite reserved. "Thank you so much Charlene. Okay...Thank you...Have a good weekend."

McCray looked more than a little surprised to find Jesse on the bench. "Are you still waiting for Karen?" At Jesse's nod, she sighed and glanced down the empty hallway from which she had just come. "I'm sorry." Grabbing her briefcase from the stand beside Jesse, she withdrew a set of keys, took one from the ring, and handed it to her. "Here. Take the Mercedes. It's still parked out front. I'll have Victor push your car into the garage until you can come back to fix it."

Jesse followed her out and grabbed a few things from her Fiat before getting into the Mercedes. For an older car it was in mint condition. It even smelled new, although it was at least eight years old, which was roughly half the age of her car.

Jesse cursed McCray's long legs while adjusting the seat and mirrors, and right when she started the luxury sedan, McCray scared the hell out of her by rapping on the window. She lowered it.

"Don't leave yet. I've got to give you some money for gas. I'll be right back."

Jesse looked from her to the gauge. "It's fine. There's over half a tank."

"Yes, but I never let it drop below a quarter. And I only fill it with Premium."

Wow! Jesse thought the woman was a bit on the anal retentive side when she apologized for the mess in her library that didn't exist, but that comment just blew her off the scale. "I'll take care of it," Jesse assured her before driving off.

Jesse had always thought that you can tell a lot about someone by the type of music they listen to. That's why she wasn't at all surprised to find that all of the presets on the Mercedes stereo were locked on easy-listening or adult contemporary stations. It took her only a few minutes to find the classic rock station she wanted.

Even though she was running late, Jesse took this opportunity to find out a little more about McCray's friend, Chris Masters. She figured from the conversation between her and McCray that the house would be empty, and from her behavior in the stable, Jesse knew she had *something* to hide.

Jesse found the house with little difficulty. On the Northeast side of Bailey's Harbor, just a few miles off the highway, the small white rambler-style ranch was nestled on a large corner lot, set among other similarly-designed homes. A huge pine took up the majority of the front yard, and Jesse pulled the Mercedes up the gravel driveway, careful not to disturb the squirrels dashing around it.

This was the part of Jesse's job that she enjoyed least. In fact, she detested digging into people's personal lives and going through their things. It just seemed wrong to her, but she came to accept it as a necessary evil of investigating. After all, it's not as if she did it for kicks. Now that'd be different, wouldn't it?

Although she was concealed somewhat by the growing darkness, there was no way to be discreet about this. She went through the unlocked service door off the attached garage, and within minutes, found herself standing in the cozy little kitchen. Wiping her feet on the carpet square at the door, she noticed the flashing red light on the answering machine on the Formica counter. She couldn't resist.

A woman's voice said, "Chris, it's me. I've been trying to reach you at the hangar and Deena told me that you haven't been there all day…Please pick up, hon…." There was a quiet sigh and the sweet voice turned more serious. "Come on, Chris. I know you're home. Quit being so stubborn, will you? What can I do to set things right between us again?" Another sigh, then the voice became very business-like and tense. "I'm calling to tell you that Linda has the flu so I'm going to take her shift tonight. I've already called Carly to tell her that I won't be there for dinner. Um, I'll be home around midnight in case you feel like waiting up for me….I love you."

Interesting. Jesse glanced into the living room on her way through the dinette. Down the narrow hall were two bedrooms. One was being used as a home office. Jesse checked that room first and noticed that Chris had the exact same computer set-up that McCray had in her library. Taking a seat behind the desk, she sorted through the clutter of papers in front of her. Under a pile of past due bills, she found a savings book. The account was held jointly by Chris Masters and Chelsea Johnson. While her mind ran wild with all kinds of lame jokes about this couple's surnames, she opened it, noting that there had been a substantial withdrawal - over thirteen thousand dollars - on July thirtieth this year.

Now her mind was running wild with other thoughts. In the top desk drawer, she found a receipt for a Certificate of Deposit worth twelve thousand dollars. Interestingly enough, it had been cashed in on the same date as the large savings withdrawal. Wow. These two were up to their eyeballs in debt. Jesse quickly noted both women's vital information in her notepad.

If the computer held the answers to the questions that had already started to flood Jesse's mind, she was desperately out of luck. Despite her technophobic tendencies, however, she glanced around the room once, then pushed the power button. Almost immediately a cheerful welcome banner appeared on the monitor.

Putting her hand over the mouse, Jesse opened a finance program, and much to her dismay, a list of file names, all gibberish to her, appeared on the screen. She brought up a few files and after a moment, fearing she might be in over her head, shut off the computer and moved to the filing cabinet in the corner to look for something on paper that might point to the source of this financial predicament. Surely there had to be something to explain what happened three months ago that cost this couple at least thirty thousand dollars.

For ten minutes, Jesse flipped through the files. She found the titles to two vehicles - a blue Ford Ranger and a black Ford Contour;

neither had been purchased within the past three months. Frustrated, she closed the filing cabinet and looked around the room, then took a slow tour of the rest of the house.

Upon leaving, even though the sky had already begun to darken substantially, Jesse paused to inspect the roof and siding of the house. They were in good shape, but neither appeared to have been recently replaced.

- Monday – Nine Days Later

Shrill ringing dragged Jesse from a sound sleep. She had spent the first full week of her investigation in Crystal Lake, Illinois, tracking down and interviewing as many of Susan's past acquaintances as possible. She figured it wouldn't be a complete waste of time. Not only is it good policy to obtain background information on the victim, it is possible that her theory was wrong. And while it seemed unlikely, she couldn't rule it out, either. Even if McCray *was* supposed to have been on the boat when it exploded, it doesn't necessarily mean that Susan wasn't the intended target.

McCray was at a technology summit in Los Angeles that week and called Jesse almost every day to check her progress - if you could call it that.

The length of those calls had grown substantially longer as the week drew to a close. While McCray seemed to get progressively more personal and more familiar, Jesse ignored her flirting and kept her part of the conversation directed solely toward the investigation.

Not to be deterred, McCray continually tested Jesse's resolve. She'd ask vague philosophical questions, hoping to hit upon something that would spark Jesse into divulging something about herself. When that didn't work, she'd ask Jesse's opinion of certain current events, but Jesse always brought her back to the investigation.

And although Jesse had never once inquired about her, McCray would go on at length about her day, how she felt about the other participants at the summit, the new technologies they'd discussed that day, how she hated being away from home, away from her horses. She had even told Jesse about her shopping binge on Rodeo Drive, which she referred to as "retail therapy", admitting that she'd gone well over her budget.

Rolling over, Jesse groped in the darkness for the phone. She had not spoken with McCray since Thursday evening. "Yeah," she murmured in her perennial rasp. "Hello."

"Jesse?"

Jesse immediately recognized the clear low voice on the other end. "Uh huh." She struggled to sit up. "What time is it?" she asked, reaching to turn on the light.

"Oh, I'm sorry. I didn't realize…it's just after two. I hope I didn't wake you."

"Two? In the morning?" Jesse yawned as she brushed a hand through her curls. "No. Of course you didn't wake me," she said with dark sarcasm. "I've been up for hours, working on my cross-stitch." She reached for her cigarettes and heard McCray chuckle.

"I'm very sorry. I didn't realize how late it was. I've been so busy since I got home, and I just now found Karen's message that you'd called earlier."

"Twelve hours ago."

"You're still in Crystal Lake?"

"Yep," Jesse replied wearily as she lit her cigarette. "Um, there's something I wanted to ask you. Hang on a minute. I gotta get my notes." On the way to the table, she tripped over Harley, her German shepherd, who had been sleeping on the floor beside the bed. "Sorry," she whispered to him. "Go back to sleep."

He sneezed at her; his way of telling her that she was forgiven.

"Here it is," Jesse sighed, coming back to the phone. "Your...."

"Are you okay?"

"Huh?"

"It sounded as though you hurt yourself."

"It was nothing," Jesse told her. "When I was at your house last Friday, you mentioned Victor, your groundskeeper. His last name is Cruz, right?"

"Yes," McCray replied. She seemed amazed that Jesse would know this.

"Did you know that he used to work for the Moriartys? They got back from Paris yesterday, and I just got a chance to talk to them."

There was a long silence on the line. Then McCray asked: "What does this have to do with the boat explosion?"

"I don't know yet. I'd like to talk to you about it. In person. I don't want to do this over the phone."

"Oh. Of course." Jesse got a kick out of the way McCray's voice dropped to a conspiratorial tone. "When will you be back?"

"Tomorrow - well, today," Jesse amended. "Probably around noon. There are a few people I need to get back to, but it shouldn't take long."

"Let me bring up my schedule. Mondays are always very hectic for me," she said distractedly. "Let's see, my staff meeting will most likely run well into the afternoon. At three-thirty I'm meeting with one of our R & D teams. At five, I'm meeting with a Legacy Scholarship candidate. I've got another interview at six, and then I'm meeting Chris and Chelsea at their anniversary party. I can't believe it's been three years."

"Pick a time!"

"Oh. Can you make it to Green Bay by, say, two? I might be able to squeeze…"

"Two's fine."

"Do you know how to get to our corporate headquarters? If you're coming from Crystal Lake, you'll want to take 94…."

"I'll find it," Jesse told her. "G'night." She abruptly hung up to avoid another long, drawn-out conversation with her.

* * * *

Jesse could tell immediately that she was nearing Green Bay. It wasn't just that the air quality had deteriorated because of the paper mills. It was because nearly every business began with the word "Titletown"; Titletown Bakery, Titletown Motel, Titletown Insurance. It's really kind of sad that the people in this, the third largest city in Wisconsin with a population of about a quarter of a million, have only a professional football team as their main source of "culture". It didn't take Jesse long to figure out just how important the Packers are to the people of this entire state. It's not just a fad to them; it's their way of life. The Packers win, everybody's happy. If they lose, look out. She had even heard that a former coach's dog was killed because he had a losing season. How frightening is that?

At one thirty, a full half-hour before her scheduled appointment, Jesse pulled into the drive of McCray Technology's corporate headquarters. Behind a massive eight-foot tall, red-brick security fence in an isolated area of one of Green Bay's growing industrial parks, it was a monstrous white marble and mirrored glass structure. It stood three and a half stories tall with four wings jutting out from the main hub. Concealed by acres and acres of wooded land between the highway and a smaller access road, it was the most impressive building in Northeast Wisconsin bar none. The building was a quarter of a mile off the road with a tree-lined boulevard leading to the circular drive at the main entrance.

Jesse turned down the stereo as she pulled up to the gate.

A man in a blue security uniform with a crew cut and a bad complexion, armed only with a clipboard, approached the Mercedes. "Hi! May I have your name, please?"

"Jesse Ferren. I have an appointment with Carly McCray." Jesse watched him check the paper on his clipboard, and then double-check it.

"I'm sorry. What'd you say your name was?"

Putz, Jesse thought. "Jesse Ferren. F-E-R-R-E-N."

"You're not on the roster. Wait here, please." He left the gate down, and Jesse lit a cigarette and turned up the stereo while he returned to his booth to call someone.

Reading his lips, Jesse muttered "Christ" when she saw that he was spelling her name for the person on the other end of the line. Obviously, he hadn't called McCray directly, and while she understood the need for someone of McCray's wealth and stature to be insulated somewhat from the general public, she was irritated that she had to go through this trouble just to keep an appointment that McCray herself had set up.

"I'm sorry, ma'am," he said, coming back to the car and leaning over to talk to Jesse. "I checked with Ms. McCray's assistant and she doesn't have any record of your appointment, so I'm afraid I'm going to have to ask you to back up and…."

No matter who was at fault, Jesse was not about to subject herself to another lecture from that woman. "I'm not backing up! I've got an appointment with Carly McCray in fifteen minutes and I intend to keep it! I'm driving her car, for Christ's sake! She called me at two this morning to set up the appointment! Now are you going to open the damn gate or am I going to have to drive through it?" Jesse knew she had him flustered and to accentuate her point, she inched forward, put the Mercedes in neutral, and revved the engine.

"Okay. Wait, okay? Let me try again. Just wait right here." He went back to the booth and got on the phone again. Within moments, the gate opened and he smiled as he waved Jesse in.

The lobby was just as Jesse imagined it would be: open and modern, perfectly befitting a tech company's corporate headquarters. Everything in the giant complex was immaculate, shiny new, done in McCray Technology's' colors of hunter green and dark purple.

Dramatic, streamline marble staircases led both up and down from the reception area. From the balcony above, rich green plants dangled down in botanical plushness, and the fountain just beyond the reception desk added a touch of warmth and class to the décor. The lobby was surprisingly quiet. Only the occasional muted trill of a phone interrupted the easy listening background music.

Jesse took a seat after announcing herself to the woman at the horse-shoe-shaped desk. She'd barely had time to choose a magazine before a woman approached her.

"Ms. Ferren?"

Not that Jesse usually noticed things like this, but the very first thing her eyes focused on were the woman's enormous breasts. They were so ridiculously gigantic it was hard not to stare at them. She was average size, yet her breasts were huge; so huge, in fact, that Jesse wondered how she got them cinched into the top of her blue dress. She rose to her feet, looking the woman in her light brown eyes and nowhere else.

"I'm Charlene, Ms. McCray's assistant. Ms. McCray is still in her staff meeting and asked me to have you wait in her office."

Jesse followed her to the glass elevator and carefully kept her gaze fixed on the reception area below as they climbed to the third floor, where Charlene led her to the executive wing.

The offices on both sides of the corridor were quite large and beautifully appointed. They all had glass walls with blinds for privacy. All of the blinds, Jesse noticed, were open, and all of the offices were unoccupied at the moment.

At the end of the hall was a corner office adjacent to an equally prestigious conference room. McCray was seated at the head of the long table talking to a group of five men and six women.

Jesse recalled having seen one of the women, the red-head on McCray's right, at services at Temple Shalom. She - Jesse believed her name was Jacey - and her husband were always there when she went. In fact, she invited Jesse to Break the Fast with her family last month after Yom Kippur. Jesse had declined. She wasn't about to go to a stranger's house and sit down and eat with her family. But Jesse thought it was kind of her to offer. That's the beauty of the Jewish people. They're all family, whether by birth or adoption/conversion; and nobody is ever truly alone. There's always room at the table.

Jacey was McCray's age, her red hair cut in a Diane Sawyer style. She looked up from her notes and gave Jesse a smile of recognition, and with her hand still down at her side, Jesse discreetly waved back. McCray had been talking to someone at the other end of the table and noticed the acknowledgment. She seemed surprised and looked at Jacey as if to ask how they knew one another.

She was facing her office, her ink-black hair swept back tightly. And while the gold-framed glasses she wore gave her a stern and studious appearance, they also made her seem more human and less intimidating. At least this woman had one tiny flaw.

"Can I get you something to drink while you wait?" Charlene asked.

"Sure." Jesse situated herself on the leather couch beside McCray's perfectly-ordered desk. "Coffee, please. Black." She adjusted her blazer and looked through the glass wall again to see if there was any indication that the meeting was about to adjourn. To her disappointment, it appeared as though she was in for a long wait because her client had a thick stack of papers in front of her and they were only two-thirds of the way through it.

Charlene returned with Jesse's coffee and as she leaned over to set it on the glass table in front of her, Jesse couldn't prevent herself from looking at her huge, pendulous breasts. The heat of discomfort rushed to her face and she quickly turned her gaze to McCray, who, to her intense embarrassment, was staring right at her, her gray eyes showing her amusement at Jesse's disconcerted expression.

Well, shit! Jesse cursed to herself. She picked up a magazine from the table and started to page through it. It wasn't a magazine per se, more like a prospectus of the company.

Beginning with a brief biography of McCray, the sole owner, it described how she had started the company from scratch, how she had built the business to what it was today - a quiet giant in the computer industry. McCray Technology, it seemed, was one of the first companies to successfully develop and market affordable encryption software for commercial and personal use with the internet.

As she read more, Jesse was amazed by the countless benefits and generous profit-sharing plan that McCray offered her employees. She was equally impressed by her client's business philosophy, her conviction to keep the company "family-friendly", and her ambitious plans for the future.

It had taken her nearly an hour to read through the prospectus, and as she returned it to the table, she looked in on McCray's meeting to see how much progress they'd made in that time. Thankfully, it looked as though they were breaking up. While most of them gathered their papers and were on their way out, McCray and Jacey remained, joined in conversation with their papers still in front of them.

They both looked at Jesse at the same time, and when McCray smiled and nodded, Jesse knew that Jacey was explaining to McCray how she and Jesse knew each other.

A voice came over the public address, paging McCray, and when she returned the call, the person on the other end of the line must have said something that upset or concerned her because in the next moment, Jesse watched her confer with Jacey, then leave the room with her, taking long, swift strides, their faces serious and urgent.

They had been gone for only twelve minutes, and Jesse looked up from the note she was about to leave for her client when she heard McCray's voice. A little more relaxed now, she stood in the doorway of Jacey's office, chatting, which really bugged Jesse. McCray knew that she was sitting there waiting for her. She knew that she'd been kept waiting for over an hour, yet she still took the time to talk to this woman about her teen-aged daughter, who was in the process of applying to colleges.

"I'm sorry to have kept you waiting," McCray apologized when she finally returned to her office. She closed the door behind herself, which caused her secretary to look up from her desk in surprise.

Now it was Jesse's turn. "From now on," she said, "when we agree to meet, I expect you to be there. On time. Most days I run on a very tight schedule. I cannot afford to sit around and wait for you."

McCray smiled a big, beautiful, genuine, open-mouthed grin. "Touché." With a quick glance in Jesse's direction, she sat behind her desk and opened her padfolio. Her long slender fingers danced over the keys on her keyboard with the same familiarity and grace as those of a concert pianist. "I should have known that today's meeting was going to run much longer than usual. And my Finance Department just informed me that they've found a problem with one of our accounts during a routine audit," she added distractedly as she took notes from the screen. "Would you mind if we talked over lunch?" She smiled up from her desk. "My treat."

Assenting, Jesse stood.

"We have excellent fare in the Atrium." She took off her glasses and checked her watch. "They stop serving at three. That gives us two minutes to get down there."

Despite its buffeteria-style service, the elegant atmosphere of the company's formal dining room made it seem like a five-star restaurant. Everything was perfect, of course; the arched transoms, the polished nickel accents, the generous use of plants, the dim lighting and the stained-glass windows that overlooked the main corridor on the first floor. The floor was carpeted with a hunter green and dark purple Berber. The design was made up of tiny squares with the McCray Technology logo. The table tops were a rich green marble. The chairs and benches to the booths were upholstered in the dark purple.

Jesse took her tray to a corner booth in the empty dining room, and after briefly socializing with the cashier, McCray slipped into the padded bench across from her. She seemed to be eyeing up the amount of food Jesse had accumulated: a bowl of chili, a hamburger, a plate of French fries, a slice of apple pie, and two cups of coffee. Her own tray contained only a garden salad, two breadsticks, and a glass of ice water.

Jesse arranged the food on her tray and started eating right away. She assumed that McCray needed to get back to work, and she certainly didn't want to hang around this place any longer than was necessary.

The silence between them must have really bothered McCray because before she even finished putting her napkin on her lap, she said, "Did you notice Charlene's tomatoes?"

Jesse had just taken a bite of her burger and nearly choked. She was astonished that someone as seemingly well-bred and sophisticated as Ms. Carly McCray would refer to a woman's breasts as *tomatoes*. God, she thought; she's a pig.

"You'd be surprised by how firm they are," she went on. "Usually when they're that big, they're squishy and tend to taste a little...salty, but hers are surprisingly firm and sweet."

Please stop, Jesse begged silently, trying with all her might to block out the mental picture of McCray and her secretary in bed together.

"When she first started working for me, she used to spread them out on her desk, but I had to ask her to stop. It got to be too distracting."

"I can imagine," Jesse muttered to herself.

"There were days when I'd come back from a meeting to find a crowd gathered around to get a look at them."

"Isn't that kinda rude?" Jesse asked at last.

"I'd take it as a compliment," McCray said. She seemed puzzled. "She's won several contests and statewide recognition because of them. People are constantly asking her for advice, wanting to know her secret." She took a sip of her ice water. "Why do you think that's rude?"

What kind of question was that? Jesse wondered. Pushing her empty plate to the far corner of her tray, she glanced up at her quickly before digging into her bowl of chili. She shrugged. "I...I don't know. I guess if she doesn't mind people making a big fuss over 'em, like she's a freak in some kind of side show, it's none of my business.

But I just don't think it's right to, you know, make such a big deal out of, um, a part of her body like that."

"A part of her body?" The confounded look on McCray's face turned into a pensive frown, then to a strange smile as she exploded with a deep robust laughter that took Jesse completely off guard.

Her shoulders convulsed. The top half of her body went limp as she nearly toppled sideways out of the booth. She was laughing so hard, she wasn't making noise anymore. Tears streaked her cheeks and she used her napkin to dab them away.

Jesse didn't get what was so damn funny. She was beginning to feel like she was in a Steven King movie, where the whole community had gone mad and she was the only sane person left. Now there's a frightening thought.

"I wasn't talking about her breasts!" Eventually McCray caught her breath enough to tell Jesse that Charlene and her husband dabble in hydroponics, that she really does grow tomatoes. "She keeps a box of them beside her desk. Didn't you see it when you passed?" she asked, trying to collect herself.

So, Jesse thought, wanting to disappear, it turns out I'm the pig. She could feel her ears burning and prayed that her face wasn't as red as it felt. "No," she muttered quietly, scooping up some chili. "I didn't." When her client's laughter finally subsided to a residual chuckling, Jesse said without preamble, "Victor's undocumented. He's here illegally, you know."

Becoming suddenly serious, McCray nodded. She set her fork

down and wiped her mouth with her napkin. She leaned forward in her seat. "He's from El Salvador. I pay him in cash." She picked up her fork again and smiled and winked at Jesse. "I don't have any political ambitions, so the fact that he's not documented has never concerned me."

"While I was in Crystal Lake..." Jesse pulled out her notepad and set it on the table, flipping open the cover. "Did you know that the Moriartys fired him in March?" Jesse glanced up to see her reaction - she was in the process of bringing a breadstick to her mouth and stopped mid-gesture. Her eyes widened in surprise. "I guess they have some pretty expensive horses. Saddlebreds, like yours, and they accused him and Susan of being in on some scheme to sell horse semen without their consent. Apparently, they'd been doing it for some time, forging the papers and then pocketing the stud fee."

"Victor?" McCray seemed truly shocked by this. "He couldn't....Susan, sure. I can see her doing something like that, but not Victor. Never Victor. He'd never get involved in something like that."

"It was rumored that they were working together, but Susan wasn't fired because she'd already started working for you. I'd like to talk to Victor and get his version."

Tension gathered around them as the silence grew deeper by degrees. Jesse finished off her chili and pushed her bowl out of the way to work on her apple pie. "Aside from that I didn't find anything unusual so far, nobody with an apparent motive to kill her. Everyone

I talked to seemed to really like her."

Staring off into the distance, seeming to have lost her appetite, McCray said in a low voice, "She was a real charmer."

"So I've gathered," Jesse said. "How many people do you have working for you at your house?"

"Karen and Victor are my only personal staff. Karen's been with my family since before I was born, and Victor...." She shook her head again as if trying to concentrate. "I, um, use private contractors for anything they can't handle. Before Victor came to work for me, Karen and Chris and I took care of everything. Mowing, raking, sweeping the walks, washing and waxing the cars, feeding the horses, cleaning the stable. Everything. When Susan came along, she convinced me that hiring someone to manage the grounds would take a huge burden off of Karen and free up a lot of my time."

Once Jesse got over the shock that her client actually did physical labor, and that she had grossly misjudged her, she asked, "How many employees do you have here?"

McCray's gaze remained on her water glass. "For tax purposes I do a lot of subcontracting here as well. Nationwide, we only employ about thirty-eight hundred people. We've already outgrown this building, so many of our associates work from home." She checked her watch as she took a sip of water. "I'm late for my meeting." Rising to her feet, she looked down at Jesse and waited for her to finish her second cup of coffee. "The staircase across the hall will take you back to the main entrance. Normally I'd walk you out, but...."

"I've gotta talk to Victor," Jesse reminded her as she wiped her upper lip. "I'll need you there to translate."

Frowning, McCray pursed her lips as she went over her options. "I'm going to Chris and Chelsea's party tonight and I don't expect to be home until late."

"The interview will probably only take a little while, an hour or so," Jesse told her. "How about before you go out?"

McCray shook her head. "I'm going directly to the party from here. Tomorrow's out of the question. I'll be here all day with the Ford execs, closing the contract. And the rest of the week...." Her gray eyes lit up as an idea occurred to her. "Why don't you write out your questions and I'll talk to him and get a transcript to you?"

"I'd rather do it in person. You can't tell from a transcript if someone's lying."

"We've got a video camera in the stable to record some of our training sessions. I'll record it for you."

"But sometimes when I interview people, they say something that leads to another question, one that I hadn't thought to write down. You might not know..."

That woman smiled. "Ms. Ferren, I've conducted thousands of interviews over the years. True, they were mostly employment interviews, but I have a firm grasp of the concept of follow-up. I understand that these things don't always follow the script."

"Okay," Jesse compromised reluctantly.

"Good. I've got to get to my meeting, but why don't you come back up to my office and write out your questions? Leave a number where I can reach you in case I have a problem with your handwriting."

Jesse filled out four sheets of legal paper - front and back - with questions for Victor. Working alone in the conference room, she checked her notepad, reviewed everything so as to leave no question unasked. She even tried to anticipate Victor's responses and wrote potential follow-up questions for her client.

Charlene was very efficient and never once let her coffee cup run dry. She paid Jesse several visits during her stay, but Jesse didn't see her client again until Charlene escorted her back to the main entrance. They took a different route this time and passed the door to the on-site day care center. Jesse thought it was an unusual place for a day care center, just off the executive wing, but when Charlene glanced in and came to a dead stop, Jesse realized why it was where it was. And she guessed that McCray had it put there for good reason.

"There she is," Charlene muttered. She turned to Jesse. "Will you excuse me for just a minute?"

Craning her neck, Jesse looked in and spied McCray in the middle of the bright and colorful room with a toddler on each knee. She was sitting on a tiny chair with a gaggle of children at her feet on the floor. She looked a little disappointed when she saw Charlene walk in.

They spoke only briefly, and when Charlene returned to Jesse in the hallway, Jesse could have sworn that she heard McCray start singing "Old McDonald Had a Farm".

That woman was just full of surprises, wasn't she? "I thought she was supposed to be in meetings all afternoon," Jesse commented.

Charlene pushed the button for the elevator. "She is. Sometimes I have to literally drag her out of there. She spoils those kids like you wouldn't believe."

* * * *

At six fifty-seven Jesse pulled the Mercedes around to the back of the Lighthouse Pub and searched for an empty spot. The place was already getting very busy. The back door was open, the van was already unloaded, and Greg, the bass player gave her a big smile when he saw her approach.

"Glad you could make it tonight," he told her. He grabbed another mic from the van and slammed the door shut. "Almost done with the sound check. Dave wants to get started soon."

"How many sets?"

"I don't know. Depends on Dave. He's the one who set this up." He looked at the Mercedes. "Nice wheels!"

Jesse grinned and tossed her spent cigarette to the ground before joining the rest of the band inside.

Her first order of business was to get a beer. After a brief chat with Dave, she took her seat behind the drums. It didn't dawn on her that she would be entertaining her new client tonight until she scanned the tavern and noticed the banner on the far wall that read "Happy Anniversary Chris and Chelsea".

"Shit," she groused as she pulled her sticks out of her back pocket.

"Oh, my God," Chris whispered to herself when she spotted Jesse. "That *was* her. I knew it!"

"That's the hot bass player, isn't it?" Chelsea asked her, suddenly appearing at her side. "We should hook her up with Carly tonight. Those two would make such a cute couple."

Chris looked at her partner. "They already know each other. That's the private detective Carly hired."

"You're kidding!" Chelsea stared at Jesse, who was getting warmed up. "What's she doing in a band?"

"I have no idea."

"Way to go, Carly," Chelsea whispered, causing Chris to give her a look.

They played eleven songs in the first set, and during their short break, Jesse asked the techies to adjust the lights before heading for the bar. She took a sip of beer and glanced around at the crowd to see if her client was there. She was relieved to find that she was not.

"We're only doing one more set. In five minutes. Greg has to get out of here early," Dave said as he passed her to meet up with his girlfriend at a nearby table.

It was during that second set when Jesse noticed a change in the atmosphere. They were playing *Flirting with Disaster* when she glanced out into the bar area to see that McCray had arrived. The crowd seemed to melt away, and Jesse found herself returning the stare of her new client. She was smiling brightly, nodding as Chris was leaning very close to her to say something. Her pale gray eyes never left Jesse, not even while Chris led her to their table in the corner.

Dave looked back at Jesse when he heard the stick clatter to the floor. He watched her recover perfectly by leaning over and grabbing a new one from the pouch near her foot.

Once settled in her seat, Carly passed the little gift package across the table to Chris and Chelsea. She was barely aware of the fact that they were already fawning over the Chihuahua puppy inside. Her focus was solely directed at Jesse, who was currently sneaking a sip of beer between songs. She watched closely as they started *Tom Sawyer*.

Throughout the entire set, Carly stared at her detective. She observed her hands, her forearms, and her biceps, which were clearly visible to her because Jesse had taken off her blazer during the first set and was now wearing only her athletic t-shirt on top. Her shoulders, beautifully freckled, were glistening with perspiration.

She watched the way Jesse's body moved when she'd use the pedal on the bass. She enjoyed the way she bit her bottom lip while performing a particularly strenuous portion of a song. All of this sucked Carly in. She wasn't just listening to the music. She was a part of it. She felt the passion, the pulse of the bass drum, the tempo of the high hat, and the fill of the toms. She felt it all over her body, most especially between her legs.

And then came the final song. Carly watched, spellbound, her heart racing in anticipation, as Jesse glanced toward the woman vocalist who had stepped up to the microphone. She saw the subtle nod between them. She saw Jesse bite her bottom lip and surreptitiously bit her own lip with the knowledge that something big was about to be unleashed.

Jesse's foot pumped the bass. It went right through Carly. The bass guitar followed, and then the singer, a fairly attractive woman with black hair and even blacker eyes, started belting out Pat Benatar's *Heartbreaker*.

But the voice, the lyrics, all of the other instruments faded away into Carly's subconscious. She was so taken by the detective's performance, the way she would quiet the cymbal with a quick and delicate touch of her hand, the way her muscles contracted and relaxed in her forearms when she rolled easily from the snare to the toms to the cymbal.

The increasing tempo matched Carly's breathing as the singer's voice rose. Carly's hand crept ever so slightly on her lap and found its way to her warm inner thigh. Just a little bit more, a little bit closer to release her inner fantasy. At the climax, Jesse stood to perform a relentless and unbelievably intense and passionate solo. The crowd was already cheering and applauding, and they grew louder the longer Jesse went on.

Before Carly could even catch her breath, the song was over. She watched as Jesse gently set the sticks on the snare, reach down for a small towel and dab her forehead with it, and sling the towel over her shoulder and walk out from under the harsh spotlight. Just like that, she was gone. The audience hadn't even stopped its applause yet.

Jesse darted out the back door with a beer in one hand, her pack of Marlboro Lights in the other. It had grown much colder since the evening began. A light mist created a haze around the lone light in the lot. Even though the juke box was now playing, Jesse enjoyed the peace just outside the rear of the pub. There were no people; no distractions, just Jesse alone with her thoughts.

"That was amazing," said a warm, low voice. "You have...you're quite talented."

Jesse turned to see her client standing there. "Thanks," she said quietly. She took a sip of beer.

"How long have you been...?"

"Hey, helluva job tonight!" Dave said as he came out carrying an amp. He noticed Carly standing there. "Oh, sorry." He carefully set it down under the awning, reached into the back pocket of his faded jeans, and pulled out an envelope. "Here ya go. That includes the last Friday you played, too."

"Thanks." Jesse tucked it into her back trouser pocket. She took another sip of beer, then lit a fresh cigarette as she watched Dave walk away to get the van.

"Aren't you cold? Do you have a jacket?"

"It's inside," Jesse told her client, gesturing. "I just came out here to cool off."

McCray nodded. "It was getting very hot in there, wasn't it?"

Jesse didn't respond. She took a long drag from her cigarette.

Dave pulled right up to them and slid open the side door. "I think Charlie will be back next week, so we'll call you when we need you fill in again. Too bad Charlie can't be gone more often," he said with a grin. "You play way better than he does."

Jesse smiled modestly and took another sip of her beer. "See ya," she told Dave. She turned to her client. "I gotta get my stuff and get going."

"You're leaving?" McCray asked.

"Yeah."

"Do you need help loading up your drums or anything?"

"They're not mine," Jesse said. "But if you want to help Dave, I'm sure he'd be grateful."

She pulled the door open to return to the bar, but Carly said, "I thought about what you'd said earlier today."

Jesse stopped and turned to look at her. She let the door swing closed.

"You said that you'd rather interview Victor in person and I was thinking - if it's not too late, that is, I was thinking that, well...I'll be leaving in a little while. You could come with me. I've already called Victor and told him that I need to speak with him tonight."

73

"Nah. I'm tired. I'm going home." She turned toward the door again.

"I just think...I think that you'd know better what to ask him," Carly said.

"I wrote all of the questions down for you. Don't you have them with you?"

"Well, yes, but...," she sighed, "The truth is that I'm not comfortable doing this alone. I'd really rather have you there with me. And you were the one who suggested that it would be better if you were there." She looked so tired. She added, "Please?"

"This doesn't have to be done tonight," Jesse said. "I could drop by tomorr..."

Carly was shaking her head. "I'll be at the office all day tomorrow." She pulled her blazer shut and hugged herself to stay warm. "Tonight is really the only time I'll be available for this."

Giving only a few moments' thought, Jesse said, "Fine." It was the way she said it, though, that made it clear to Carly that it wasn't fine. "Let me get my stuff."

They entered the bar, and Carly waited for Jesse to pick up her blazer. She said, "I'll tell Chris and Chelsea that we're leaving."

They waded through the crowd together to the table in an out-of-the-way corner.

Chris and Chelsea were sitting together, alone, talking quietly to one another. Their conversation died immediately when Carly put her hand on Chris' shoulder.

"We're leaving," she told them, causing them both to look up at her.

"You can't leave yet!" Chris insisted as she rose to her feet. "C'mon, Carly! You just got here!"

"Yeah," Chelsea chimed in. "Stay for a little while!" She looked at Jesse. "You were great tonight, by the way! We saw you play a few weeks ago, too, at the Mariner. You were playing bass. You're wicked good!"

"Thanks."

"I'm Chelsea, by the way." She stuck her hand out. Chelsea was a nice-looking woman, a bit on the heavy side, with long straight auburn hair and pleasant hazel eyes

Jesse shook her hand. "It's nice to meet you. I'm Jesse." She turned to Carly. "We really should be leaving," she said politely.

"We can stay for a few minutes, can't we?" She pulled out a chair for the detective. "Here. Sit here." She gave Jesse very little choice in the matter and took the only remaining seat at the table, next to Jesse, directly across from Chelsea.

"Carly told us about Victor," Chelsea said, leaning in so they could hear her above the music. "You don't think he had anything to do with Susan's accident, do you?" She must have sensed from Jesse's reproachful glare at her client that she had said something wrong. Smiling uneasily, she stood. "Can I get you something to drink, Jesse?"

While reaching into her trouser pocket for some money, she

asked for a Miller, and Chelsea and Chris threw startled looks at McCray, who simply leaned over and reminded Jesse that she was driving. She suggested a club soda instead.

"I don't like club soda." Jesse handed Chelsea a ten. "Miller." The troubled look that loomed on McCray's face was so overwhelming that Jesse felt obliged to defend her choice of beverage. "It's only one beer. It's not going to kill me." Chris mumbled something that sounded like "too bad", but Jesse ignored it. Instead, staring at her client, she pulled out her cigarettes and said, "I thought I told you not to discuss the case with anyone."

Chris jumped to her friend's defense before McCray had a chance to reply. "Lighten up, Miss Marple! She just told Chelsea and me. It's not like she held a press conference, for Christ's sake. We're family. We don't keep anything from each other."

Jesse felt the small vein in her temple start to twitch while she turned her laser-like stare to Chris. Her first instinct was to ask her if she'd "shared" the reason for her large and recent debt with McCray because Jesse would bet her life that she hadn't. She was also pretty sure that her fear of Jesse discovering her debt was the source of her unpleasantness toward Jesse. But this was neither the time nor the place to get into that. So Jesse kept her peace, but her look of granite never left her as she brought a Marlboro to her lips, lit it, and sank back in her chair.

Chris was the first to look away. Jesse knew she would be. She kept staring at her as Chris looked down into her jean jacket and made a face as she pulled something out. It was so small, Jesse couldn't tell what it was until she lifted it up to the table.

"I think she peed on me," she said, chuckling in surprise as she held a tiny little Chihuahua in her arms like a baby, petting it. It was reddish-tan with huge helicopter blades for ears and bulging brown eyes. Chris' large hand covered the puppy completely. "She's cold,' she told McCray, holding the dog in one hand while using the other to wipe her shirt with a napkin. "She's shaking."

"Ohh! That reminds me…" Leaning for her briefcase, McCray pulled out a small gift bag and reached inside. She took out a small purple and green knit sweater for the dog. By the way she slipped it over her fingers, it looked like a deformed glove. "Jacey made this for her. Isn't it adorable? When I told her what kind of dog I'd finally decided upon for you, she asked me to give it to you." As she leaned to slide the sweater over the dog's head, she must have noticed Jesse's expression.

At that moment, the bartender arrived with Jesse's beer. Funny, Jesse thought, I gave Chelsea a ten. Shouldn't there be change? Taking a sip, she glanced over and saw Chelsea at the juke box, making important musical selections. It seemed that the tension at the table had been too much for her and she wasn't coming back.

Chris straightened the sweater on the dog, and McCray inclined her head toward Jesse. "You don't like dogs?"

Jesse made a face and took another sip of her beer. The little dog jumped when she set her empty bottle down on the table. "Real dogs, sure. Not bug-eyed rat dogs."

Chris heard Jesse's remark and saw McCray's hurt expression. "Well Chelsea and I love her, Carly. She's great! And I'll be able to take her flying with me." She lifted the tiny dog high in the air, causing it to shake and whimper. "We're going to call her Mickey," she said, giving McCray a knowing grin, which McCray returned with a chuckle.

While Chris went back to fussing over the new addition to her family, Jesse swiveled her head back to give her client a bored look. "Are you ready?"

"You can't leave yet!" Chris told McCray. "Jake's coming. He'll be here any minute! He's really looking forward to seeing you tonight! And there's cake! Won't you at least stay for a piece?" She leaned closer to Carly. "It's marble cake. Your favorite."

McCray and Jesse maintained eye contact for several moments until she finally made up her mind. She released a deep breath and turned to her friend. "I'm sorry, Chris. I've really got to be going."

Jesse was stunned. She thought for sure that McCray would decide to stay a little longer and try to convince Jesse to do the same. Chris seemed equally stunned. Stunned and disappointed.

"I'll get your coat," she told McCray, safely tucking Mickey into her jean jacket and walking away.

Jesse watched her approach Chelsea at the juke box. She showed her the dog tucked in her jacket, whispered something that brought a warm smile from her, took her by the hand, and led her to the small parquet dance floor across the room.

"I thought she was getting your coat," Jesse complained.

But McCray didn't answer. She was watching her friends, clearly enthralled by their closeness. She didn't take her eyes from them once. The song on the juke box had come to an end, but Chris and Chelsea continued their dance, dancing to music that - apparently - only they could hear. McCray seemed absolutely amazed by them, maybe even a little envious. Taking a swallow of her water, she looked at Jesse and caught her staring at her, watching her friends.

She gave Jesse a nice smile, but Jesse just blinked and looked away, distracted suddenly by the two flamboyant women who had just entered through the rear of the lounge. One of them, the shorter of the two, had to be at least forty. She was provocatively dressed and adorned with so much jewelry that she appeared to glow. The woman with her was similarly dressed and couldn't have been more than twenty. Jesse wondered if they were mother and daughter.

"What is she doing here?" McCray grumbled quietly, so quietly that Jesse could barely make it out. "It's Donna; Donna Meyer." She said that name with a tone of evil presentiment as her tired eyes slid to Jesse. "That's how she always introduces herself."

"Which one is she?" Jesse asked, glancing at the woman and her adolescent companion. She recognized the name from Susan's address book.

In a voice so caustic that Jesse actually felt its heat, McCray replied, "She's the whore in the leather pants." From her body language, the way she crossed her legs and leaned forward, it wasn't too difficult for Jesse to realize that there were some pretty intense feelings between her client and this Donna Meyer character. "She raises Saddlebreds, too. She married Robert Meyer, The Robert Meyer, seven years ago." She huffed out a laugh, shaking her head as she ran her fingertip along the rim of her glass. "I'm sure she never imagined that the old man would live this long." Looking at Donna, her smile vanished. "Susan detested her almost as much as I do. Donna had been coming on to her since she moved in with me."

Jesse turned her glance from her client to Donna. "She's married? And she was coming on to Susan? You mean making sexual advances?"

McCray nodded and took another sip of water. "She's got four stables of saddlebreds and two stables of young women. She wanted to make Susan a member of her harem. We've never gotten along. Ever since….Well, despite the fact that I've never participated in her little games, she seems to be in some sort of contest with me. She's very competitive about everything: the horses, money, women, you name it." She waved her elegant hand to punctuate her comment. Then, with a rather smug look on her face, she told Jesse that her horses had consistently beaten Donna's horses in competition and that with Susan's expert riding her prized horse Damien won the World Championship. "Donna was furious," she told Jesse with a smirk. "Her pitiful nags didn't even place."

"Well if it isn't her highness, the widow McCray," said a sharp voice from behind Jesse. Of course it was loud enough to get just about every head to turn in her direction.

"Donna," McCray said cordially. The hint of contempt in her voice came nowhere close to matching the fury behind her eyes.

"What are you doing here, princess? Slumming? I didn't think you socialized with the locals." There was an evil, grating laugh. "Isn't it a little soon to be starting up with someone new? Susan's not even cold yet."

As Jesse crushed out her cigarette, she felt a cool hand come to rest on her shoulder. Turning, she looked up at the little woman standing over her. She was probably a fraction of an inch over five feet, only a few inches shorter than Jesse. Along with her green satin blouse and black leather pants that outlined her figure like a second skin, she wore a haughty smile on her thin lips. Her dark, almond-shaped eyes exuded not one iota of kindness.

"Where'd you find this cute little filly?" Donna asked, eyeing Jesse as a USDA inspector would study a choice piece of meat. "My God, look at you! You're a beauty!"

Turning back, Jesse felt a different hand skim her shoulder. When she realized that it was McCray's hand, she looked at her and saw her expression change from that of revulsion to one of cunning inspiration.

"She's a dear old classmate of mine from Madison," McCray told Donna, doing a good job of hiding her satisfaction at her improvisational skills. "We met during a Philosophy course in our junior year." She smiled and gripped Jesse's shoulder. Jesse's body tensed as McCray pulled her to her chest and planted a kiss on the side of her head. "She taught me the meaning of the word 'hedonism', didn't you, darling?"

Jesse leaned out of her embrace to light another cigarette and made it clear to her with her expression just how unhappy she was with her client's little charade.

Donna sat in the chair that Chris had vacated. "How are you tonight, gorgeous? I'm Donna, Donna Meyer." Reaching across the table, she took Jesse's free hand and rather than shaking it, held it to her nonexistent lips and kissed it. She turned her glance to McCray. "This new finger puppet of yours is much smaller than the others. You'll have to buy all new costumes for her."

"This is a private party, Donna. I don't believe your name is on the guest list."

Donna reached for Jesse's Marlboros and shook one out and brought it to her mouth. She motioned for Jesse to light it for her.

When Jesse obliged, McCray glared at her. "Don't you have a husband waiting for you at home?" she asked without bothering to disguise her hostility. She still had her arm around the back of Jesse's chair, and although Jesse was leaning forward, McCray's hand was able to reach her. Through her blazer, Jesse could feel McCray's fingers making tiny circles on her shoulder.

Donna smiled slyly, checked her watch. "Donna's not due home for hours." Blowing a puff of smoke in McCray's face, she looked her up and down. Under the table, a foot ran up Jesse's leg. Jesse assumed it was Donna's. Backing up a little, she used her hand to push it away, but when she moved back, McCray's hand caught her shoulder and held on tight this time.

"You look like hell," Donna told McCray. "You could stamp 'Samsonite' on those bags under your eyes. Why don't you loosen up a little? Have a drink. Come on, baby, just one. I'll buy." She stood and took a few steps toward the bar, then turned back. "What was it you used to drink? Martinis? Or, better yet, how about a margarita?" she asked, rolling the *r*'s and shaking her hips a little.

A towering man approached the table at that moment. "Hey, stranger." He was probably a few years older than McCray. His brunette hair was mixed with gray and cut very short. He had the same dark, deep-set eyes that Chris had.

McCray tipped back her head, and a huge smile consumed her face. It took five years off her appearance. "Jake!"

"Mom told me you were here," he told her. "How've you been?"

"Fine. Just fine." She stood to hug him and returned the wave of an older woman across the room who had been watching him.

"I'm sorry I missed the memorial service. Chris called right away when it happened, but I couldn't get back in time. I'm really sorry."

McCray told him that she understood and thanked him for the beautiful flowers. She invited him to join them at the table. Mindful of her manners, she introduced him to Jesse, and when she sat down again, her hand returned to Jesse's shoulder. Her fingers moved to Jesse's hair to play in her curls.

That did it. Jesse backed her chair away from the table and left to find an empty spot at the bar - well away from Donna Meyer - and ordered another beer. And then another. And another. McCray seemed to have forgotten that she was even there.

"This is bullshit," Jesse grumbled as she put out her cigarette in the ashtray and got up to find the bathroom.

She was washing her hands at the sink and was startled by two hands winding themselves around her waist. They came to rest just inches above her crotch.

"Hey!" Jesse spun around so fast that her hair slapped Donna Meyer across the face. She removed Donna's hands from her hips. "Don't touch me!"

"Relax, cutie," Donna whispered lustily in her ear. She used her hips to pin Jesse in the corner, up against the countertop and the wall. Her sweet, heavy perfume gagged Jesse. "Donna's not going to hurt you. She just wants to get to know you a little better." She pulled her hands from Jesse's and gripped Jesse's shoulders. "Ohhh, muscles. Donna likes strong women. But you're so tense, dear. Must be the company you've been keeping lately. It's a pity you're involved with the likes of Carly McCray. You realize that she goes through women faster than she goes through toilet paper."

Jesse's head was swimming from the loud music vibrating through the door, the bad perfume and various other odors from the restroom. And Donna certainly wasn't helping.

She talked as fast as her hands moved, and Jesse really had to exert herself to keep up with them. At last, she got a grip on Donna's arms. Holding her firmly by the elbows, a safe distance away, Jesse turned her just enough to break free from the corner.

"My, you're a spirited one." Somehow Donna wriggled out of Jesse's grasp, and when her hands found their way to Jesse's breasts, Jesse wasted no time in forcibly restraining her. She twisted both of Donna's arms behind her back and shoved her up against the counter.

"What the hell's the matter with you?" Jesse demanded.

To her horror, Donna seemed to like it. "Ohhh, that's nice," she moaned. She arched her body back and rubbed her shoulders up and down on Jesse. "Very nice, baby." She moaned as she rubbed her front against the counter.

"Jesus Christ! Stop it! What are you doing?"

Jesse's grip tightened, and Donna moaned again. "Yeah, oh, yeah, Donna likes it rough. Come on, honey. Don't make Donna do all the work."

Horrified that she was participating - albeit unintentionally - in some sort of sick sexual foreplay with Donna, Jesse didn't move. She didn't know quite what to do. If she released her, Jesse was certain that the ensuing race for the door would only prolong Donna's pleasure. And if she didn't release her, Jesse was equally certain that Donna would finish whatever it was she had started. And she definitely didn't want any part of that.

In order to buy enough time to get out of there, Jesse looked around, then pulled Donna away from the counter and jammed her hands up into the paper towel dispenser. A couple of her rings got caught up in there, and once she was absolutely sure that she was good and stuck, Jesse let go and got the hell out of there.

As she walked down the dark back hall back toward the bar, she could hear Donna's throaty laugh coming from the restroom.

Enraged, Jesse stomped past her client on the way out. Chris and Chelsea had rejoined her at the table. "I'm leaving," she told her client. Peripherally, she saw Chris' menacing glare move to the back of the lounge near the restrooms. She glanced back to see what had shifted her attention and was mortified to see Donna walking toward her with her hair disheveled. Her green blouse was askew and untucked, unbuttoned far enough to reveal her black lace bra.

"Buckle your belt, love," Donna hollered out as she slinked up to her date at the bar.

Jesse stopped dead. Scorching heat rushed to her face as she looked down and saw that both parts of her thin leather belt were dangling from the loops in her trousers. Right away, while adjusting it, she glanced at Chris, Chelsea, Jake, and McCray and saw them all exchange a look. Chris was snickering.

One gaze around the bar told Jesse that she was now the center of attention. Everyone was staring at her, eyebrows raised, no doubt thinking the same thing. "Crazy bitch," she muttered on the way out the door. She was so pissed off that she'd forgotten that she'd parked the Mercedes in the lot behind the bar.

Taking the sidewalk around the building, she stopped to light a cigarette. The light mist had turned into a soft shower. The music grew louder as the Pub's door opened behind her, and Jesse knew that her client had followed her out.

"Jesse, wait!"

Determined not to give in, Jesse kept walking. "Forget it!" she yelled over her shoulder. "I don't need this shit!" How could she have let things get so out of hand? Who's in charge here, her or me? She wondered angrily. Well if she thinks she's going to get away with this, she's got another thing coming.

"Please, Jesse! Wait!" Carly had caught up with her and grabbed her arm to stop her.

Jesse pulled free. "Don't touch me!" She looked up at her client and saw the determination - or was it fear? - in her eyes. The rain shimmering off the lights made it appear that there was a halo above Carly's head.

Damn! Jesse cursed silently. Life was so much easier when she didn't give a shit about anyone or anything. Turning to fully face her, she got right up in Carly's face. "Let's get one thing straight right now," she said. To underscore her reprimand, she used a gesture made famous by George H. W. Bush, pointing the index fingers of both hands at her as if they were weapons. "I'm a detective and you're my client. That's all. I'm not a paid escort. I'm not your psychologist. I'm not your friend. And no matter how rich you are,

I'm not going to ask 'how high' every time you say 'jump'. Understand? What you did in there was…was…"

"I know," McCray interrupted. "I'm sorry."

"You used me to get back at her!" Jesse charged. "You knew she'd come after me the way she did!"

"I'm sorry," she repeated, staring into Jesse's eyes.

"And you've been telling Chris and Chelsea everything, haven't you? Did you think my rules were just something you could break without consequence?"

Carly shook her head. "No. Of course not. I'm sorry, Jesse. Truly, I am. It won't happen again."

"Damn right it won't happen again." Jesse puffed angrily on her cigarette while staring at her. She couldn't even fathom why she was going to stick with this case. "You two were lovers, you and Donna Meyer. That's why there's so much hostility between you, right?" By McCray's silence and the way her glaze slid away, Jesse knew she'd been right all along. She huffed out a scornful laugh and shook her head. Still staring at her client, she took a long drag on her cigarette.

"It's a long story," McCray told her. She sounded like she was on the verge of tears. "She…shortly after we broke up, she started playing all kinds of practical jokes on me." She didn't look up as she tied the belt on her beige overcoat. "They were harmless at first: sending me dead flowers on my birthday, having my car towed while I was shopping, emptying a box of nails on my driveway, calling a moving company while I was out of town and having all of my furniture put in storage, that kind of thing. But these practical jokes of hers have escalated over the years." She was still looking down, watching the rain drops hit the sidewalk at her feet. "This past summer at a horse show....I was...I was in the trailer with Damien. She knew I was in there. She *knew* I was in there, and she lit a firecracker near the rear of the trailer. It spooked Damien so badly, he nearly trampled me. Luckily, I escaped with only a broken arm, but..." She looked meaningfully at Jesse, running her right hand up and down her left forearm. "He could have killed me."

So there it was. She finally trusted Jesse enough to give her the cue she had been waiting for. Jesse shifted her weight to her left side, took another drag from her cigarette. "You didn't hire me to find out what happened to Susan," she said calmly, without accusing her. "You think someone's trying to kill you, don't you? That's why you hired me?"

Carly looked at Jesse with the shock of recognition, and Jesse knew that she had just put into words something that Carly could not bring herself to believe. Her hands left her coat pockets to toy with the strap of her briefcase. She watched Jesse inhale on her cigarette again. Her face was stone serious, and Jesse could hear her breathing quicken. "I haven't told a soul about this - not even Chris...I...I need you to keep this to yourself," she said in something near a whisper. "If word got out that my life might be in danger...."

Jesse nodded her understanding. After a moment and another

drag on her cigarette, Jesse asked thoughtfully, "Is there something that makes you think the boat explosion was meant for you and not for Susan? Have you gotten threats?"

Carly shook her head. "No. But there was something…In…I think it was June or July. I was on my way to pick up Doug, my nephew, from the airport. He'd just gotten back from Dallas and…and on the way there, my car, the Mercedes was running funny. Then I developed this headache. I…It wasn't one of my migraines, this was different. I pulled off the road and called Jake, Chris' brother. He found a rag stuffed in my tailpipe."

"So the headache was from carbon monoxide," Jesse concluded. She saw a new silver BMW speed past and caught a glimpse of the driver, Donna Meyer. "Did Susan ever drive the Mercedes?" she asked, keeping her eyes on the BMW.

"No. Never. She…I bought the Lexus for her shortly after she moved in with me, and she always used that. But that's not all. Maybe a month after that incident, while Susan and I were at a wedding reception for some friends of mine, well, I don't know if I was poisoned, or if…I don't know." She shrugged helplessly. "I was never so sick in all my life. I became so violently ill, I…I was throwing up, I was dizzy, I had dia…gastrointestinal problems. I honestly thought I was going to die."

The BMW was gone now, and Jesse turned her attention back to Carly. "Did anyone else get sick?"

"I don't know. I thought it would have been rude to ask."

"How 'bout Susan. Did she get sick?"

Carly paused for a moment to reflect. "She…we'd shared a plate of hors d'oeuvres, and I know I commented to her that the crab salad had an odd taste, so I don't think she had any of it. I think she was fine. I don't recall, to tell you the truth."

"Sounds like the crab salad had been sitting out too long. Did you see a doctor?"

By the look on her face and the way she was shaking her head, Jesse knew that she had taken offense to her tone, which had been meant to ease her concerns, not disparage her.

"Look," McCray said, wiping the rain-soaked hair from her forehead, "I'm not saying that any of those incidents were intended to kill me, but when my boat exploded, when I saw Susan's body in the morgue, those little incidents that I just mentioned to you started to appear much bigger to me."

"I understand. But even if the boat and the other things are related, how do you know that you were the intended target and not Susan? I mean, Victor might have…"

Although Jesse was empathetic and sincere, Carly had clearly lost patience, evidenced by her faltering speech pattern, the way her lips barely moved when she spoke. "I don't know that I *was* the target, detective. That's what I want you to investigate, don't you see?"

Now it was Jesse's turn to lose her patience. "Well then why the hell didn't you tell me that from the start?" That shut her up. Jesse puffed on her cigarette while enjoying her victory. "Do you think

Donna's got something to do with the boat explosion?"

McCray nodded uncertainly. "It's quite possible that she did. She was at my house earlier that week. She was at the horse show, she was at the wedding."

"Why would she want to kill you?"

"Isn't it obvious?" Carly charged. "She's psychotic! I...I don't know if she meant to kill me or Susan in the boat. Last month, when Susan finally told her off, Donna assaulted her." She flung an arm out. "Right there in my tack room, pinned her up against the wall and tore at her clothes, grabbed her everywhere. Poor Susan was horrified. There's no telling what Donna would have done if I hadn't walked in." Jesse's brow furrowed, and McCray added, "She doesn't assault all women, only the ones who are with me. That's why I pretended that you were my....that we were...I just assumed that you knew that I didn't...that I was trying to give you a reason to talk to her." She paused for a moment before adding, "And I knew you could handle her."

Her clear discomfort and fear worked to ebb Jesse's anger. "From now on," she said, tossing her spent cigarette to the pavement and stepping on it, "I'll do the strategizing on this case, understand?"

A chilling breeze kicked up. Under the light from the street lamp, McCray nodded her agreement, and they both just stood there staring at each other.

Jesse used her stare to convey her unhappiness with her. She had no idea what McCray was trying to convey with hers, but it was starting to bother her. "We should get going," Jesse said finally. She nodded toward the dark green Jeep Grand Cherokee parked at the curb. "Is that yours?"

McCray looked over at it. "Yes." She pulled a set of keys from her pocket and looked up and down the street for the Mercedes. "Where are you parked?"

"In the lot in back," Jesse said, jerking her head in that direction.

"Are you okay to drive?"

"What?"

"You've been drinking," she reminded Jesse. "Why don't you ride with me? You can stay the night and we'll pick up the Mercedes tomorrow."

Was she serious? Did she honestly think Jesse was drunk? Jesse never had a problem handling her alcohol. Never. And what did she mean by "stay the night"? Jesse wondered. "I'm fine," she assured her.

She didn't seem too happy about Jesse's decision, but she wisely let it go. "I have to stop for gas. Will you be able to find my driveway in the dark, or would you rather follow me?"

Jesse turned to walk away. "I'll meet you there." She paused before turning the corner of the building and looked back at McCray, who was leaning near the rear of her Jeep, looking at the tailpipe. "Shit," she muttered, chuckling.

Reaching the half-way point between town and McCray's house, Jesse rolled down her window as she pulled yet another cigarette from the pack. There were no street lights, no other cars, no houses visible from the highway. The song *Brown-Eyed Girl* came on the stereo and instantly reminded her of Abby. For over six years, she was Jesse's Brown-Eyed Girl, and Jesse used to sing this song to her all the time.

It's funny, Jesse thought, how music and scents and things can trigger memories. She wanted to hear the song, to think of Abby, but at the same time, it was a dangerous prospect. Could she handle the sadness? She doubted it. Their parting was the lowest point in Jesse's life.

Hoping the sheer volume would drown out the painful memory, Jesse touched the tiny button and cranked the music.

Abby would love it here, she thought, staring out into the darkness as the wipers gently swept the rain from the windshield. She'd especially love spending the winter here. We'd live in our very own cozy little cabin, tromp through the snow together, and snuggle up in front of the fire. Jesse smiled and lit her cigarette, picturing the scene in her mind, indulging in a fantasy that she knew was just that - fantasy. She knew Abby would not be coming to see her. Not for the winter. Not ever.

The song ended. Jesse topped a small hill and when she glanced into the rear-view mirror, noticed that the car behind her had come out of nowhere and was closing in on her with alarming speed. She wondered if it was McCray, hurrying to catch up to her. Unfamiliar with the terrain, Jesse slowed the Mercedes to urge it around a tight curve. The glaring lights of the car trailing her were momentarily trained on the road's shoulder as it, too, took the curve. Jesse alternated between watching the road and watching her pursuer. She made out that it was a red vehicle, a TrailBlazer or Excursion, she wasn't sure which.

Whatever it was, it was at her bumper by the time they reached the straight-a-way. Jesse accelerated slowly, expecting the car to pass. But it didn't. It kept perfect pace with her. Jesse slowed. The other vehicle slowed at the same rate. And when she sped up again, clipping along at a dangerous eighty-eight miles an hour, the other car stayed right on her fender.

Jesse slowed again. At forty-five, she was going ten miles under the speed limit, and there was no sign that the car behind her had any intention of passing. This was not good.

The road was narrow. There wasn't room on the shoulder to pull off safely. Jesse was fast-approaching another close curve. She had to do something.

The Mercedes quaked as the other car made contact. Jesse looked in the mirror.

The car shuddered as it was hit again, and Jesse struggled to keep it under control. The cigarette dangled from her mouth. Her hands, moistened with perspiration, gripped the wheel tighter. She spit her half-smoked cigarette out the window and let the wind carry it off.

Her assailant hit her again, much harder. And this time, it sustained contact and actually pushed the Mercedes along. Jesse hit the brakes, but the car wouldn't slow.

Her heart was in her throat, rapping hard. She felt the car gain speed as they closed in on the curve.

Suddenly the headlights went out on the other vehicle.

"What the…." Jesse narrowed her eyes and checked her mirror again. Nothing. Blackness. By the time her gaze returned to the road, it was too late.

"Fuck!" She veered to the left. Then bracing herself, she stood on the brake. For a moment, she thought she might have a chance. The car was actually slowing. Maybe it wasn't too late.

Then realization hit. Almost simultaneously, the other vehicle hit her again.

This time she was jolted from the side. It was a jarring impact, a horrible thundering of the two vehicles colliding. Airbags exploded from everywhere, punching Jesse with the force of a heavyweight boxer. Then came another bump. Just a little one this time. But that was all it took.

Jesse felt it. She felt the moment she lost control. She felt the tires leave the pavement. It was the last thing she felt before her world fell silent.

* * * *

"Jesse, can you hear me? Jesse?"

Jesse came to just long enough to see that she was about to die. She saw Carly's face through the smoky interior of the car. Flames shot up behind her and she was choking hard. One of them was upside-down, and Jesse realized that it must have been her because she couldn't figure out how else Carly could be kneeling on the ceiling of the Mercedes. She tried to say something. She tried to move, but couldn't. My god, she thought, mortified, what an awful way to die.

"Jesse!" Carly cried in desperation, trying to tug the detective's foot free from under the seat.

* * * *

Soft sorrowful music played, and somewhere between unconsciousness and death, Jesse saw Abby. She was standing in the doorway, clear as day, and Jesse couldn't believe her eyes. *Maybe the accident was worse than I thought, she reasoned in her delusional state. Maybe Abby knows something I don't know. Maybe I'm dying. Maybe I've already died. Or, maybe now that Abby's here, she'll realize that we belong together. Maybe she'll take me back.*

The last thing Jesse remembered was the painful coughing fit she had when someone stuck smelling salts under her nose. She had no idea where she was or how she got there. The one thing she did know was that she wasn't in a hospital. She seemed to recall something Carly said about the hospital being too far away. She vaguely remembered telling an older woman that she couldn't feel her right side. She heard Carly gasp, and she was sure she mentioned something about her boy, Harley, that he was alone at home.

Maybe that's why Abby was here, Jesse thought. She came to take care of him. That's good. Abby's always been good with animals. Harley never had a chance to meet her, but Jesse was convinced that he'd really love her.

Instantly comforted by her presence, Jesse had somehow forgotten the emptiness and utter despair Abby caused when she left. All she could feel right now was her heart beating faster as Abby drew closer to the bed. Tears formed in her eyes, she was so grateful to see her again.

She sat beside Jesse on the bed and held her hand, and as Jesse stared into those beautiful familiar dark eyes, she prayed that this wasn't just another one of her dreams.

"How'd you know where to find me?"

"I have my sources," Abby told her with her enigmatic smile. "You'd be surprised how far-reaching my network is." She patted Jesse's hand, but Jesse couldn't feel it. The accident must have paralyzed me, she thought. But it didn't matter. Abby was here with her, and she was positive that everything would be fine.

Encouraging her to slide over, Abby moved to hold Jesse in her arms. Her sweet scent invaded Jesse's nostrils, and she took a long, deep breath, remembering. "God, I've missed you," she whispered.

"I'm missed you, too, hon," Abby replied sweetly. She kissed Jesse's forehead.

"What are you doing here? Have you seen Harley? Is he okay?"

"He's fine," Abby assured her. A look of concern hardened her features. "But I don't know what I'm going to do with him if you don't get better. You know I can't take him back with me."

With the realization that Abby had no intention of reuniting with her after all, Jesse looked away. "You told me we'd be together forever."

"Come on, Jess. Let's not get into that right now." Abby slid down further on the bed and draped her arm over Jesse. "You just concentrate on getting better."

"I can't," Jesse whispered, tears flowing. "Not without you. Abby, I'm so lost without you. Take me back. Please say you'll take me back. Please? I don't want to live without you. Please take me back."

She held Jesse close and kissed her tenderly on the cheek, not unlike the way a parent would kiss their wounded child. "You know I can't do that, babe."

Abby held her a moment longer, then sat up, and terrified of losing her again, Jesse clung to her in desperation. She squeezed her eyes shut as if to will her to stay. "Wait! Don't go!" she cried, hugging her beloved with all her might. "Please don't go!"

Warm arms hugged back. A soft, sweet voice whispered, "Shhh. It's okay, Jesse. I'm right here. I'm not going anywhere." But when Jesse opened her eyes again, anticipating seeing Abby's face, she was shocked to see a pair of pale gray eyes staring down at her.

"No!" Bewildered, gasping, she pulled away and sat bolt upright. Her eyes flashed wildly about the room in search of Abby.

"Shhh. It's okay, Jesse." Carly looked over at her maid, who was cleaning up after the doctor's visit. "Will you bring her a glass of water, please?" Turning back to Jesse, she pulled the blankets up a little. "It was just a bad dream. You're okay." With her arm around the back of Jesse's shoulder, Carly guided her back down to the mattress.

Jesse looked up at her, looked right through her eyes to her soul, it seemed, then let her head fall back on the pillows. She was asleep instantly.

- Tuesday -

Pale morning light seeped in through the French doors and the huge windows in the room. Jesse's aching body was enveloped in a warmth that encompassed all of her senses. Most especially, she was aware of the soothing classical music in the room and the enduring scent of perfume on the comforter, the same tangy herbal aroma from the Mercedes. Jesse breathed it in and immediately regretted it because of the wave of shock it sent to her ribs.

She was on her back with an ice pack under her neck and shoulders. Harley's head rested protectively on her chest. Turning her head, Jesse opened her eyes to see McCray sitting on the loveseat near the French doors. Her eyes were closed, her head tilted to the left. Her long ebony hair fell over the front of her shoulders. Her hands, cut and raw, dangled over the arm of the loveseat. The sleeve of her black thermal Henley was pulled up to her elbow, and a wide gauze bandage was wrapped around her wrist. Her notebook computer and her cell phone rested beside her, both folded and quiet.

Harley scooted up on his elbows and started his ritual of bathing Jesse's face with his tongue, and Jesse tried to move to pet him, but he had her pinned under the covers.

The events of the past evening replayed in her mind, including the final time Carly woke her. At that time, though they were both exhausted, emotionally and physically, they discussed the accident.

Carly was shocked as Jesse recounted how she had been forced off the road, and Jesse was equally as shocked to hear every horrifying detail of every horrifying moment afterward, as Carly came upon the accident. Jesse listened intently, without interrupting; sensing that this was something that Carly needed, that just talking about it was having a cathartic effect on her.

She explained how she'd seen the white pillar of smoke off the side of the road, described how the guard rail had been bent and twisted, and told of her panic when she smelled the gasoline and saw Jesse tangled in the back seat of the Mercedes.

Toward the end of the story, Carly took Jesse's hand in hers and entwined their fingers. She breathed out slowly, gently running her thumb along Jesse's thumb. Her tired gray eyes glistened like jewels in the dim light as she shifted them from their hands to Jesse. "When I first saw you, saw that you were still in the car, I thought I'd lost y....I thought you were dead."

"It takes a lot more than that to kill me," Jesse had replied, pulling her hand from Carly's grip. Even to her own ears it sounded as if her statement had been meant to dare the fates rather than to alleviate her client's concerns.

And she was sure that her client had many, many concerns. Her hands fiddled with the damp washcloth she'd been holding. "Jesse, will you be able to find out who's behind all of this?" she asked. "Can you help me?"

Jesse didn't remember answering her. The next thing she knew, the maid had come in to test her alertness. It was in stark contrast to Carly's technique. Like a drill sergeant, Karen stood over her in her pink bathrobe, curlers in her hair, hands on her hips, rifling questions at Jesse: "What's the date?", "Who's our President?", "What's your telephone number?" To that point, Jesse had answered correctly, but then Karen asked, "Who won Super Bowl twenty-one, the Redskins or the Broncos?"

Jesse thought about it for a moment and replied, "Neither. The Giants beat the Broncos 39-20."

"Wrong," Karen said automatically. "It was a trick question." Then, once she realized what Jesse had said, and realized further that she was correct, her eyes grew, and she looked at Jesse in utter surprise as she lifted Jesse's head to place another ice pack under her shoulders. She gave her a quick wink. "A girl after my own heart."

Thinking back to Karen's expression and her odd attempt at tripping her up, Jesse chuckled. She worked a hand free from under Harley and guided his head away. She'd had enough of his kisses. She rolled onto her side and groaned from the piercing jolt that shot up her neck. "Shit," she muttered, squeezing her eyes closed as if that would somehow shut out the pain.

"How do you feel?" a soft voice asked.

When Jesse opened her eyes again to half-mast, Carly was the only thing in her line of vision. She was beside the bed, staring down at her, her face drawn and gaunt. "Like my skull's about sixty sizes too small for its contents."

Carly smiled sympathetically at that. "Can I get you anything? Are you hungry? Would you like breakfast?" Jesse slowly shook her head, and Carly leaned to pet Harley. "I wish you'd have mentioned that Harley was a dog, not a small child. You kept saying, 'my boy Harley', and I just assumed he was your son." She laughed a little and held out her injured wrist. "Imagine my surprise when I stepped into your cabin and was mauled by this huge beast."

Jesse had to smile at that. Not the part about Carly being mauled, the part about her having a son. Now that was funny.

"Oh, and while I was at your cabin, your sister called."

"Oh, no," Jesse groaned. "You didn't tell her about the accident, did you?" Jesse pushed Harley away a little and tried to sit up despite the strong objections of her body.

"Well, yes. And she's been calling every hour to check on you."

"Shit," Jesse mumbled.

"She was so relieved after Dr. Moreland did some neurological tests and checked your reflexes. You kept saying that you couldn't feel your right side. You had me so scared. I was so afraid you might be paralyzed." She added, "You're very lucky to have a sister who cares so much about you. My sister and I were never close. Of course, we weren't twins like you and Lauren. Anne and I were eleven years apart. I'm sure that made a big difference. That, and the fact that she blamed me for Mother's death." She looked at Jesse with a kind of wonder. "I've always been fascinated by twins. It must have been so nice growing up with a built-in confidant, having such a close bond with someone, sharing everything with them."

"I have to put him outside," Jesse responded, gesturing toward her dog. She moved her right arm around and was gratified that she was getting a little more feeling in it.

"I'll take care of him," Carly offered. "And I'll get more ice for your neck while I'm downstairs."

"Don't bother," Jesse said as a tidal wave of nausea rolled over her and threatened to consume her. She put her head in her hands, waiting for the sensation to pass. Lightly touching the stitches on her forehead, she felt the crusted blood in her hair.

McCray picked up a dvd from her night table. "I spoke with Victor earlier and asked him the questions you'd given me." She handed it to Jesse, and Jesse set it back on the night table as she pulled the covers back and swung her legs over the edge of the bed.

"Does he drive a red Excursion or TrailBlazer?"

"No. He drives my old pick-up. And it's not red, it's dark green. He did tell me something, though, when I brought up your accident last night, about being run off the road by a red sport utility vehicle."

Jesse looked at her in expectation.

"He told me that he'd seen a red Excursion in the driveway the day before the boat explosion. He said he'd completely forgotten about it until I brought it up. I suppose it didn't really mean anything to him at the time because people sometimes mistake my driveway for a road. Or sometimes they're curious to see what's back here. Or sometimes they're lost and need directions."

"I don't suppose he got the tags, huh?"

"Pardon?"

"The tags. The license plate number."

"Oh, no," she replied. "He didn't get that. He did tell me that the driver, a brunette woman, talked to Susan for quite a while."

Out of curiosity, Jesse asked, "What'd he say about being fired by the Moriartys?"

Carly shrugged. Her hands fidgeted with the hem of her shirt.

"Didn't you ask?"

"Well, yes." She paused, but when Jesse gave her a look that urged her continue, she added, "Apparently he...he *was* working with Susan."

"And that's why she convinced you to hire him when she came here. I'll bet a million dollars they were doing it here, too." Carly replied with a disillusioned nod, and Jesse asked, "Did you fire him?"

Carly shook her head.

She can't be serious, Jesse thought. "But you're going to, right?"

"No," Carly answered. She must have read the astonishment on Jesse's face. She frowned. "It wasn't his fault, Jesse. Susan forced him into it. He obtained the semen from the horses. That was all. Susan had all of the contacts. She did the rest."

"And how'd she force him into it?" Jesse asked.

"He said that she'd threatened to call INS and have him deported. She told him that if he told anyone or refused her anything, he would be on his way back to El Salvador." She shrugged. "He didn't have a choice."

Jesse chuckled her sarcastic little laugh. "Of course he had a choice," she insisted. "And instead of making the right one, he made the easy one."

"Yes, but now that Susan's gone I'm quite sure he'll never do it again."

"Until he has the opportunity," Jesse jumped in. "Or until someone else comes along and threatens to have him deported."

"He's an honest person, Jesse."

"Whatever," she mumbled.

"He was a victim of circumstance. I trust him. I think he was very relieved to finally have gotten this off his chest. I think he deserves another chance."

Jesse grunted. "Suit yourself. He's your employee, not mine."

"Maybe you'll feel differently once you watch the dvd. It's all there. You can watch it while you're recuperating."

"I don't have time to recuperate. I've got to find the driver of that Excursion."

Jesse misjudged the distance to the floor as she pushed herself into a standing position. Carly must have seen her waver because her hand shot out to grip Jesse's arm. "I applaud your determination, Jesse, but you're not doing anything today. After I take you to the hospital for x-rays, you're going to call your sister and tell her you're okay, and then you're going to spend the rest of the day in bed. Dr. Moreland said that your concussion was…" She looked directly into

Jesse's eyes and stopped talking, and Jesse wondered if she was aware of the fact that her grasp had tightened on her arm and that she was pulling her closer.

"I'm fine," Jesse lied, untangling herself from Carly.

She looked down at the nightshirt she was wearing and knew that she had nothing on underneath. She could feel Carly staring at her, and couldn't describe the relief she felt when Carly answered her unasked question.

"Karen and Dr. Moreland changed you out of your clothes while I went to pick up Harley."

To support herself, Jesse grabbed the thick oak footboard of the king-sized sleigh bed and gazed around the bedroom for the first time.

The warm comfort and elegance from the lower level had clearly been carried throughout the house. The white marble fireplace on the wall across from the bed looked as though it had never been used. The furniture was also spotless, and the white sheer drapes over the multi-paned French doors that overlooked the Lake were tied open, giving Jesse her first glimpse of the breathtaking view of the cove. "Those should be closed," Jesse told her, motioning toward the drapes.

"Oh, I'm sorry. Is the light bothering you?" Carly hurried to close them.

"No," Jesse said. "I don't want you to be an easy target for a sniper." Jesse saw her terror when she snapped her head around to look at her. Without saying anything, she seemed to be asking Jesse if she honestly believed that there was a serious threat of something like that. Jesse responded with an expression that said, "You never know."

The nausea rose again, and Jesse took a few deep breaths to try to send it into remission. "Can you point me in the direction of a bathroom?" she asked urgently.

"You don't remember where it is?" Carly's voice was wrought with concern. "I showed you where it was twice last night, remember? It's right through here." Rushing up to her, Carly held onto Jesse's elbow and slowly led her across the room. "I set out some towels and a toothbrush and things. Had I been thinking clearly, I'd have packed a change of clothes for you while I was at your place. Karen is still soaking the clothes you wore last night so I left a sweatshirt and a pair of jeans on the counter for you. They'll probably be big on you, but you can roll up the sleeves and the legs. At least you'll have something to wear until your clothes are clean and dry. I don't even know if Karen will be able to get all of the blood off your blazer. And your pants were so stained with mud…Of course I'll reimburse you for everything…."

"It's okay," Jesse assured her, cutting off her nervous rambling.

"Let me know if you need anything." Carly opened the door to her changing room and as Jesse traveled through, she was awed by the expensive dresses and tailor-made business suits with both slacks and skirts.

There were hundreds of them in this mini-warehouse, all in

conservative, neutral shades, hanging uniformly on racks to Jesse's right. Off to her left was a collection of shoes that would put Imelda Marcos to shame. The cosmetic table, with its foreign-made skin care products near the mirrored vanity with lights all around it gave the room the appearance of a movie star's dressing room. How could she not have remembered any of this?

At last she came to the gray-tiled bathroom. Closing the door, she limped to the toilet and leaned way over, waiting. Nothing came, so she made her way to the counter and clung to it as she carefully slid the long nightshirt over her head. She looked over the luxurious sunken bathtub, the huge glass-enclosed shower stall, the skylight, and then made the mistake of looking at herself in the mirror.

"Oh, shit," she moaned. What a sight. She leaned over the counter and pulled her blood-coated hair off her forehead to get a better look at the row of fresh stitches that went all the way across, just above the hairline. A dark purple bruise had already formed around it. Jesse's tawny loose curls were more wild than usual. She looked like a mad scientist. Her green eyes were glazed and bloodshot as if she was stoned.

Aside from a few other scrapes and bruises, the rest of her body seemed intact. Sore, but intact. She took one of the fresh white towels from the stack that Carly had left for her, hung it on the brass hook near the shower stall, stepped in, and turned the dial, full blast, to hot.

"Aaaagh!" Eight separate shower heads were aimed right at her and pummeled her body with powerful jets of hot water that felt like zillions of tiny little needles piercing her skin.

Carly flew into the room. "Are you okay?"

Jesse saw her through the glass and made a hasty, bashful retreat to the far corner of the stall. "Why the hell didn't you warn me about this shower? Christ! I could've had a heart attack!"

Jesse was serious, but Carly laughed. "I'm sorry. I suppose it can be quite shocking if you're not accustomed to it."

"No shit," Jesse concurred.

"Um, Dr. Moreland said that you shouldn't get your stitches wet."

"They always say that," Jesse told her. The only movement she made was to lift her head to see if Carly was still in the room. "You can leave now."

Once she was fully clothed, Jesse returned to the shower and placed her hand on one side of the glass door while looking at it from the other side. "Shit," she grumbled. She could see her hand perfectly. No doubt Carly had a similar view of her.

While she rolled up the legs of her jeans to a point where she wouldn't be stepping on them, she spotted her cigarettes, along with the other contents of her pockets, on a gold plate at the other end of the counter. Thank God. Using the toilet as an ashtray, she enjoyed her morning smoke before going in search of something to eat.

She was on her way down the stairs and came upon a young man wiping up the dirty paw prints on the wooden steps of the grand staircase. He was at the mid-way point and looked up from his task as she approached.

"She doesn't let dogs in the house," he grumbled. He was dressed in khaki trousers and a long-sleeve navy t-shirt.

Jesse assumed by the family resemblance that he was Doug Heller, Carly's nephew. Both he and Carly were classically beautiful with very similar facial features: a slender nose, a delicately defined chin, a perfect mouth composed of sensuous lips which were neither too full nor too thin. It was no wonder that they both had the reputation of being popular with the ladies - even though he's engaged to be married. His dark hair was cut short, above the ears, well above the collar, with every strand in place.

It was hard to judge from Jesse's vantage point, but he looked as though he was well over six and a half feet tall. And he was built like a linebacker, very solid. From what Jesse had gathered from the newspaper articles regarding the explosion and the subsequent town gossip, he is a recent college graduate, now working for his aunt. His grandfather, Carly's father, had made Carly guardian of a substantial trust account, which will become his in its entirety on his twenty-fifth birthday.

Using the railing for support, Jesse made her way down to him. "I'll finish," she said, holding her hand out. Sure, she was sore and tired, and Carly could have hired just about anyone to clean the stairs, but Harley *was* her dog, her responsibility. The least she could do was clean up after him.

Doug straightened up and gladly handed her the cleaning supplies. "So you're the detective, huh? You don't look like a detective."

Jesse didn't know what people expected a detective to look like. She sometimes wondered if they'd take her more seriously if she took up smoking cigars. From this young man's tone, Jesse suspected that his comment wasn't meant as a compliment. She sat on the step and started wiping. She waited until he was at the top of the stairs and said something to the effect that he'd have a lot to gain if his aunt were to suffer an untimely death.

He stopped and turned around.

"All this would become yours, wouldn't it?"

"If this is your clever way of asking me if I had anything to do with the Mercedes being run off the road last night, I assure you, I didn't," he replied in his smooth Tom Brokaw voice. "I couldn't have. I was at the Lighthouse Pub when it happened."

"I didn't see you there."

"Stephanie - my fiancée - and I stopped in after a late dinner. We must have just missed you." He smiled. "She's right in here," he said, gesturing down the hallway toward a door. "You can ask her yourself if you don't believe me."

The front door opened at that moment, and Harley came dashing up the stairs to Jesse. Carly followed him in and spotted Jesse on the step as she closed the door.

"What are you doing?" she asked, surprised and angry.

"I'm cleaning his mess," Jesse told her, patting Harley's rear-end.

Her powerful glare went all the way up the stairs to her nephew. "Doug, I want to see you in the library." To Jesse, she said kindly, "Karen's making breakfast. Why don't you wait for us in the dining room?"

The maid was in the kitchen alone, cutting mushrooms and grating cheese. She glanced up when she heard the door from the dining room swing open. Her eyes grew wide. "Get that dog out of here!" she yelled, backing up against the counter. "He doesn't belong in the kitchen! Get him out!"

Startled, Jesse spun around and pushed the door open and pointed. "Out," she said. Harley understood and immediately obeyed, returning to the dining room. "Stay," Jesse told him, knowing that he would.

"He shouldn't even be in the house," the maid told Jesse. "We've never had dogs in the house. They've always stayed in the stable, but when Carly came home with him last night, he started scratching the front door. He wouldn't budge - he wouldn't stop scratching the door until she finally let him in."

Jesse smiled to herself. "Sorry."

"We just replaced that door last year. Now it's all scratched."

"I'm sorry," Jesse repeated. "I'll pay for the damages."

"Oh, that won't be necessary," Karen said, blowing it off. Jesse didn't get it. If she didn't want her to take care of it, why'd she make such a big issue out of it? What a strange woman.

"Breakfast will be ready in ten minutes," she told Jesse as she crossed to the pantry for a can of black olives. "Can I get you some coffee or juice?"

"Coffee'd be great. If you show me where the cups are, I'll get it."

"Nonsense. Sit."

Feeling slightly intimidated by this flinty old woman, Jesse did as she was told. She took a seat at the breakfast nook and watched her pour. "You weren't here at all the day of Susan's accident?"

Karen shook her head. "My sister-in-law had just been diagnosed with Hodgkin's disease and I went to Madison to be with her."

"You didn't notice anything unusual around here before that, did you? Any unusual phone calls or visitors?"

"I didn't see a thing."

"I get the feeling you didn't care for her all that much."

"For who, Susan? I didn't," Karen told her plainly. She set the cup of coffee in front of Jesse. "Cream or sugar?"

"No thanks." Jesse took a cautious sip and studied her. "Why didn't you like her?"

"I had my reasons," the maid responded simply.

"Can you be a little more specific?"

"Susan's gone. There's no sense dredging up things that are only going to disturb the peace around here."

"But if I'm going to find out the truth about what happened, I need to know what you're talking about."

Jesse's badgering was obviously irritating the maid. She looked up from the green pepper she was dicing. "I'll be serving breakfast in the dining room, not in here." She pointed to the door with the knife, and since it has always been Jesse's policy to never argue with someone wielding a sharp instrument, she left the room.

The table in the formal dining room looked so bare. There was room to seat at least twenty, but there were only three place settings. As Jesse pulled out a chair, she called Harley over to her and gave him some love. "I'm taking the money for the front door out of your allowance," she told him. He playfully bit her hand, and she slipped him a piece of bread that she swiped when the maid wasn't looking. He was still smacking it around in his lips when Carly walked in.

She smiled down at him as she took the chair right next to Jesse, at the head of the table. "Did you phone your sister?" she asked.

"Not yet," Jesse replied. Her voice, weaker than usual, crackled. She plucked a Marlboro from the pack and brought it to her lips.

"I'd prefer if you wouldn't smoke in my house."

"Oh." Jesse retracted the cigarette. *Should I confess that I smoked in the bathroom? Nah.*

"If you need to smoke, I'd rather you do it outside and not in the bathroom." Smiling at the guilty look on Jesse's face, she seemed to be inspecting her closely. "You're going back to bed when we get home from the hospital. You look awful." Jesse gave her a look feigning hurt feelings, and Carly quickly added, "That's not what I meant to say. What I meant to say was that you....you...look like...like..."

Jesse held back her laugh. "I know," she said, letting her off the hook. She opened her notepad and looked at her. "Are you going to work today?"

The doorbell rang, and Carly shook her head as she stood to get it. "Jacey's taking care of things this morning," she told Jesse on her way out of the room. "I'll either work from here or drive down later."

Jesse heard a man's voice talking in a kind and gentle manner with Carly. They came into the room together, and Carly invited him to join them.

"Jesse, this is Sheriff Richmond," she told her. "He wants to get your statement."

"That was quite an accident last night," he commented as he pulled out a chair. He was an older man with thinning gray hair, the stubby beginnings of a beard and mustache, and a big stomach that lapped over his belt. He nodded his thanks to Karen when she set a cup of coffee in front of him. Pulling a pen from the pocket of his uniform shirt, he wrote down the date on the form he'd brought with him. "Let's start with your name."

"Jesse Ferren," Jesse told him. She didn't particularly feel like talking, so she plucked her driver's license from her notepad and slid it across the table for him to copy. She glanced at her client and noticed how her features had tightened. She was staring intently at him, looking nervous.

"Want to tell me what happened last night?" he asked while filling out her address.

Jesse looked at Carly again. She was so tense. Her eyes seemed to be pleading with her, and Jesse understood immediately what she wanted. In the next moment, Jesse heard herself answer, "I swerved to avoid hitting a deer and lost control." She watched Carly breathe out slowly and look at the sheriff.

To Jesse's surprise, he didn't question the validity of her statement one bit. He just nodded and kept writing. "The road was slick with rain," he commented. "I'm sure that didn't help. Were ya wearin' your seat belt?"

"No."

He looked up. "You're lucky you weren't more seriously injured or killed, young lady. I hope you realize what Carly went through to get you out of that car. You owe her your life. If she hadn't come across you when she did, you most likely would have perished in that fire." He gave Carly a fatherly smile, and Carly glanced at Jesse before dropping her gaze in humility. "God, that's good coffee," he said, replacing his cup. He looked at Jesse. "Why were you driving her car?"

"Her car broke down when she came to visit me," Carly replied quickly.

The Sheriff nodded and finished writing something. "I'll need you to sign by the X," he told Jesse, passing the form over to her. To Carly, he said, "I'll have Mabel get you a copy of this for your

118

insurance."

Carly invited him to stay for breakfast, but he put his hands on his big belly and joked that he'd better not or his wife would have to let out the Santa suit a few more inches come Christmas.

Karen served breakfast while Carly walked the Sheriff to the door. Jesse couldn't wait and had half her omelet down by the time she got back. "For the next few weeks, I want you to keep a low profile," Jesse told her as she sat down. "I want you to close all of the drapes in the house. Don't follow your normal routine, don't take the same route to work, don't drive the same car, don't spend too much time outside, especially if you're in the open. Don't put your schedule on the computer or anyplace where someone might be able to see it. Don't tell anyone anything. You're going to start using the security system and close the gates at the end of your drive. I also want a list of people you know, anyone who might have some kind of motive to want you dead. That includes everyone," Jesse emphasized. "Friends, family, employees, former employees, customers, former lovers, everyone. I want names, addresses, phone numbers, anything you think might be important."

Carly nodded. Her expression told Jesse that she understood the gravity of the situation, but then she disappointed Jesse by saying, "I'll do my best to maintain a low profile, as you say, but I refuse to be held captive in my own home."

Jesse took a bite of toast and pretended to give her statement serious thought. "You're right," she said as if she was. "I wouldn't want to inconvenience you too much. Just go on with your normal activities. After all, what's the worst that could happen?"

Carly frowned at her. "All I'm saying is that I'm not....Do you honestly think all of this is necessary? Isn't it possible that last night's incident was....I don't know, random?"

How could it be possible that this woman was still in denial? Jesse gave her a look that assured her that it was not a random occurrence, but Carly continued: "Could it have had something to do with the fact that your judgment was impaired because you'd been drinking?" she picked up her cup and took a sip, glancing at Jesse over the rim.

Jesse saw her do that, saw the look on her face, and felt herself grow angry, not only because of her comment, but because her gesture reminded her so much of Abby. The woman didn't resemble Abby at all, but that one simple motion reminded Jesse of her, reminded her of how Abby had left her. That made Jesse even angrier, and she took it out on her client. "Jesus Christ," she muttered. "A few beers did not impair my fucking judgment!"

"First of all, you had *seven* beers! And secondly, there's no call for such profanity."

The volume of Jesse's voice was not helping her massive headache. "The hell there's not! You're making it sound like it was my fault! For your information, lady, I didn't just putter along until I flipped off the road!" Jesse tapped her cigarettes on the table, seriously considering lighting up right here, right now. "Whoever

120

was driving that Excursion wanted whoever was in that Mercedes dead! And it was your Mercedes, not mine! You do the math! I just happened to be in it at the time, just like Susan with the boat!"

Nice going, Jesse, she scolded herself, noting her client's look of horror. *You've got her scared to death. Well, maybe that's what she needed.* Jesse sighed and softened her tone just a bit. "Look, I know it's not a pleasant thing to acknowledge, but you've got to accept the fact that someone wants you dead. Your instinct was right. That's what sent you to me in the first place. But you've got to trust me. I know what I'm doing."

Jesse excused herself and went outside for a cigarette. Harley followed her out. They walked together to the McCray boathouse, which was a gigantic old structure at the bottom of the slope from the driveway. For an older building, it was well-preserved. The wide vertical gray boards appeared to have been recently painted. Birds chirped in the rafters as Jesse turned to look up to the house. Only someone standing in the driveway or garage would be able to see her. She tried the knob, and the birds fluttered above at the disturbance, squealing madly.

On a sunny day, light might have found its way through the knotholes and cracks in the walls, but not today. She found a light switch and flipped it, but the darkness endured. The echo of her boots on the planks joined the chorus of the birds and the waves slapping the sides of the building.

Along the deck were motorized winches and cables and chains

used to hoist the boats out of the water during the off-season. Two boats were suspended above her; one a small outboard, the other a good-sized cruiser.

The air felt cooler in here, thinner, as if it was at a high altitude. Under her heavy McCray Technology sweatshirt, she felt goose bumps up and down her arms. The old planks creaked below them as she and Harley crossed them together. Harley alternated between lifting his nose in the air and sweeping it along the wood, sniffing.

Jesse felt uneasy. To abate her anxiety, she pulled out her penlight and clicked it on, waving it back and forth on the boards just in front of them. She was about to take another step when she spotted small brown stains on the wood. Drops of something. Blood, perhaps?

Getting on her knees to inspect it more closely, she groaned. Her body was still so tender she had to use both hands to support herself, so she was on all fours with the penlight hanging out of her mouth. Harley seemed to think that they were playing some sort of game because he would charge at her, bring his front end down with his paws extended, ruff at her once, and then bounce backwards.

"Cut it out," she told him. Slowly, she moved her head back and forth, back and forth, pointing the light on the planks. There, wedged under a slightly protruding nail, was a scrap of torn cloth. It was a dark, thick material, denim.

Directing the penlight on it, Jesse bent over and saw the tiny brown specs on it. Reaching into her jeans pocket, she pulled out her small Swiss Army knife and drew out a blade. It took her only a moment to work the object free. Holding it between her fingers, she brought it up to the light. A fleck of dried blood came free when she touched the end of the cloth.

The cellophane wrapper from around her cigarette box made an innovative receptacle for it. Jesse crimped it closed on top, looked at the fabric once more through the clear plastic, and put it deep into her pocket before continuing with her search of the area. Just up ahead, she spotted a tiny white object that she initially assumed was a pebble, but it was too perfectly shaped to have been a small stone. Crawling up to it, she picked it up. It was a part of a tooth that had apparently been chipped off.

Harley's whine broke her out of her thought process. She looked out the service door and saw her client walking down the sloping path from the driveway. "Go ahead," Jesse told her dog, and Harley took off running toward Carly. Jesse tucked the tooth fragment into the cellophane wrapper with the denim material and closed the door to the boathouse. She lit a cigarette as she crossed the dock. Harley was walking with Carly, who was taking long fast strides on her way to Jesse, who was now leaning up against the railing, watching the water.

"I'm normally very slow to anger, Ms. Ferren, but you've crossed the line. How dare you invade my friends' privacy! And my nephew just informed me that you questioned him about the accident last night. What on earth possessed you to do that? What possible motive could he have to hurt you or me or anyone?"

Disappointed that she hadn't been able to figure that one out by herself, Jesse just looked at her. "Who's the primary beneficiary in your will?"

"That's personal! Other than my attorney, I'm the only one who knows what I'm bequeathing to whom, and I intend to keep it that way!"

Taking a puff of her cigarette, Jesse turned her gaze back to the turbulent waves of Lake Michigan.

"I also want to know why Chris and Chelsea are mentioned in here!" She waved Jesse's notepad at her. "Why were you in their house on the day I first met with you? They couldn't possibly have known that you were there because Chelsea was working and Chris was here! How could you invade my friends' privacy?" She threw the notepad at Jesse. It hit her on the knee and dropped to the wooden planks at her feet.

Bitch, Jesse thought. *Hypocritical Bitch.* She stepped on her notepad to keep it from blowing into the water, and then held her hand over her ribs as she stooped to pick it up. *Count to ten, Jesse, she instructed herself - count to ten. She's upset. She's scared. She's just blowing off steam.* This was all she could do to keep herself from telling this woman to take a flying leap. The wind whirled her hair around her head, and she pulled it out of her face as she slowly straightened up.

"Answer me! Is this how you conduct business? Wasting your

time and your client's money?" McCray ranted. "If you're going to continue working for me, you'd better start treating my friends and family with the respect they deserve!"

"Your friends and family haven't done anything to earn my respect," Jesse replied calmly, not at all intimidated by her veiled threat. "They don't automatically gain it by virtue of their relationship to you. And I couldn't possibly be wasting your money because you haven't paid me yet."

Although Jesse had scored an obvious point with that last remark, Carly was unmoved. She towered over Jesse, using her height to intimidate. "When are you going to have answers for me? You haven't even found Susan's parents yet, have you?"

"No,' Jesse replied angrily. "I haven't. That wasn't my number one priority. It's not relevant to the investigation, and I wanted to work on more important…."

"More important?" Carly asked shrilly. "So what have you done? You've been working on this case for over a week and there's nothing in your notes. Nothing! You've got a whole lot of questions but no answers."

"If you would have been honest with me from the start, maybe I'd be a lot farther along. Did you ever think of that? You're the one who wasted my fucking time!" Taking a step forward, Jesse got right in her face with a deadly, chilling expression. She tried to make her voice as penetrating as her stare. "And if you ever touch my notes again, I'll break every bone in your hand. Understand?"

Like protons and neutrons in the nucleus of an atom, they seemed to circle each other, both radiating mighty currents of energy. "Oh, I see. Respecting the privacy of others means nothing to you, but if someone should dare to invade your privacy…"

"I was doing my job! I had a reason to be at your friends' house. You had no reason to look through my notes. They're mine. They're private, and they're none of your business. Got it?" Carly's expression cut Jesse off. Wiping the dust from the brown leather cover, Jesse tucked her notepad into the back pocket of her jeans and backed up a step or two. Her tone became subdued, almost compassionate. "Look, I know you're frustrated. I know you're scared. But you're taking your anger and frustration out on the wrong person. I know that all I've got is a lot of questions, but that's good. That's my job. If I don't ask questions, I don't get answers." Jesse looked hard at her as if willing her to understand. "And I wouldn't be doing my job if I didn't at least suspect Chris and Chelsea or Doug. In a case like this, nobody is above suspicion. If someone did kill Susan and is gunning for you, too, it seems to me that it has to be someone who's fairly close to you, someone who knows your routine, someone who would have a lot to gain by your death." Jesse took a quick, final drag on her cigarette. "Tell me this: Do you think Susan would have left quietly if you had broken up with her?"

"What?"

Jesse made a face. *Does she think I'm stupid?* "You were planning to break up with her, right? But then she got sick and you

126

decided to wait until she was feeling better." Carly looked up at her house as Jesse went on. "You were with her for, what, seven months? She worked for you. Don't you think things could have gotten a little sticky? Do you think she might have sued you for palimony?"

She gave the matter very little thought. "I'm fairly certain that she would have pursued some sort of legal recourse if she wasn't happy with her severance."

"Is it possible that Chris, who would do 'anything in the world for you', took it upon herself to spare you the trouble, that she killed Susan, knowing that it might damage your reputation if you and Susan became involved in a long and ugly and public court battle?"

"Don't be ridiculous. Chris doesn't have a violent bone in her body."

"She's been nothing but hostile toward me. And she knew that you weren't driving the Mercedes last night. What if she did kill Susan, and now that you've hired me, she's getting scared?" Jesse pulled out another cigarette. "Has she been acting differently?"

An enraged expression clouded McCray's features, and Jesse made the quick decision to change the subject and move on to a different theory. "Was Susan in your will?"

"Of course not."

"Is it possible that whoever's trying to kill you thought that she might have been, that you might be leaving her a sizable amount, and decided to kill her first so they'd get a bigger piece of the pie?"

"I suppose that's possible, but..."

Jesse pulled out the cellophane wrapper. "I think Susan might have been dead - or at least wounded - before she even got on the boat."

"What is that?"

"Some ripped fabric and part of a tooth."

McCray took it from her. Pushing her hair behind her ears, she held it up to inspect it closely. "Where did you find this?"

"In there," Jesse told her, nodding toward the boathouse. "There were stains - I'm assuming blood stains - near it, so I'm thinking Susan might have been in a struggle with someone before she even got onto the boat. That might explain why she didn't answer when you tried to call her." While McCray continued to examine the package from every conceivable angle, Jesse said, "I doubt if a dentist would be able to tell anything from this; it's such a tiny piece. Maybe, if the coroner saved some tissue or blood or something, we could send this off to a lab and see if they could somehow confirm or refute that it was hers."

With a shaky hand, Carly gave the small package back to Jesse. "I don't want anyone involved in this," Carly told her. "I can't imagine who else would have lost a tooth in there without me knowing about it. And if there are stains on the boards, they had to have gotten there fairly recently, because I just had the dock, the boathouse, everything cleaned in August before I had the weatherproofing applied. It must have been hers. But…"

"Okay. Let's assume that it is. So now with Susan out of the picture, it seems to me that Chris, Chelsea, and Doug would all have a lot to gain financially - or at least *think* they'd have a lot to gain - if you were to die."

Unwilling to see Jesse's point, Carly shook her head vigorously. "I've known Chris for twenty-seven years and Chelsea for the past three years. I love and trust them both. And I've known Doug since the day he was born. I helped raise him after my sister died. If any of them wanted to kill me for my money, why would they have waited this long to do it?"

Jesse immediately thought of Chris' current financial situation. "Maybe Chris and Chelsea need the money," she suggested gently.

"Don't be ridiculous. They don't need money. They're living comfortably," she replied. "And if they were having financial difficulties, they know I'd gladly help them."

"Have they made any major purchases lately? Taken a long vacation?"

McCray's eyes narrowed for a second, then returned to normal. Along with her curious expression, she was beginning to look a little uncomfortable, and Jesse knew she'd have to tread lightly here. At last, Carly shook her head. "They were supposed to have vacationed with Susan and me in late May, but Chelsea had to spend eight weeks in Minneapolis at a nursing seminar." Sighing heavily with exasperation, she tucked her hands in her pockets.

Jesse quickly changed the subject again. "What about Doug?"

"What about him?" Obviously troubled, Carly folded her arms

across her chest and scrutinized Jesse. "You don't trust anyone, do you?" she asked with reproach.

"You're not paying me to trust people." Jesse took a drag of her Marlboro, which she had neglected for so long, it had almost gone out already. "Actually, you're not paying me at all," she said, grinning, trying to keep the conversation from declining into another shout-fest.

"Tell me," Carly said, showing an inane interest in her philosophy, "is it your line of work that has made you such a cynic? Or have you always had an unhealthy degree of distrust in people?"

Despite her gallant efforts, Jesse could not fend off her client's unrelenting and misdirected antagonism. "I've always had it. That's what makes me so good at what I do. I call it reality. And if you think that people won't lie, cheat, and steal to serve their own interests, then you're living in some kind of fantasy world." The creases in Jesse's forehead deepened. "And speaking of trust and distrust, did you ever consider that you might have an unhealthy degree of trust in the wrong people? You sit there and tell your friends and your nephew every detail of this case, yet it never occurred to you that one of them might have killed Susan, and that you might be next. You won't fire a man whose been stealing from you and lying to you since the day he came to work for you. And you come to me for help, practically beg me to take this case, but you don't bother to tell me that I wasn't really supposed to be looking into Susan's death, that the real reason you hired me was to find out if someone was trying to kill you." Using her hand to shield the wind as she lit yet another cigarette, she continued, holding the cigarette between her teeth, "And then you have the nerve to tell me that I'm wasting your time and money?"

Abby had often told Jesse that she had a wicked stare and that she knew precisely how to use it. And she was using it now, boring those intense green eyes deep into her client. Jesse made sure to give her a good long look that she was sure stretched well beyond her comfort level. "You've pretty much broken all of my rules. If you're going to keep breaking them, tell me right now, and I'll be happy to leave."

The air was taut. Both women sensed the palpable buzzing between them. McCray shivered, whether from her own inner turmoil or the breeze, Jesse couldn't be sure. She watched her pull her hands out of the pockets of her nylon jacket and zip it to her chin. She looked down at Harley and said quietly, "I don't want you to leave."

* * * *

It was going to be a short day. Despite Jesse's feeble condition, she worked on her car for the rest of the morning. It was a compromise that she and Carly had come to - without argument. Jesse refused to go to the hospital for x-rays, insisting she was fine -- and Carly wouldn't let her out of the house until she was confident that Jesse was okay. According to Carly, Jesse still "did not look well at all."

By eleven thirty, Jesse had pin-pointed the problem with her Fiat and walked into the house through the door from the garage and found Karen in the bright, warm laundry room off the back hallway. The scent of fabric softener hit her as she stepped in. "Where's Carly?" she asked over the low hum of the commercial, stainless-steel washing machine.

"She's in the library," Karen replied, folding a pair of jeans and setting them on the table in front of her. "She's in the middle of a video conference with her office and asked not to be disturbed. Is there something I can do for you?"

Jesse chuckled, faint, quick, humorless. "Not unless you know how to rebuild the starter on a '79 Fiat."

Through Karen, Jesse relayed the problem to her client, and Carly agreed to let her use the gold Lexus that was parked in the garage stall next to her ailing Fiat.

As she slid in behind the wheel, before she even put the key in the ignition, she froze. Abby's image flashed into her mind. It was as if she had transcended the boundaries of time and reality and found herself huddled with Abby before a campfire, having one of their intimate talks. Jesse was on the ground at Abby's feet. Her back was to Abby, sitting between her legs. Her arms rested on Abby's thighs, and Abby was leaning over to whisper something to her, something about the clear night sky, the stars, eternity, and Jesse felt the heat from her breath as it brushed past her ear. It was so real Jesse could actually feel the pressure of Abby's breasts on her back. She turned to see Abby's beautiful face, which seemed to undulate with the light from the fire. She was inextricably trapped in Abby's eyes, her warm, loving smile, but just as she reached her hand out to touch her, the image vanished. Abby was gone.

A cold chill cut through Jesse's body, and she was frozen in that spot for another long moment, blinking several times, half expecting Abby to return. "God," she muttered, shaking, "I'm losing my mind. Now it's happening when I'm awake."

Her first stop was back on Washington Island, where she went to her cabin to change her clothes and feed Harley as she dropped him off. She also called the Indiana Department of Vital Statistics in Indianapolis to arrange for Susan's birth certificate to be sent to her.

While she was on the phone, she looked across the room. The picture of her with Abby on the table next to the sofa had been moved. It was a few inches from its original position, at a different angle, and she assumed Carly had looked at it while she was there to pick up Harley.

After hanging up, she plopped down on the chair next to the sofa-bed and put her feet up on the mattress. She picked up the picture and stared at it for a long time. It was taken eight years ago, a week after Abby's twenty-first birthday, while they were visiting Joan and Lauren in Phoenix. They were still in school at ASU, and Jesse and Abby had gone to help them move to a different apartment. They had taken Jesse's motorcycle from their place in Santa Barbara, and Abby's face was red from wind-burn. Jesse couldn't help but notice how young they both looked in the photo. So young. And so happy.

Abby was sitting beside her on Lauren's couch, a glass of wine in one hand, a book in the other. She was looking directly into the camera and couldn't have looked more beautiful. Her smile always seemed to come from within, and Jesse was thrilled every time she directed it at her. Even now, all these years later, just looking at her in the photo gave Jesse a warm feeling inside.

All of a sudden, though, a deep sadness started to creep in, so she hurried to put the picture back. She looked around the cabin to see what else Carly might have found while she was snooping last night. There wasn't much there. Nobody could accuse Jesse of being materialistic. Everything she owned, she could carry in her duffle bag.

The phone rang as she was on her way out.

"Why didn't you call me? Didn't Carly give you the message? God, I've been worried sick!" Recognizing her twin sister's voice, Jesse rolled her eyes. "You get to a hospital today, Jess. Have them take x-rays. You could have broken something. Or you might have internal injuries. And if your side's still numb, make sure...."

"It's not numb anymore, Lauren. It's fine. I'm fine. What the hell were you thinking, calling my client every hour last night?"

"I was worried, Jess. And she...Carly didn't seem to mind."

"Well I mind! How'd you like it if I called your patients in the middle of the night and told them that I was worried about you? Think they'd have any confidence in you at all after that? Christ, Lauren!"

"I wasn't thinking about it in those terms, Jesse. All I knew was that something was wrong, and I had to know that you were okay before I could go to sleep. I'm sorry if I embarrassed you in front of your client. That wasn't my intent."

Jesse lit a cigarette. "You didn't tell her anything, did you?"

"No, nothing. I promise."

"How'd she find out we're twins?"

"Oh, well I didn't see any harm in telling her *that*. Besides, she asked how I knew you - she wanted to know why I was calling. When I told her, and when she told me that you'd been in an accident, all I did was ask her how you were; that's all. Except the last time I talked to her, a little while ago, I think she might have heard something on the television in the background and thought we had kids or something so she asked about my family. That's how we got to talking about how Joan and I were going to have a baby."

"Oh, Jesus," Jesse muttered, bringing her hand to her head.

"All those times I talked to her last night, it never occurred to me that she was gay. We must have talked for over an hour. She talked about how she's always wanted a big family and lots of kids, and she asked tons of questions about artificial insemination, how Joan and I chose the donor, how we decided which of us would carry the baby. I really like her, Jess. She seems nice."

"Yeah, she's a real peach," Jesse said sarcastically. "Just do me a favor and don't call her anymore."

"I won't. Oh, but I promised to e-mail her with some information about AI. And she's going to send me the name of an accountant friend of hers so we can get a grip on our finances and set up a real plan, you know, for our clinic." There was a protracted silence between them until Lauren cleared her throat and said, "Uh, Jess?"

"What?"

"Um, Joan and I are going to take some time off before the baby comes. We were thinking maybe you could come here..."

"I'm not coming back, Lauren."

"Well maybe we could come see you," Lauren suggested. "We could bring Nanna!"

"We'll see. I'm not making any promises, though."

Lauren was pleasantly surprised that Jesse had conceded that much. She was aware that Jesse never made a promise that she couldn't keep, so she knew better than to push it. But she couldn't resist the opportunity to add, "Great! It'd be nice to meet Carly, too. She seems so..."

"I've got to get to work, Lauren. I'll call you Saturday, okay? Say 'hi' to Joan and dad and Nanna for me." And she hung up.

She filled Harley's water bowl and left to retrace her steps of the previous evening, canvassing the area where the Excursion had first started following her. She stopped to speak with people at the gas station/convenience store, neighboring houses, and came up empty. Nobody had seen a red Excursion.

Next, she went to the bank to cash the check that Carly had given her after their tiff on the dock. She glanced again at the amount and shook her head, chuckling to herself. It was more than most people make in a year.

"And if there's anything left when you're through with your investigation," McCray had told her as she handed it to her, "I want you to keep it - as compensation for your injuries."

Of course, Jesse had objected, recoiling from the check as if it was some sort of venomous snake, but Carly insisted. And somehow, her way of insisting made it impossible to refuse. Jesse was puzzled and disturbed that she had such a hard time saying "no" to her.

"I'm sorry, ma'am, but I can't cash this for you."

"Huh?" That brought Jesse back.

"There's a problem with this account," the teller told her, flipping the check over in his hand. "You'll have to talk to the person who wrote..." He noticed the name on the front. "Hang on a minute. Let me get the Manager."

Jesse watched him talk with another man, both of them operating the keyboard and then looking at the monitor as if they were trying to figure out what they were doing wrong. Ten minutes Jesse waited, drumming her fingers on the counter, sighing. Her stomach growled. She wanted to growl.

"Look," she finally blurted, "why don't you just give me back the check and I'll talk to Carly about it, okay?"

* * * *

137

A black Contour was parked in the driveway of Chris Masters' house, its trunk open, and Jesse pulled in behind it just as Chelsea came out the front door. In a way, Jesse was relieved to find Chelsea there and not Chris, because in Jesse's frame of mind, she was not looking forward to talking to Carly's contentious friend.

Chelsea was wearing her nurse's uniform, white cotton slacks and a white blouse under a red cardigan. She smiled big when she saw Jesse. "Hi! Jesse, right?" She pulled out two eight-packs of Diet Coke, set one on the gravel driveway, and slammed the trunk. "I heard what happened last night. Are you okay?"

"How'd you hear about it?" Jesse followed her into the house.

Closing the door behind them with her foot, Chelsea smiled over her shoulder on the way to the kitchen. "From Chris. Carly called this morning and told her that you'd been in an accident with the Mercedes, that someone forced you off the road." She set the Cokes on the counter and started unloading the other groceries.

"What time did Doug and Stephanie get there? Do you remember?"

"Oh, they got there right after Carly left. Like ten minutes later."

"And what time did they leave?"

Chelsea paused to think about it, tilting her head backwards a little. "I don't know for sure. They were still there when we left. Doug was playing poker with some of Chris' brothers, so probably not until two-thirty, maybe three."

"What was Stephanie doing?"

"She was at the table with Chris' sisters-in-law and Ella." She turned with a smile and explained, "That's Chris' mom."

"When did you and Chris leave?"

"About an hour after you and Carly left. Chris knew I had to get up early this morning." Chelsea's kind smile faded. "Why are you asking me all these questions? You don't think…"

"It's routine," Jesse fibbed just a little. "I always start with those most familiar to the victim and then work my way out. So where's Chris now?"

Turning to put a box of Tender Vittles into the cupboard, Chelsea glanced at the clock on the microwave. "She's either on her way home or she went to see Carly."

"Those two sure spend a lot of time together," Jesse commented causally.

"Making up for lost time, I guess."

"What do you mean?"

"They didn't see much of each other while Carly was with Susan because Carly started spending a lot of time at the office after Susan moved in with her. She worked probably eighty or ninety hours a week. Now that Susan's gone, though, she's spending a lot more time at home."

Jesse was confused. "If she didn't like spending time with Susan, why did she stay with her for seven months? Why didn't she break up with her?"

Favoring Jesse with an ironic little laugh, Chelsea leaned her large frame against the counter. "I think that was Chris' doing. Before Carly even met Susan, she and Doug had been badgering her to settle down with someone and I think Carly took that as a challenge. I think she wanted to show them - and herself - that she could sustain a relationship with a woman for longer than one night or a weekend. But Susan and Carly never really had a relationship. I'm sure Carly cared for her, but I think she was just a....I don't know, a weekend fling that lasted seven months."

Jesse squinted, trying to bring Chelsea into focus. Her headache was growing progressively worse. And the nausea was returning. She took a seat at the table in the dinette. "So how did Chris and Susan get along?"

"They didn't exactly hit it off. For Carly's sake, they tolerated each other when we all went somewhere together but I don't think Chris approved of Susan." Jesse was hardly surprised by that. "I don't think it was anything she did or said, it's just....Well, I don't think anyone Carly went out with would ever measure up to Chris' standards."

"Was she jealous of Susan?"

Chelsea frowned at her. "Why would she have been jealous of her?"

Jesse shrugged.

"Chris never had to compete with her for Carly's time, if that's what you're getting at." Chelsea turned on the chandelier over the dining room table. "She knew Carly was there for her no matter what."

Jesse propped her head up with her hands. "Has their relationship ever come between you and Chris?"

"Not really," Chelsea replied indefinitely, turning to put a gallon of milk in the refrigerator. "I mean, when we first started going out, it took me a while to figure out their relationship. I couldn't believe that, as close as those two are that it was always strictly platonic. But it is. And for a while, when Chris spent more time with Carly than she did with me, I...I'll admit I was jealous. But now Carly and I have become good friends, too. And I know where I stand with Chris."

Jesse watched her pull the Coke bottles one-by-one from the plastic rings that held them together. "Where is that exactly?"

Lining the Coke bottles on the top shelf of the refrigerator, faced away from Jesse, Chelsea paused for a split-second, and catching it, Jesse knew that she was on to something.

Chelsea turned to look at her. "We've been together happily for three years now. I think that speaks for itself."

Jesse watched her cut up the plastic that held the bottles together. "Did Chris fly out to see you a lot this past summer when you were in Minneapolis?"

Visibly shaken by that question, Chelsea turned to the sink and ran water over the pile of fresh vegetables she'd just dumped in. "Once or twice," she replied with her back to Jesse. Her voice was unusually high and quiet.

"Carly told me you were gone for eight weeks, at a seminar." In hot pursuit, she moved to a stool on the other side of the snack counter. "What kind of seminar was it?"

"It had to do with patient relations," Chelsea told her quietly.

"Where was it?"

"Minnesota State."

"Must've cost you a fortune," Jesse commented.

"Not really. My, um, the hospital reimbursed me for it." Chelsea glanced at Jesse over her shoulder. She looked like a spooked horse. "Look, I'm kind of busy. We're baby-sitting Chris' nieces and nephews tonight and I've got to change and get dinner started, so if you don't mind...."

* * * *

The police file, photos, everything Jesse had gathered so far in the case was neatly spread out on the table in her cabin. While waiting for her frozen pizza to finish baking in the next cabin, wearing only trousers and a t-shirt, Jesse took notes on her interview with Chelsea. It was still early, only four-fifteen, but Jesse was tired. And sore. Everything ached, and all she wanted to do was eat and go to bed.

Propping the phone between her shoulder and ear, she dialed the number for the Bursar's office at Minnesota State and turned the page in her notepad.

Someone finally answered after six rings, and Jesse picked up her pen. Pretending to be Chelsea Johnson, she requested a receipt for the nursing seminar she attended in May, explaining that she needed it in order to get reimbursed for it by her employer.

"Give me your student ID number," the woman on the other end of the line sighed.

"I don't have it with me. I'm calling from work."

"It's your social security number," she told Jesse.

"Oh." Turning to that page in her notepad, Jesse read Chelsea Johnson's social security number to her and heard the tapping of keys on a keyboard. When the woman told Jesse that she didn't show up, Jesse requested to be transferred to the Registrar's office.

Harley's whine diverted her attention, and she glanced at him, noting that his ears were perked as he hopped down from his spot on the couch and trotted to the door. Jesse put her hand over the mouthpiece. "Knock it off. I just walked you."

A woman named Kelly came on the line and Jesse explained that she was updating her resume and that she needed the name of the nursing seminar she attended in May. She told Kelly that it dealt with patient relations, but she couldn't recall the exact title.

Harley scratched at the door and whined again, and Jesse frowned at him. "Stop it! What is wrong with you?"

"Ma'am, the only nursing seminar offered during the summer session was OR Techniques. It had nothing to do with patient relations."

"Thanks." Jesse hung up and muttered, "I knew it."

There was a noise just outside her cabin door. Glancing at Harley, Jesse got up to check on it. Much to her surprise, Carly was standing right there in front of her when she flung open the door.

Her hand flew to her throat. "You scared me half to death! You didn't even give me a chance to knock." She looked tired, overworked, troubled, but she still managed a warm, shy smile when their eyes met. "You, um, I received a call from the bank. Gerald told me that you'd been there with the check I'd given you and, uh, I don't know what to say. This has never happened to me before."

"Now you know why I prefer cash," Jesse commented lightly.

Carly looked offended, as if Jesse had assumed that bouncing checks was an on-going problem of hers. "There was some sort of mix-up with the computer either at the bank or from my office and some of my deposits were never posted and...I'm so sorry. I..." She blew out a long breath. She seemed so embarrassed Jesse thought she might actually cry.

Instead, she thrust out an envelope. It was full of cash, mostly hundreds and fifties. Jesse took it from her and motioned her in, glimpsing into the parking lot as she closed the door.

"Oh, and you forgot this at the house and I thought you might want to watch it tonight." Seeming strangely unsure of herself, Carly held out a dvd, then started digging into her briefcase for something. "It's the, um, the interview with Victor. I didn't know if you had a dvd player, so I brought this, too." She found what she was looking for and held out a portable dvd player.

"Thanks," Jesse took everything from her and put it on the money on the countertop in the kitchen.

Carly fidgeted with the strap on her briefcase, shifting her gaze from Jesse to her hands and back again. "I, uh, also want to apologize for this morning. I don't know why I unloaded all of my frustration on you." She smiled a quick, self-conscious grin. "Maybe Chris is right. Maybe I should see a psychologist."

Maybe you should, Jesse thought privately. The timer on the microwave went off, and Jesse wisely closed the cover to her notepad as she excused herself to retrieve her pizza from the cabin next door. Carly was standing near the table when she came back with her cheese pizza.

"My oven doesn't work," she explained while crossing in front of her, "so I have to use the one next door."

Looking a little disoriented, McCray checked her watch. "I'm sorry. I didn't realize how late...that you were about to have dinner. I should have called first."

"It's okay," Jesse told her, pulling out a chair for her at her worn card table before crossing to the kitchen area again. She left the pizza on the cardboard circle while she sliced it, then tossed it on the table. On her way to the refrigerator for a beer, she hesitated. "Want some? I could get a plate."

Lowering herself into the chair, McCray appraised the food that Jesse set out in front of her. "No thank you. Karen fixed a light lunch for me earlier." She reached into her briefcase and withdrew a manila folder. "I've brought my list. It took me nearly all afternoon to merge the proper files to compose it, but I believe I've included just about everyone." Opening the front cover, she tapped her perfectly manicured finger on the bottom of the first page. "There's a key to let you know how I know each of these people."

Of course there is, Jesse thought. She nodded, taking a look at it as she sat down to eat. Little red hearts, she noticed, were used to designate past lovers. Cute. But it wasn't so cute anymore when Jesse noticed that twelve of those tiny hearts dotted the first page alone. And there appeared to be a minimum of fifty pages, each with approximately one hundred names. Jesse did the math in her head as she browsed through the pages. Pausing at one name with a heart beside it, she looked at her client. "Isn't she a model?"

Carly nodded, and Jesse fixed her with an indistinct look as she slid the folder back to her. "It's nice that you've got them all in alphabetical order with addresses and phone numbers and everything, but I want you to narrow it down. Just give me the names of the people who know your daily routine or have access to your schedule, anyone who you think might have motive or opportunity to kill you or to have killed Susan."

"I'll work on it tonight."

"I want to show you something," Jesse said, wiping her hands on a napkin before handling one of the photos. It was a gruesome picture of the head, and Jesse was sure that Carly was wondering how she could bear to look at it while she ate. Truthfully, it was making Jesse a little sick. She couldn't imagine ever getting accustomed to looking at photos like this without feeling queasy. Most of the flesh on the face and scalp was seared off, and the skull was partially charred.

Jesse tapped her finger on the victim's mouth. "Look at this. See there? Looks like she's missing a tooth, doesn't it?"

Carly reluctantly leaned in for a better view. "Which one?"

"Right there, the cuspid. It looks like it's gone." Jesse brought the photo closer. "It's hard to tell from this picture, but it looks like there are a couple of teeth missing." Jesse paused to think about that for a moment. "I doubt that the explosion would have blown them out." She took a bite of pizza, wiping her mouth. Finally, she said, "Did she have false teeth or crowns or something?"

Carly apparently didn't have the stomach to look at the photo any longer. "I...I don't know." She gazed around the cabin, while Jesse continued to stare at the picture, eating her dinner. The silence around them grew deeper by degrees.

Several long moments passed. Carly sighed. She drummed her fingernails on the table. When that didn't get Jesse's attention, she said, "Chelsea called me a little while ago and told me that you'd been to see her." Slowly, Jesse looked from the photo to her client. "She was concerned because you...you looked a bit pale. Now that I'm here, now that I see you, I must admit that she was right to be concerned. You look worse now than you did this morning." Her fingers fussed with a rip in the vinyl table top. "Please don't take this the wrong way: I want you to stay at my house tonight so I'll know you're okay. Karen's already prepared a guest room for..."

"I can take care of myself." Jesse hoped the defensive edge in her voice wasn't as obvious to Carly as it was to her.

It must have been, because Carly's tone softened considerably. "I didn't mean to imply that you can't, Jesse. You were seriously injured last night, and I merely thought it would be better for you, in your condition...."

"I said I can take care of myself." Jesse took a long sip of beer and returned to her dinner.

Silence again gathered around them. Harley seemed to sense the tension. He picked up a rolled up sock and dropped it in Carly's lap, plunking his enormous body on the floor at her feet. She smiled down at him, and in a high-pitched voice that adults normally reserve for small children, said, "Well hello, Mr. Harley! It's so nice to see you again! You're such a beautiful dog! Yes, you are!" As she rubbed his neck, his tags jingled against his collar. "I love his colors," she told Jesse. "I don't think I've ever seen a German shepherd with so much black. Usually they have the black in the face and the sock and the saddle area, but he's almost completely black. Is he a purebred?"

Jesse shook her head. "Part Lab."

Carly combed her fingers through is thick coat. "But he's got the size and expressive face of a shepherd," she said absently, staring at him, petting him. "Very intelligent, beautiful dark eyes. So dark."

She didn't seem to notice that she was working up the big tumbleweeds of hair that surrounded him on the floor. "How old is he?"

Jesse's mouth was full of food so she held up three fingers.

"Did you train him yourself?"

Swallowing, Jesse nodded, flipping her curls over her shoulder in the process.

Then Carly said something that took Jesse completely by surprise. "And you won the custody battle for him when you and that woman separated?" She gestured toward the picture of Abby across the room.

Hurt, angry, offended, Jesse lifted her head from her dinner. She was sure that Carly had no trouble reading each of those emotions in her eyes because Carly looked like she suddenly regretted having made such a personal inquiry.

Neither of them spoke again for a long, long while as Carly continued to pet Harley, watching Jesse eat. Abby used to tease Jesse about how vigorously she attacked her food, and she was right - Jesse had always enjoyed a healthy appetite. It wasn't that she was ill-mannered, necessarily; she's just always eaten with great enthusiasm. She'd never been self-conscious about it. Until now. Carly was making her very uncomfortable, the way she was looking at her. She was probably trying to figure out how Jesse could eat as much as she did and still weigh less than Harley.

It hadn't always been that way. While with Abby, although they were both very active, Jesse's weight increased little by little. She had been a good twenty-five pounds overweight and happier than she ever thought she deserved to be. Abby loved to cook and was great at it. But then everything changed. In a matter of weeks after Abby's departure, Jesse lost more than fifty pounds. She doubted if Abby knew how shattered she left her.

"I was thinking about hiring a bodyguard," Carly said, taking Jesse from her brooding.

Jesse popped the last piece of pizza into her mouth and got up from the table to throw her plate in the garbage. "That's probably not a bad idea," she said, swallowing. She lit a cigarette and leaned back against the counter, folding her arms across her chest.

"I thought perhaps you...."

Jesse's expression took on an ironic twist. "Just a few minutes ago," she said, "you were so concerned about me that you wanted me to stay with you. Now you want me to throw myself in front of a bullet for you?" She exhaled smoke with a little laugh. "Which is it?"

Jesse enjoyed how Carly looked so flustered. She loved doing that to people.

"No! That's...I *am* concerned..."

Jesse broke her off with a cynical chuckle. "I'm an investigator, Carly. Not a bodyguard. I can't watch you twenty-four hours a day and conduct a proper investigation at the same time."

"Well, yes." Carly's hand fidgeted with Harley's ear. "Of course.

I just thought, um, we have excellent security at the office…it's…at home. Even if I activate the alarm system, anybody could break in and kill me before the police arrived. And Doug's going to be in and out of town for the next two weeks and…"

Jesse inhaled on her cigarette. While she was concerned for Carly's safety - and her own - she was also concerned that Carly might interpret her presence in her home as an invitation to make their relationship more intimate. "I don't think so," Jesse said, blowing smoke through her nose and mouth. "Why don't you see if Beth can find one for you?"

"I suppose that's what I'll end up doing if…It's just…the idea of living under the same roof with some stranger, some muscle-bound, brainless thug doesn't appeal to me in the least. That's why I thought I'd ask you first."

"If you're just looking for someone to stay with you, why don't you ask Chris to move in with you for a while?"

Carly smiled briefly, shaking her head. "I know she'd do anything for me, but she's so opposed to any kind of violence, she'd probably freeze if someone actually broke in." Breathing out slowly, she looked at Jesse, her fearful expression a desperate appeal.

But despite her compelling facial cast, despite her apparent vulnerability, Jesse stood firm in her denial. She turned away, flicking her ashes into the stainless steel sink.

"It's not as though I'm asking you to risk your life for me, Jesse. I'd merely like you to be there with me in case…"

"No."

"I'll double your salary," she offered.

"Money's not an issue."

"I'll let you smoke in the house."

With a discouraging yet not unpleasant closed-mouth smile, Jesse refused again, but Carly, apparently, wasn't about to back down. Jesse guessed that she wasn't used to people saying "no" to her. Her fingers continued to play with Harley's pointy ears as she thought of a different approach. "Well," she said at last, "if you won't help me, may I at least borrow your dog until you find out who is trying to kill me?" She seemed half-serious, half-joking as she tried to affect her most influential pout.

They looked at each other then, and Jesse was sure she sensed by her tiny sneer that her resolve was melting. Carly's pout grew more dramatic as she ran her hand down the dog's back. "What do you say, Mr. Harley, will you live with me for a few weeks?"

He stretched his neck to lick her cheek. His tail thumped hard on the linoleum, and Carly playfully replied for him, giving him a deep and dopey voice, like Bullwinkle's. "A few weeks? I don't think I can make that kind of commitment to a woman."

"I understand," Carly told him, grinning. Jesse was sure she did understand. She was also sure that Carly knew that Jesse was staring at her in astonishment as she made an ass of herself, but Carly didn't seem to care. At this point, it was clear that her determination had taken over.

Taking the dog's face in her hands, she spoke to Jesse through him. "If you did come to live with me, you'd have your own bedroom, of course, plenty of good food, and the run of the house. We'll have all of your phone calls forwarded so you won't have to run back here to check your messages."

Using the dog as a puppet, she tilted his head toward Jesse. "What would I do with her if I decided to go?" Harley asked in the dopey voice that Carly had given him.

Carly looked over at Jesse as if giving the matter serious consideration. "You could put her in a kennel."

"No. I couldn't do that," Jesse's dog replied heavily. "It'd be cruel to cage her up like that. Besides, she probably wouldn't get along with the other dogs."

"Hmmmm." While giving Jesse a long look, Carly touched her index finger to her chin, thinking. "I guess you'll just have to take her with you. She's small, keeps to herself, probably won't be too much trouble."

Even though Jesse rolled her eyes and grunted, she had to admit that she was genuinely entertained by this performance. And when she asked Harley if Jesse was house-broken, Jesse nearly laughed out loud.

"Oh, for Christ's sake," Jesse groaned, walking toward the bathroom. "Let me pack a few things."

Carly looked at Jesse's dog. "Is she always this grumpy?"

This time Jesse answered for him, using the very same

Bullwinkle voice, except hers came out a little growly. "Lady, you haven't seen grumpy."

* * * *

"Why don't I give you a tour of the house while Karen brings your bag to your room? You didn't have a chance to see everything before you left this morning."

After a quick journey through the lower level, which included the library, the kitchen, Karen's living quarters, the laundry room and an indoor pool adjoined by a work-out room, Carly led Jesse to the staircase off the front entrance and preceded her up the steps. "Upstairs there are seven bedrooms, each with adjoining bathrooms." She opened the first door on her right and turned on the light. "This is - was - Susan's room."

"You had separate bedrooms?" Jesse could tell that her tone embarrassed Carly.

She dropped her gaze to her hands. "I wanted to make sure that we both had enough privacy."

From Jesse's vantage point at the door, she looked past the empty boxes and nodded, taking everything in, the Aztec design with the pale walls, the oak furniture, and a ton of plants in various stages of life.

The next room was Doug's room which Carly acknowledged with a nod toward the door. She did not open it to show Jesse. "He's done all of the corporate traveling for me for the past couple of months, so I haven't seen much of him lately. When he is around, he either stays with Stephanie or at my house in Green Bay." She led Jesse to the room across the hall from her own bedroom and opened the door. "You'll be staying in here. Karen's already brought in your bag," she told her, gesturing toward the battered, military-style duffel bag that Jesse had packed for herself.

Jesse shouldered her way past Carly and into the enormous mint-green room. A majestic canopy bed was the main attraction. It was gorgeous, rich dark wood, a truly remarkable piece of furniture, covered with a hunter green comforter and countless pillows arranged symmetrically at its head.

The bathroom door was open and Jesse saw the new white robe, pajamas, and the assorted toiletries laid out for her on the counter. Overwhelmed by everything, she crossed the room to look out the window, feeling like she was in the Presidential Suite of a five-star resort.

Harley sauntered past her, sniffed his way into the bathroom, and in the next moment, Jesse heard him lapping water out of the toilet. "Shit," she muttered under her breath. She snapped her fingers loudly, and Carly smiled as the dog came out with his head down, looked at Jesse out of the corner of his eyes, and jumped up on the bed, making himself right at home.

"There's a remote for the television and the stereo in the top drawer of the night table. Karen will do your laundry for you; just leave it in the hamper in the bathroom. Call me if you need anything," she instructed, nodding toward the intercom. She stood there for a precarious moment, watching Jesse sit on the bed and lean to pull off her cowboy boots. "Thank you for agreeing to this," she said at last. "I can't tell you how…."

"It's no big deal," Jesse said bluntly without looking up.

"I know you've already eaten, but would you like to join me for dinner later?"

"No."

"Oh." Carly stared at her. "Please don't feel as though you're confined to this room, Jesse. You're more than welcome to come downstairs. Karen's made chocolate…."

"I'm tired," Jesse told her. "I'm going to bed."

Holding the doorknob, Carly reached for the overhead light switch. "Would you like this on or off?"

"Off, please."

With the exception of the golden beam from the light of the hallway, the room fell black when she flipped the switch. "Good night."

Jesse briefly glanced over to see Carly, backlit, smiling warmly, about to close the door, but waiting for her reply. "Yeah. G'night."

Once the door closed, Jesse flopped backward on the bed and closed her eyes, absently petting her dog. "Shit," she muttered. "I never should have agreed to this." She looked over at Harley. Her eyes had adjusted to the darkness, and she could just make out his form. "And you weren't much help, you know, the way you were flirting with her." In shame, Harley covered his face with his front paws, and Jesse jabbed him lightly in the side. "Don't give me that. It's not gonna work. You owe me for this. You owe me big time."

- Wednesday -

Like spring-loaded window shades, Jesse's eyes flew open when she heard the tapping on her door. "I'm up," she said groggily.

"May I come in?" The door opened before she could say anything, and Carly turned on the light and took a step into the room. The double-breasted gray suit she wore was perfectly coordinated with her high-heeled shoes, which emphasized her calf muscles beautifully.

"Christ," Jesse said, squinting, shading her eyes as she sat up and scratched her head. "What time is it?"

"It's four-fifteen."

"Four fifteen?" Jesse groaned, looking over at her. "Don't you ever sleep?"

Carly brushed a speck of invisible lint from her skirt and held up a manila folder. "It took me most of the night, but I've managed to highlight a few names for you." Setting the folder on the dresser, she turned to leave. "And your sister phoned for you last night, but you didn't answer the intercom, so I assumed that you were already asleep."

For some inexplicable reason, her entire demeanor toward Jesse seemed to have changed overnight. She wasn't nearly as warm and friendly as she had been earlier - and that not-so-subtle flirting was gone, too. While Jesse was grateful for that, she wondered what had happened to make her entire personality change so drastically.

Lauren, she thought. Lauren told her something about me, about my past. She opened her big mouth and now my client is freaked out. "Is everything okay?" Jesse asked.

Harley's whole back side wiggled as he jumped down from the bed and trotted up to greet her. She glanced at Jesse as she leaned to pet him. "Yes, fine," she said stiffly.

"So you talked to Lauren last night?"

"Just for a few moments," Carly replied vaguely without looking at Jesse. "I, um, can you be ready in about a half hour? I've got to get to the office early today."

Did Jesse hear her correctly? She was so busy wondering what it was that Lauren had told Carly about her, that she wasn't really paying attention. "You want me to come with you?" she asked.

"If you don't mind. You don't have to stay. It's just to make sure I get there in one piece. I, uh, won't be home until very late, so unless you want to be stuck in Green Bay all day, I suggest we take separate cars."

"Fine," Jesse told her in a none-too-pleasant tone. "Give me a few minutes."

* * * *

Six hours later, at ten-thirty, Jesse awoke again. She was mostly clothed, everything but her blazer, her socks and her boots. Somebody had come in and covered her. She concluded that it must have been Carly. She probably came in to find out what was keeping her, and when she saw that Jesse had fallen back to sleep after her shower, decided to let her keep dozing.

If that was the case and she drove to her office in Green Bay alone, Jesse guessed that Carly was pretty upset with her. And who could blame her?

Climbing into her socks and boots, Jesse grabbed her blazer and hustled downstairs. Karen caught her just as she was on her way through the back door and informed her that Carly was home again today, in the library, and that she wanted to see Jesse.

Carly flicked a glance at her watch when she saw Jesse standing at the door. Since she was working from home today, she had changed her clothes and was now wearing jeans and a comfortable sweatshirt with her company's logo on it.

Jesse opened her mouth to speak, but Carly held up a finger to her and said, "Tell David that I want a status report by this afternoon," while turning back to her computer. "And before I let you go, Charlene, please remind Tina to close the Atrium tomorrow afternoon so she'll have enough time to set up for Friday's reception. And please ask her not to use the helium balloons for centerpieces. They're tacky. I want floral arrangements. And send something out to let everyone know that Friday is *not* a casual day."

"Yes, Carly," Charlene's voice replied over the speaker. "Oh,

Ted from Finance told me to tell you that he found more irregularities in the accounts. He wants to schedule a meeting with you. Do you want me to take care of that?"

"If you don't mind. Set it up for first thing tomorrow morning. If it's serious, though, I want to know about it right away."

After pressing the button to hang up, Carly motioned Jesse in, and Jesse quickly apologized for having fallen back to sleep. She took the chair across the desk from Carly.

"It's no problem," Carly said kindly. "You needed your rest. I shouldn't have woken you earlier. Under the circumstances, I suppose it's better that I work from home for a while." She sighed while straightening a stack of documents.

"If you've got some free time, I'd like to go over your list," Jesse said. Carly nodded, and Jesse quickly excused herself to retrieve the folder from her bedroom.

She met up with Karen in the doorway when she returned. "Would you like breakfast?"

Jesse peeked into the library. Carly was waiting patiently for her at the conference table in the middle of the room with a pen and a legal pad in front of her. She had just poured them each a cup of coffee and glanced over. "Do you like pancakes?"

"Sure," Jesse replied. "That'd be great." Taking the seat next to her client, Jesse opened her notepad. "How many names have you highlighted?"

"I believe there are sixteen or seventeen." She hesitated before moving her chair in closer to Jesse and pulling the folder between them. Harley sauntered in and hopped up on the couch across the room. He started turning in circles, making a night nest, lightly scratching the leather cushions until Jesse told him to knock it off. He circled once more, then groaned loudly as he flopped down for a nap.

Convinced that he wouldn't be a distraction for a while, Jesse got right down to business. For each person highlighted, she asked Carly numerous, probing questions; how long it had been since she'd last heard from them, what kind of motive they might have to kill her; did that person have access to her schedule, to her house, to her boathouse?

They'd finished breakfast, exhausted two pots of coffee, and were only about half-way through the list when Carly stood to stretch. "I need a break," she sighed.

Jesse was busy finishing up on the notes she'd been making and didn't bother to look up at her when she asked if Jesse wanted to go swimming with her. "No thanks," Jesse told her. "I really want to finish up here."

Carly looked at her for a long time, then asked, "What do you do to relax?"

"Huh?" This time Jesse looked up at her.

"How do you relieve stress?" she asked, turning her head from side to side. "Do you have a hobby that you enjoy? Do you walk?"

"Look," Jesse said. She put her pen down and rubbed her eyes. "I…Why don't we just finish up here, okay? Let's just….Let's not go there."

Carly's face dropped. "Fine," she muttered under her breath like a spoiled child, frustrated, falling back down into her chair. She started to restlessly swivel from side to side, while tapping her hand on the table, the whole time staring at Jesse, watching her work.

"Carly?" Chris Masters came strolling into the house, whistling.

Harley growled from deep within his chest, and out of the corner of her eye, Jesse saw a black flash shoot out the library door.

The deep and menacing growl intensified as he flew down the hall. In a second, he was both barking and growling at the intruder.

Carly jumped to her feet. "Chris?"

"Hey!" came a startled cry from the foyer. "What the hell? Back, Cujo!"

"Release!" Jesse yelled out, and within a matter of seconds, Harley came trotting back into the library, Chris trailing him, her startled expression fresh on her face.

Jesse directed him back to his spot on the couch, while Chris kept her eye on him as she crossed the room to take a seat on the other side of the table.

"That's the biggest dog I've ever seen," she said, a little out of breath. "His teeth are enormous." She propped her big feet, clad in new Fila tennis shoes, up on the table. She finally took her eyes off Harley and looked up at her friend. "Playing hooky again?" she asked, grinning.

Carly swatted her feet down with her legal pad. "Look who's

talking," she said. "Aren't you supposed to be on your way to New York?"

"Jake took my place. Said he had something to do there anyway. I'm taking his lessons for the rest of the week. I came to ride Hoosier and saw your Jeep in the driveway. So do you want to knock off and go riding with me?" She tilted her head in Jesse's direction. "Or do you two have other plans?"

The tone behind that question gave it a totally different meaning, and Jesse knew that Carly caught it, too, because her surprised expression changed to a worried and embarrassed frown.

"We have other plans," Jesse couldn't help but tell her. "We're working."

"Good," Chris said, grinning at Carly. "Then it'll just be me and you."

Jesse stopped writing again and looked up at her client, who was already on her feet, getting ready to leave with Chris. "I don't think you should go." She stared at her, watched her debate the situation in her mind, then reach a decision.

Chris prodded her along. "C'mon. The fresh air will do you some good. You can't stay cooped up in here. We'll take one of our marathon rides. We haven't done that for so long, just the two of us."

Carly frowned, looking from Jesse to Chris and back again, clearly torn. "Why don't you come with us?" she asked Jesse. She looked scared again, and Jesse knew that if she didn't go, Carly wouldn't go, either. But she wasn't going to let that influence her decision. They had work to do.

Chris seemed to be reading the situation correctly and knew exactly which button to push to settle the matter. "Think she'd be able to keep up with us on Mr. Billy?"

After a remark like that, what choice did Jesse have? She excused herself and headed for her bedroom to get her gun. On her way up the stairs, she overheard Carly say, "Why must you do that?"

"Do what?" Chris asked innocently.

Carly gave her a stern look, and Chris laughed. "Oh, relax," she said, glancing at the papers on the table. "I was just giving her shit. She might be a cranky little troll, but she looks like she can take it. You wouldn't want to deprive me of my one true joy in life, would you?"

McCray said irritably, "Don't call her that."

"What, cranky little troll? Okay. How 'bout nasty gnome. Is that acceptable?"

"Grow up, Chris."

* * * *

Rolling Thunder was a huge Saddlebred - seventeen hands, according to Carly - and Jesse had never ridden before in her life. She was, to put it mildly, a bit apprehensive. She couldn't believe that she let Chris provoke her into doing this.

The horse was one giant muscle. His coat was light gray, his mane and tail a shade darker. As scared as she was, Jesse had to admit that he was a magnificent animal.

She was grateful that instead of using a tiny little English saddle, Carly had outfitted him in a great big western one. It looked like something Gary Cooper would have used, and Jesse liked that a lot. It was black leather with a dark green upholstered seat, comfortable stirrups, and perhaps most importantly to Jesse, a big saddle horn. At least she'd have something other than two flimsy straps of leather to hold on to if the going got tough.

"Where's Victor?" Chris asked, coming out of the tack room with a saddle slung over her shoulder.

"I had to let him go," Carly replied.

"What? Why?" Chris stared at Jesse while Carly explained what he and Susan had been doing. She didn't seem all that surprised and agreed with Carly's decision to fire Victor, but she said to Jesse, "What if Victor had nothing to do with the boat explosion?"

"I'm pretty sure he didn't," Jesse told her simply.

"So your investigation cost him his job?"

"Her investigation didn't cost him his job," Carly corrected her friend. "His own actions cost him his job."

Chris stared at Jesse for a long moment before returning to her horse.

Coming up beside Jesse, having just finished saddling up her own horse, Carly helped her climb aboard Rolling Thunder. "Don't worry," she whispered, knowing that Jesse was scared shitless. "He's very tame and he knows the trails. And he's got the smoothest gait of all my horses so you won't get too sore."

Jesse nodded that she'd be okay as she situated herself in the saddle. She waited for Carly to adjust the stirrups before sticking her feet in them.

"Just your toes," Carly instructed, touching Jesse's leg and pulling the stirrup to the very tip of her boot. "You don't ever want to put your entire foot in there. If you lose your balance, you don't want the horse to drag you."

"Thanks for that image," Jesse said quietly.

"Relax. You'll be fine." Carly winked up at her and patted her boot.

Jesse held onto the saddle horn with one hand as she walked the horse out of the stable's back door, trying to get a feel for the animal and trying to become more relaxed and comfortable on him.

The sky was one dark gray cloud above the bare treetops. The thermometer on the outside of the stable read forty-seven degrees, but the strong breeze from the North made it seem much colder.

Harley followed them out and was running figure eights around the horse's legs. It was making both Jesse and the horse nervous, so Jesse put an abrupt end to his shenanigans by whistling once. He seemed hurt, but he obeyed immediately by dropping to the ground just outside the stable.

Five acres of low-cut grass led to the wooded area through which they were about to ride. A cold gust of wind cut through Jesse's thick black wool blazer. Her hair whirled around her face, and the cries of the gulls overhead combined with the roar of waves crashing up on the shore.

Carly and her friend finally came out, and Carly rode up alongside Jesse. "Are you okay?" She was on a young chestnut Saddlebred, Santana, who was only a few inches taller than Rolling Thunder.

"Yeah," Jesse replied, gaining a little confidence.

Chris pulled up on her other side. Her horse was a Palomino quarter horse, much smaller than Rolling Thunder, and not nearly as pretty. "Just try to keep up, will you? I don't want to have to stop every ten minutes and wait for you."

Jesse glared at her. She hated her. She hated the taunts. Her problem with people like Chris was that she let them get under her skin. She knew she shouldn't, but she did. And that's what started it. She sat up taller in her saddle, using her rare height advantage to intimidate. "If anyone will have to wait," Jesse told her, "it's going to be me, waiting for you."

It was too late to shut her mouth. The words had already come out, and the moment they passed over her lips, she knew that she had made a huge mistake. There was no question from the jaunty grin on Chris' face exactly what was coming.

"We'll see about that." Sure enough, Chris raised her hand and said, "I'll give you a head start!"

"Chris, don't you dare…" Carly began to say, but it was too late.

Chris had already brought her hand down and slapped Rolling Thunder's rear flank. Hard. It made a loud cracking noise that was bound to haunt Jesse for a long time to come.

"Shit!" Jesse yelled. But because her horse had taken off on a wild gallop and bounced her high and hard in the saddle, it came out more like "Shi-I-I-I-t!"

I'm going to die, Jesse thought, holding on for dear life. *I'm going to die.* Her hair went straight back from her head. Her feet shot out of the stirrups and were sticking out to the sides. She fought to catch her breath. Each jarring step the horse took vibrated through her body, painfully reminding her that she was not yet recovered from her recent injuries. She felt the massive animal beneath her, running at full speed. She felt how each muscle worked to make the horse go faster and faster.

To her terror, the horse didn't slow at all as he charged up a small hill. They had reached the edge of the pasture and were heading into the woods. Thankfully the horse seemed to know where to go because he was the one in control, not Jesse. Nervous perspiration on her hands made the reins slippery. She was practically laying on her stomach on the horse's back, clinging with both hands to the saddle horn, the mane, anything she could hold onto.

The horse followed a worn dirt path. It was about five feet wide and littered with dead and broken branches and leaves. Some of them were fairly large, but Rolling Thunder just rolled over them as if they were mere twigs.

"Jesse, pull back on the reins!" Carly shouted. "Pull back on the reins!" She was making a mad dash to get to them and was gaining fast. She ducked under some low-hanging branches and prodded Santana to move in beside them.

Jesse was too scared to look back. They had to be moving twenty-five or thirty miles an hour, but it felt much faster. She nearly went flying off when Rolling Thunder stumbled on a loose rock. In a way, Jesse would have preferred to have been thrown because at least then her body wouldn't have still been subjected to this pounding.

Santana's approach only seemed to make Rolling Thunder move faster. It was as if he sensed that they were racing and he didn't want Santana getting too close. He even seemed to swerve from side to side on the trail so Carly wouldn't be able to pull up alongside, but Carly was no novice.

She maneuvered her horse perfectly and was right beside them now. "Hold on," she said as she leaned out of her saddle. For a moment, Jesse thought she was going to join her on Rolling Thunder's back, but then she reached over and grabbed the knotted reins above Rolling Thunder's withers. Pulling his huge head to one side, while keeping perfect pace and control of her own horse, she gradually brought the huge animal under control to a manageable trot.

"Whew! Are you okay?" she asked, breathing heavily as she handed the reins to Jesse.

Waiting a moment to catch her breath before answering, Jesse glanced back to see that Chris was a fair distance back. She sat taller in her saddle and said with a straight face, absolute deadpan tone, "I knew I'd end up having to wait for *her*."

Carly threw her head back and laughed a hearty, full-throated laugh. "You are too funny."

Chris eventually caught up to them and smirked as she passed Jesse. "Pull back on the reins to get him to stop," she jeered.

"That's enough, Chris." Carly encouraged her friend to come up beside her, leaving Jesse alone to bring up the rear.

As Jesse continued to gather her senses, she came to realize that as frightful as her wild romp through the woods was, she felt exhilarated by it. For the first time in a long time, she felt really alive. It gave her an incredibly intense sense of freedom, of release. It was no wonder Carly enjoyed it so much.

The scenery was gorgeous despite the weather. The vivid fall colors and the sounds of the hooves and snapping twigs and the various scents lulled Jesse into a state of tranquility. Little did she know that the tranquility was about to be snapped like the tiny branches under Rolling Thunder's hooves.

The trail they were on, under a canopy of mostly-bare branches, began to narrow a little as they came upon the ravine that traversed Carly's estate. This bridge was similar to the one on the driveway leading up to the estate, a big, sturdy structure, planked by two-by-sixes, with untreated two-by-four railings. It was almost fifty feet long, supported by a complex system of thick, hardy braces that crisscrossed underneath.

There wasn't enough room to go across the bridge two abreast, so Chris glanced back at Jesse as she slowed her horse to let Carly go first. Jesse was busy getting a good grip on her reins and trying not to let Chris see her trepidation.

Santana took a few plodding steps onto the bridge, and Jesse wasn't sure what exactly happened next, but all of a sudden, she heard a loud bang, like a gunshot. In the next moment, she saw her client's horse rear up. The loud bang must have spooked him because he went absolutely wild. Carly managed to hang on for a good couple of seconds, but it seemed hopeless. She was never going to get him under control because each time he landed, it caused another loud bang, which only frightened him more. He jolted her so hard that with each bounce her head snapped back and forth like she was a rag doll. Eventually, she lost the battle.

Her hip clipped the railing. There was very little time to react; very little she could have done to have stopped herself. Jesse watched in horror as her client disappeared over the side of the bridge.

Santana reared up several more times, creating more booming snaps from the planks on the bridge. Then he, too, simply disappeared. He dropped straight down, making an unearthly thud. The giant horse released a terrifying wheeze when he landed at the bottom of the ravine.

Someone screamed. Jesse didn't know if it had come out of her mouth, Carly's mouth, or Chris'. But once the echo died, the woods fell silent. It was as if they were in a vacuum, as if all the birds, all the little forest animals, and even Jesse and Chris were too stunned to move.

But Jesse did move. She jumped down from Rolling Thunder and raced over to the bridge. Some of the planks were actually missing at the point where Santana had gone down.

The bottom of the ravine was a good sixty feet down. The side was really steep, almost straight down. It was dotted with jagged rocks. Parts of it had become overgrown with wandering foliage.

Jesse looked down and saw the horse lying motionless on its side, but her client was nowhere in sight. She heard labored breathing and wondered if it was hers or Carly's. "Carly?" she called.

Chris was on the bridge now, walking carefully on the planks that were still there, holding onto the railing as she looked down into the ravine for her friend. "Carly? Can you hear me?" She strained to find her friend. "Carly? Are you okay?"

Now Jesse spotted something moving in the underbrush about a third of the way down, maybe fifteen or twenty feet below. She heard Carly groan in pain.

Jesse leaned farther over, being careful not to get too close to the edge. "Can you climb back up?"

"I….No. It's…Oh!"

Both Chris and Jesse heard a struggle, the whooshing of branches and leaves, the sound of loose stones and dirt falling.

"What?" Chris cried. "What's wrong?"

"I'm slipping! Chris! Help!"

Jesse took off for Rolling Thunder. She snapped a blade out of her Swiss army knife and quickly sliced the leather reins from the bit. There were two of them, one on each side, each about five feet long. They weren't very thick, but it was all she had. She tied the two together on her way to Chris' horse. He backed away from her, but she fearlessly pursued and caught him in the next moment. With all of the reins tied together, Jesse now had twenty feet of leather, give or take a few inches.

Chris, who had been shouting down words of encouragement to Carly, helped her secure one end of the leather to the beam of the bridge. "Don't move, hon," she told her friend. "It'll be okay. I'm coming down for you."

"I'm going," Jesse told her, pulling the reins from Chris' large hands.

"No way!" Chris objected. She made a move to get the reins back, but Jesse ripped them away. "She could be seriously hurt! She might need to be carried and you're not strong enough to get her back up here!"

"Well it's not like this little strap is going to hold your weight!" Jesse snapped back. Muttering, she began her slow descent, propelling her way down carefully and slowly so she wouldn't burn her hands or, worse, slip and fall.

She found Carly about eighteen feet down. She was in a semi-standing position hugging a tiny mound of earth that stuck out from the ravine wall by no more than six inches. Using both hands, she hung on for dear life. The only reason she hadn't fallen the rest of the way was because she'd somehow managed to dig the toes of her riding boots into the dirt. How she managed to land in this position, Jesse would never know. It didn't really matter anyway. What mattered was getting her up safely.

Jesse made her way over to her, trying to find a place to situate herself so she could tie the leather around her client without making them both take the long dive to the bottom. There was a rock that stood out about eight inches from the wall like a shelf. It was on the other side of Carly, about three feet away, at waist level.

Perfect, Jesse thought. If she could get to it, that is. Holding the rein securely, she pushed off the ravine wall with her legs to get on Carly's other side. Once she got her footing, she took off her belt and pulled up the little bit of excess leather and tied the two together. "I'm going to have Chris pull you up," she said, her gaze going from Carly's toes to her hands, which were reaching up clutching a thick vine. The sleeve had been ripped on her jacket and sweatshirt, and Jesse saw the strain this was putting on Carly's arm muscles. But it was straining her in other ways as well, because when Jesse looked into her gray eyes, she didn't have to look hard to see the sheer panic.

Carly's head was turned to the right; the left side of her face was scratched and pressed up against the dirt. Every part of her body was adhered to the rocky earth as if she'd somehow become a part of it. She didn't move a muscle, just her eyes, as she watched Jesse work quickly to make the knot.

The trick was going to be getting it around her without having either one or both of them fall to the rocky bottom forty feet below. Standing with her feet sideways on the protruding rock, Jesse leaned into the ravine wall to support herself. She tried to reassure Carly with her look. "Can you grab this if I toss it to you?" she asked.

"I don't know," Carly replied, her voice a terrified whisper.

"Maybe I can..." Jesse reached way over with the belt in her outstretched hand. But it was no use. She came up almost a full foot short. "Shit!"

Growing more and more concerned, Jesse searched for a different way to get to her. She looked up, but that was no good. Carly couldn't climb, and there was no way she could let go long enough for Jesse to get the belt around her.

"Jesse," Carly cried, and Jesse knew that time was running short. She was losing the battle against gravity. The urgency in her voice sent Jesse into action. There wasn't time to fully think through her plan. If there had been, she might never have done it.

Slipping the make-do harness over her head and shoulders, she pulled it tight to her chest and tugged on it once to make sure it was still securely fastened above.

Then she did it. She leaned way back and kicked herself from the security of her perch, lunging backward in Carly's direction. The leather holding her weight gave a little, and then dug into her ribcage, which was sore to begin with. It squeezed the breath from Jesse, and she groaned in pain. It hugged her like a giant boa constrictor, and if she hadn't gotten lucky the first time, there most probably wouldn't have been a second time.

Letting all of her weight rest on the reins, she let go and reached out with both hands to grab Carly around the waist. When she made contact with her, Carly's right hand let go of the branches that she had been clutching, and Jesse heard her panicked gasp.

"I've got you," Jesse told her from behind with her arms wrapped securely around her waist. Her plan was to pull Carly back with her to the little ledge, put the belt around her, and have Chris pull her up. She figured Carly was smart enough to figure that out for herself, but for some reason, she wouldn't cooperate when Jesse tried to move her.

The terror that seized her seemed to have transferred itself to her hand, and neither would let go. She had a death-grip on that root and no matter how hard she tried to persuade her hand to release it, it would not.

Acknowledging her reluctance, Jesse tightened her grip around Carly's waist as if making a soundless promise to get her to the ledge safely. Perspiration dripped from Jesse's forehead and down the sides of her face.

Her feet slipped on the loose rocks and dirt as she pulled herself up a little higher. She pulled Carly backwards so that Carly was leaning into her, and tried to pry her fingers from the root. "Come on, god dammit! I've got you!" Jesse wheezed in her ear as she tugged on her arm.

But still, Carly's fingers held tight. They were white; her whole hand was white, the thin veins bulging on the backside. And she was shaking. Every part of her body was shaking.

Jesse wasn't having much fun, either. She knew that they'd have to do this the hard way. Having no other choice, she held onto a small rock and hung there by one arm while she used the tip of her cowboy boot to dig in a foot-hold for herself. Once it was deep enough, she unhooked the belt from around her chest.

At one point, while working to get the belt around Carly's waist, she felt the dirt around her foot start to give. She grunted. Her hand on the small rock was sweating. It was cramping, and she was well aware of the fact that her life literally depended upon her grip and that one tiny piece of stone.

"I've gotta get this around you," she told Carly, breathing hard and working fast.

Carly managed to provide a small space between herself and the earth so Jesse could slip one end of the belt through the opening. Once it was though, Carly pressed herself up against the wall to hold it in place.

Taking the other end, Jesse brought the belt around the other side, and still using that one hand, managed to buckle it.

There. Carly was okay, provided Jesse's make-do harness held up. Now all Jesse had to do was find a way back to her perch and wait for her turn to go up.

Holding her breath, she inched away from Carly slowly, then

swung in mid-air like a monkey and grabbed a vine with her free hand.

But the vine didn't hold. Down she went - five feet, ten feet - and, try as she might to grab onto something, anything, she couldn't stop the free-fall. She slammed against the earth a few times, further injuring her body.

All of the air gushed out of her when she landed hard on her stomach. She was a good thirty feet down, just over half way. Grabbing her ribs, sucking in greedy gasps of wind, Jesse carefully turned over onto her side and looked up to see that Chris was still struggling to pull Carly to the top.

Jesse looked down and realized that she only had one option. Even though she was closer to the bottom of the ravine than the top, she had to go up. The wall was simply too steep. She wouldn't have a chance.

This was when those rock-climbing lessons would have come in handy, she thought bitterly. If only she'd taken them. If only Abby would have stayed with her a little longer, she was sure that was something they would have done together. But the point was moot now. She never did learn to rock-climb. And Abby's gone.

"Fuck" she groaned.

She started climbing. Her arms were as weak as water. Her hands were stiff. Her ribs were killing her. Her holster, hidden beneath her blazer, caught on a shrub. She only needed to go up about ten feet on her own. After that, once she made it to the shelf safely, she'd be able to tie the belt around herself and have Chris pull her up.

Slowly, carefully, painfully, she made her way up inch by inch. When the harness was finally tossed down, she slipped her shoulders through and started her climb. Chris, she noticed, was tending to Carly and made very little effort to pull her up.

Finally, Jesse rolled onto solid ground. Lying on her back, exhausted, she undid the belt with one hand while turning her head to take in the situation. Chris' horse and Rolling Thunder were nowhere in sight. Chris and Carly were sitting on a fallen tree about twenty feet from her. While lying on her back looking skyward, struggling to catch her breath, she wiped her hands on her trousers and reached into her blazer pocket for a Marlboro. Something jabbed into her finger, and when she looked in to see what it was she grew ill. She was devastated.

It was her sunglasses. These weren't just any sunglasses. These were her very favorite sunglasses. Abby had bought them for her six years ago while they vacationed in Acapulco on her birthday. And now they were destroyed. There was no way to replace them - or the sentiment behind them. Even if they could be repaired, they wouldn't be the same. Nothing would ever be the same, she lamented privately, trying frantically to piece them together again.

When it became apparent to her that there was no hope in their regeneration, she sat up and heaved them over the ravine's edge. "Fuck."

A low moan, a soul-wrenching groan from below made Jesse's heart sink. She had a sneaking suspicion that she knew what it was and crawled over to the edge to get confirmation.

She was horrified by what she saw. Santana's head was moving. His hind legs were tangled beneath him in a way that horse's legs don't normally bend. He was struggling, thrashing his head back and forth. Jesse rose to her feet and reached into her blazer.

This was where the lines of Judaism and her own beliefs didn't meet. Rabbi Glickman once told her that mercy killing was contrary to God's law. But while the Tradition prohibited euthanasia, Jesse could not stand idly by and watch another soul suffer.

She recalled very clearly her argument with the Rabbi on this issue. "Only God can give and take life," he had told her.

To which Jesse responded, "God might deal with life and death, but once death is the only option, when a case is terminal, we must step in to prevent further suffering." She reminded him of the story that he had told her at her first conversion class, whereby a Pagan challenged Hillel, a great sage, to explain all about Judaism in the few short moments during which a man might stand on one foot. Hillel responded by saying, "That which is hurtful to thee do not do to thy neighbor. This is the whole doctrine. The rest is commentary. Now go forth and learn."

Jesse had argued that it would be hurtful to her to die a slow and painful death, that it wasn't just her *choice* to end someone's life when they were suffering, but, according to her interpretation of

181

God's will, it was her *duty* to end their suffering.

Rabbi had thought about it for a moment, but wasn't entirely convinced.

And now, all these years later, Jesse was faced with that same issue. Santana's fate was sealed. Jesse's responsibility was to see to it that his suffering was kept to a minimum.

To herself, she said, "God, let Santana find refuge forever in the shadow of your wings, and let his soul be bound in eternal life. May he rest in peace. Amen."

Taking aim, she inhaled slowly, trying to steady her shaky hands. Slowly, she pulled the trigger, shooting two rounds into the horse's head, killing him. Jesse exhaled and dropped her arms to her sides.

Chris jumped up from the log. "What the hell are you doing?" she demanded.

Jesse turned to look at Carly, and Carly knew exactly what she'd just done. "He was suffering," she told her friend quietly, staring at Jesse. Tears streaked down her face. "He wasn't going to make it." She put her head down. Her shoulders trembled, and Jesse watched Chris move to hold her.

Before checking out the bridge for herself, Jesse stayed back for a while, had another cigarette, and watched and listened to Chris consoling and comforting her friend. It seemed genuine and sincere, but there was something about the way she kept looking back at Jesse that made Jesse uncomfortable.

Jesse put out her cigarette and turned her attention to the bridge.

There was no way to cross it now. Several boards, fourteen according to Jesse's count, were missing. They had fallen through the beams and were scattered haphazardly around the dead horse. She checked the railing, which seemed secure, and sidestepped her way across the right beam to get a look at the remaining planks.

Determined not to look down, she made her way to the half-way point of the bridge and settled herself on the first solid plank that she came upon. Five of the planks that she had passed had been loosened. There were hammer marks on the undersides of them. Some of them were missing nails altogether.

This was no accident.

"Chelsea and I will stay with you tonight," Chris told Carly on the walk back to Carly's house.

Carly had been holding her left wrist in her right hand. She shook her head. "That won't be necessary," she told her friend, making small circles with her left hand, testing it. "Jesse will be here."

"I don't know why you're not having her look into Donna Meyer," Chris said. Apparently she understood the new direction Jesse's investigation had taken. "Did you tell her about the firecracker? This little stunt has her name written all over it. She probably used the North Drive to get back here so nobody would see her."

"Sounds like you have it all figured out," Jesse commented.

Chris stopped. "What's that supposed to mean? Listen,

Sherlock, if you think I…"

Carly's stern features and sharp look told Chris to stop it, and Chris replied with a frustrated and angry sigh.

Both Carly and Jesse showered and changed clothes when they returned to Carly's house. At Carly's insistence, Chris left once she got Rolling Thunder and Hoosier back to the safety of the stable.

Apparently, Carly didn't want to have to listen to Chris and Jesse go at it all afternoon. In the library, after making arrangements to have Santana's body removed from the ravine, Carly asked her housekeeper to bring them a pot of coffee and joined Jesse at the conference table again.

"I'm really sorry about your horse," Jesse said, looking up from her notes.

Carly nodded solemnly. Her eyes were still red and puffy. "Thank you for not letting him languish."

"Do you want to finish this now?" she asked, gesturing toward their unfinished work. "It can wait if you're not up to it."

She nodded and shook her head at the same time. "Let's get it done." Her somber mood remained with them throughout the rest of afternoon. The room had grown dark now, and the light over the table gave Carly an eerie profile.

"Last one," Jesse told her, watching her rise to stretch again. She was still gingerly testing her left wrist, which, from Jesse's perspective, seemed to be quite swollen. "You should put some ice on that."

"Let's just get through this," Carly said quietly. Clearly, she needed something to get her mind off her grief. "What's the last name?"

"Jack Walthorp. How do you know him?"

"He was a computer expert who used to work for me, one of the first people Jacey and I hired. He and Jacey developed our first product and then he turned around and sued us for every penny we'd made on it. And then some."

"Did he win?" Jesse asked, looking over at her. She was standing at the desk now, parting the drapes to look out at the Lake.

Carly shook her head. "He knew when he was hired that he was under exclusive contract with us, that the company would own the copyright. We made that very clear to him at his interview. I haven't heard from him for, oh, six or seven years."

"Think he'd wait all that time to get his revenge?"

Carly turned and wrapped her arms around herself. "I doubt it. I don't know. I'm just so perplexed by this whole thing. I can't believe this is happening. I can't believe that somebody I know has such animosity toward me that they'd try to kill me!"

"How about family? Was he married? Did he have any kids?"

"I think he was divorced. I don't know if he had any...."

The phone interrupted her, and while she took the call, Jesse got up to go to the bathroom. Carly was off the phone when she returned, busily typing something at the keyboard.

"I have to go to the office," she told Jesse grimly, turning to face her. "Someone has hacked into almost all of our accounts. Money is missing. A lot of money." She turned in her seat and picked up a folder from the credenza. "I think you should meet with Donna Meyer tonight. I think Chris might be right. It's Wednesday, Donna's dart night. She'll be at the Eastland in Sister Bay."

"I'm going to look into Jack Walthorp first."

"But…"

"He's a computer expert, right? Don't you think it's possible that he found a way into your mainframe, that he's finally getting his revenge? And if there's money missing…"

Carly shook her head. "I think Donna…."

"Listen to me, Carly," Jesse insisted, cutting her off. "From what you've told me and from what I know about her, she doesn't have a reason to kill you." Carly opened her mouth to object, but Jesse wouldn't allow the interruption. "She's been pulling these pranks - as you call them - for the past, what, seven or eight years? She does it to get a charge out of you, to get your attention. That's all. If she killed you, the game would be over, wouldn't it?" Tucking her notepad into the back pocket of her trousers, she added, "I don't believe she's as dangerous as you make her out to be. I think your past might be clouding your judgment just a little."

"Well there's only one way to find out, isn't there?"

They finally agreed, after yet another heated discussion, that Jesse would drive Carly to her office in Green Bay to make sure she got there, and then drive back to the Eastland Bar for a convenient "chance" encounter with Donna Meyer.

Although Jesse was still uneasy about leaving her client alone in Green Bay, Carly assured her that she would be fine and that she would take one of her fleet cars home so as to remain low-key.

It was nearing six-thirty in the evening by the time they were both ready to leave, and since neither of them had eaten since breakfast, Carly suggested that they dine together at Luigi's in Green Bay before Jesse dropped her off.

Jesse noticed, as they walked into the dining room at Luigi's, that the small group of diners all seemed to stop what they were doing to look at Carly. It was then that Jesse realized just how popular this woman was. Carly didn't seem to notice. Jesse supposed that she had other things weighing heavily on her mind. That, and she was probably used to the attention, but Jesse certainly wasn't. Nor was she accustomed to the quiet murmuring that seemed to follow them as they were quickly escorted past the tables.

They were seated at an out-of-the-way table that had a *reserved* tag on it. The waitress was there immediately with ice water and menus. Carly asked for a club soda. Jesse ordered a beer, and when the waitress walked away, she detected a definite change in her client.

"What?" she prompted.

"Nothing."

"Don't say 'nothing'. Why'd you look at me like that?" She stared at her over the flickering candle between them as she lit a cigarette.

Carly took her time. She glanced around the restaurant, fiddled with her napkin, then returned Jesse's stare. "Do you have a drinking problem?"

Jesse smiled and laughed a little. "No." She inhaled from her cigarette. "I like to have a drink every now and then to relax. Sometimes I like to relax a lot. So what?"

"So you're driving tonight."

"I'm a big girl, Carly. I know my limits." Jesse struck an oppositional pose, leaning forward in her chair, her chin in her hand. "What are you, one of those recovering alcoholics who've sworn off booze forever, who have to walk around all holier than thou and tell everyone how long they've been sober and make them feel guilty for taking a sip of beer every now and then?"

"No," Carly said simply.

"So what's your problem?" She blew out a puff of smoke as the waitress returned with their drinks.

Carly watched her take a big gulp of beer, nearly finishing it off in one sip. Her gaze suddenly sharpened. "Do you want to know what my problem is? I'll tell you: There's simply no room in my life for people who drink or do drugs or have any kind of addiction for that matter," she said, waving the smoke from in front of her face. "I have absolutely no tolerance for people who participate in that kind of destructive and self-destructive behavior, no tolerance at all."

Jesse smacked her with a vile grin as she inhaled deeply on her cigarette. "Yeah," she rasped, blowing smoke across the table at her,

"Well hopefully you won't have to tolerate me much longer." She drained her glass and motioned for the waitress to bring her another. Noting Carly's disgust, Jesse huffed out a laugh and said, "Oh, relax, will you? Why don't you have one? Christ, after what you've been through lately, you deserve it."

Carly refused to look at her, and Jesse studied her while taking a final drag on her cigarette.

* * * *

Carly arrived home at two-thirty in the morning and went directly to her library where she used the intercom to summon her housekeeper. She was sorting through her briefcase and looked up as Karen, in her bathrobe, pushed open the door. "Has Jesse gone to bed already?"

"She's not home yet," Karen told her. "After she left, that mutt of hers tore apart your bedroom and when I tried to get him to stop, he growled at me and wouldn't let me get close to him so I had Doug take him outside. He somehow got into your bureau and shredded several of your undergarments. The dog, that is, not Doug."

Frowning, Carly unbuttoned her blazer and leaned forward as Karen helped her out of it.

"Are you hungry? Would you like me to fix you something?"

"No, thank you." She ran a hand through her hair, clearly troubled. When she had passed the Eastland on her way home, the

Lexus was not there, and she assumed that Jesse would be here when she got home. She had not even considered driving past Donna's house. Jesse wouldn't have gone home with Donna, would she?

Carly picked up the phone, hesitated, then slammed it down.

"You look so tired, dear. Why don't you go to bed?"

Taken briefly from her thoughts, Carly shook her head. She replaced the papers she had just unpacked from her briefcase. "I'm going to change and go back to the office," she announced, standing.

- Thursday -

"You can't come barging in here like this! Carly isn't even home!"

"Relax, honey. I'm not here to see that wench!"

Recognizing the harsh voice in the hallway, Jesse sat up in bed just as Donna Meyer burst into her bedroom with Karen on her heels.

The clock told Jesse that it was ten-fifteen. She'd only gotten home three hours earlier. It wasn't completely Jesse's fault. Her evening with Donna Meyer had not gone exactly as Jesse had planned. What she intended to do was to get a quick interview in the safety of the Eastland Bar and leave. She had assumed that the real Donna Meyer wasn't the obnoxious unpleasant psycho hussy she portrayed herself as when they had first met. Turns out, Jesse assumed incorrectly. A good part of the evening was spent fending off her assaults, but Jesse eventually got her to talk openly. They had gone back to Donna's house when the bar closed, and once there, Jesse completely lost track of time.

"There you are, sweetie," Donna said with her haughty little smile as she stalked her way to Jesse's bed. Over her shoulder, Jesse saw Karen's angry look of concern. "I should have known you'd be catching up on your beauty sleep."

"It's okay, Karen," Jesse told the maid who'd been standing in

191

the doorway with her hands on her hips.

Donna turned and smiled at the housekeeper. "Yes, Karen. We have some unfinished business and would like to be left alone. Don't you have windows to clean or clothes to press?"

Karen stepped away, leaving the wooden door standing open, and Jesse turned her gaze to Donna. How could she look so refreshed after a sleepless night? "Do you have the money?" Jesse asked.

"Of course, my dear. Donna is a woman of her word. She had to wait until the bank opened." She reached into her purse and pulled out a large roll of cash. "How much?"

"Twelve thousand, eight hundred."

Donna waved a handful of hundred-dollar bills in front of her, teasing her with them. "Just promise me you won't sleep with the tramp," Donna said. "Believe me, she's not worth it. She has no idea how to satisfy a woman."

"Just give me the money, Donna."

"Oh, darling, I'll give it to you. You certainly earned it, didn't you? And last night was worth every penny, my dear. Every penny."

Jesse's focus shifted as Harley came running into the bedroom and jumped up on the bed. She looked toward the doorway and was more than a little shocked to see Carly standing there.

To the untrained eye, Carly might have appeared calm and collected, but Jesse knew that she was shaking with unrestrained anger on the inside as she stepped into the room with her natural poise and dignity. "What are you doing here?"

Donna turned quickly and broke up laughing, and Jesse knew that Donna had been saying what she had been saying because she knew Carly was standing there. "Look, Bashful!" she exclaimed, looking from Carly to Jesse. "Snow White is home!"

Carly's atom-splitting glare went from Jesse to Donna. Stepping closer to the bed with her clenched fists in the pockets of her blazer, her jaw tight, she said in a remarkably controlled voice, "Get out of my house." She extended her arm toward the door. "Right now, or I'll call the police."

Donna chuckled. "Oh, calm yourself, dear. You'll give yourself a migraine. Donna's leaving. She just came to settle a debt." Turning to Jesse, Donna puckered up her lips and blew her a kiss. "As for you, my love, Donna would love to have you more often. You're more than welcome to spend the night any time you want." She turned on her heel and swaggered out of the room.

Carly stood in the middle of the hallway and watched her all the way to the front door. It took her four strides to return to Jesse's bedroom where she took the chair next to the bed. Their eyes made contact, and in that brief glimpse, Jesse got a real sense of just how painfully absorbed Carly's deep-seated loneliness was.

"Why was that woman in my house? Why did she give you money?"

"I won it," Jesse told her frankly, patting the stack of bills. Carly seemed a bit leery of that, so Jesse elaborated. "We shot pool all night. It was the only way I could get her to stop groping me and talk.

193

Sometimes I have to get people on their own turf and use a distraction to make them comfortable enough to talk to me. And if I let them talk long enough, they'll eventually tell on themselves."

"You couldn't possibly have won that much money from her." Carly looked Jesse right in the eye as if trying to find a reason to believe her. "Donna's excellent at billiards."

Jesse just stared back. She didn't say a word as Carly scrutinized her, agitation clouding her features. "Do you honestly expect me to believe that you spent an entire night with her and did nothing but shoot pool?"

Instead of being deeply insulted or angry, Jesse just laughed. "Christ! Give me a little credit, will you?" She leaned forward and rested her elbows on her knees, petting her dog's head playfully. "I know how competitive she is and used it against her. We played the first game for a hundred bucks and then played double or nothing for the rest of the night. I let her win the first five games, but she lost every game after that."

Carly suddenly felt foolish for having convinced herself that Jesse had slept with Donna, that her gripping obsession with that one irrational thought had overruled her better judgment and sent her home early. "You must be very good," she said quietly.

"Yeah. My one marketable skill." Jesse huffed out a doleful laugh and looked away. "That's how I made my way across the country - shooting pool in run down old biker bars."

Carly looked at her with a combination of pity and horror. "What about your music? You...."

Jesse just shrugged that off, shaking her head. "I...you have to talk to people to get a gig. I...uh, I traveled alone."

"Wasn't that dangerous?"

"Not as dangerous as spending a night with Donna Meyer. She's quite a piece of work, that woman. It's like she's an octopus or something. Hands everywhere."

"She's always been very aggressive," Carly commented, enjoying Jesse's talkative mood.

"I've met packs of wolverines more passive than her. And did you ever notice when she smiles it's like she's not really smiling, but more like baring teeth?"

Carly smiled at that, but the loneliness remained. "Karen was convinced that Victor and Donna had conspired to kill Susan."

Laughing with Carly at that, Jesse made a derisive face. She set the money aside and scratched her head. "I don't think she's behind any of this, Carly. I really don't. I think once we find out who's breaking into your computers and stealing your money, then we'll know who killed Susan and who's trying to kill you."

"I have people working on the security problems we've been having."

"Any luck so far?"

She shook her head. "We'll have more information later this afternoon. But Jesse," she said, leaning forward in her chair, "I don't think you should cross Donna off your list just yet. She might have fooled you last night, but believe me…"

"Carly," Jesse said calmly, trying desperately to avoid another verbal boxing match with this woman, "she denied ever touching your car, the bridge, and she swore up and down that she didn't light the firecracker while you were in the trailer with your horse."

"Well of course she'd deny those things, Jesse. Any fool…."

"She said she thought Chelsea lit the firecracker."

"Chelsea? That's ridiculous. She and Chris are the ones who pulled me out the trap door." She shook her head stubbornly. "No. Donna did it. I'm absolutely certain of that. In the ambulance on the way to the hospital, Susan told me that she saw Donna walk right past at the moment it went off. It was one of her pranks."

The room turned silent as Jesse stared at her. "She admitted everything else, though; the dead flowers, the nails, the towing, and the movers."

"None of those incidents threatened my life, Jesse," Carly pointed out. Jesse could tell that she, too, was trying to keep things calm even though she got up to pace at the foot of the bed. "I should have put an end to this long ago. I thought that if I ignored her antics she'd eventually give up and leave me alone, but it obviously hasn't worked."

"According to her, you're the one who started the whole thing when you broke up with her."

"I…?" Overwhelmed, Carly brought her hand to her throat, and then stretched it toward the door. "I didn't break up with her! She left me!" Blotches of red appeared on her chest, up her neck, on her cheeks. "She married the man whose son decided to drink a case of beer and get behind the wheel of a car. The accident he caused killed my father, and nearly killed my nephew and she thinks *I* started it? Poor, poor Donna has a few scrapes, a few broken bones and expects me to drop everything to be with her. My God, I'd just lost my Father in the same crash. Doug was in intensive care for over a month, and all she could think about was herself. This was my *family*! My only remaining relatives, and I was supposed to forget about them and visit her?" She crossed the room again, pacing, and Jesse followed her with her eyes. "She called me once after she was released from the hospital and accused me of cheating on her with Chris. Can you imagine? She didn't even ask about Doug.

"And three years with her, for over three years, Father bent over backwards so we could be together while I was going to school. He paid her way when we went to Rome, he gave her a job, a new car, he offered her a ride any time he came to visit me in Madison, and not once, not one time did she bother to call or send flowers or even a letter to say that she missed him or that she'd been thinking about him. Meanwhile, Robert feels guilty for what his son did, visits her a few times in the hospital, pays attention to her, and six months later, she's walking down the aisle with the old bastard to spite me for an affair that I never had. And she thinks *I* started this? She's insane!"

"It seems to me she married Robert for his money, not to spite you." "Whatever the reason, it was unforgivable." Carly stopped her pacing and turned to face Jesse. "Do you believe she had the audacity to send me a wedding invitation?"

After having spent an evening with Donna, Jesse responded, "Uh huh." She paused for a moment. "I think she still really cares about you," she told her, bringing a scoffing scowl to Carly's face. "I mean it. You were all she talked about - you and the time the two of you spent together."

This obviously took Carly by surprise. She opened her mouth to say something, but Karen's voice over the intercom cut her off.

"Carly, Jacey Elder's on the phone. She says it's urgent."

Carly sighed and reached over to pat Harley on the head. "I probably should have just stayed at the office today," she said quietly, "but I've been told that I make some of my people nervous when we're under deadline. I have a tendency to hover." She took a few steps toward the door and stopped. She turned back. "I hope I'm not doing that to you."

"Nah. I'd let you know if you were."

Carly smiled as if to say *yes you would, wouldn't you?* And left the room.

A short time later, while Jesse was out in front of the house with Harley, a delivery van pulled into the drive. Finally, her rebuilt starter had arrived.

She was in the garage working on her Fiat when her client startled her. "There you are. They finally delivered the part you needed?"

Now Jesse knew what she meant about her hovering problem. "Uh huh. Just a few minutes ago." Wearing only her baggy trousers and a plain white t-shirt, she was leaning over, standing on her tip-toes, straining to loosen a bolt. She banged her head on the hood when she turned to look at her. "Ouch!"

"Ohhh!" Carly hurried to her side. "Are you okay?"

"Yeah," Jesse told her, rubbing her head. "I've been blessed with a thick skull."

With a fascinated expression, Carly examined her car. Jesse couldn't blame her. It was quite a site. Most of it was covered in rust. There were only a few spots of paint to indicate that it had once been red. The California license plate in the back dangled by one bolt and read 24kauk9.

Jesse had nearly everything torn apart and scattered across the floor.

"Are you going to be able to put all of this together again?" she asked.

"Yeah. And hopefully I won't have any spare parts."

Carly smiled, watching her. "While I was talking to Jacey on the phone just now, she reminded me of the fund-raiser Saturday night for the Service League. It's at the Carlton. I don't suppose you've ever been there?"

"Nope."

"Father used to take me there when I was a child. It's a beautiful old building, once a theater, but the new owners, friends of mine, bought the restaurant next door and have just finished the renovations that joined the two buildings, turning it into a convention center/banquet hall. I can't wait to see what they've done with it."

"Are there going to be a lot of people there?"

"Yes. A few hundred I would guess. From what I've read, the new Carlton can accommodate up to twelve hundred."

"You can't go."

"I beg your pardon?"

Jesse stopped what she was doing and turned full around to face her and said louder, speaking slowly: "You can't go."

"I didn't realize that I needed your permission."

Jesse couldn't tell by Carly's tone how she had meant that remark so she took a quick glance over her shoulder as she groaned to loosen the last bolt that held her old starter in place. "You'd be taking a big risk. With all those people, you'd be an easy target."

From the tone of her next comment, Jesse knew immediately that this was going to go the full ten rounds.

"You don't understand, Jesse. I am going. It's a celebrity fashion show, and I've already agreed to host it. I understand that you're not an escort or a bodyguard, so I won't pressure you into going with me. Chris and Chelsea will be there, Doug and Stephanie and Jacey and her husband, so I'm sure I'll be perfectly safe. I just thought…I agreed to do this before Susan died and I ….I thought that perhaps you'd enjoy spending an evening with my friends and me rather than staying home alone."

"Fine," Jesse said, making a quick decision and hoping to avoid further conflict. She pulled the old starter from her car and shook her head as she set it on the floor.

Carly looked down at it. She didn't seem to know what to make of Jesse's concession. She was shocked and confused, maybe even a little hurt that Jesse didn't prolong their bickering. Quickly shifting gears, she said, "I don't mean to sound presumptuous, but I'd be happy to give the Lexus to you. I bought it for Susan and I know I'll never use it."

"No thanks."

"If you'd rather, I'll lend you the money for a new car."

"I don't need money and I don't need a new car. Once I get this in, it'll run fine." She smiled quickly at Carly. "But thanks for the offer."

"Where'd you learn so much about cars?"

"From my dad," Jesse told her. "The problem is, now they make cars so you have to be some kind of computer nerd to fix them. They've got chips running everything. I hate that. I like the older cars better, the kind where everything's right there, not hidden away in some microchip." Wiping her hands on her shirt, she leaned on the car. "I've always hated computers," she said. "They're nothing but trouble. Portals to hell."

Jesse couldn't tell if Carly was offended or astonished. "Once," she confessed, "when I was six, my parents took us to a petting zoo. They had a computer there that told you what kind of pet most closely matched your personality. My sister…"

"Lauren," Carly interrupted.

"Yeah. We…"

"Is she your only sibling?"

Jesse looked at her. "No. I also have a brother, Scott."

"Are you the oldest, middle, youngest?"

"Oldest. By twelve minutes."

Jesse opened her mouth to continue her story, but Carly broke in again. "So you're older than Lauren?"

"Uh huh," Jesse said slowly in a tone that ridiculed her for having stated the obvious. "Anyway, we answered all of the questions, and according to the computer, our best bet was a guinea pig, so, of course, we begged our parents for one."

"And did they buy one for you?" Carly asked, nodding her encouragement, clearly caught up in the story.

"Yeah. Mary." Jesse grinned. "Lauren named him before we figured out what sex he was. We only had him a couple of days because we kept arguing over him. We shared a double bed at the time, and Lauren wanted him to sleep with us, but I thought he was ugly and didn't want him in bed with me. One night - without telling me - she took him out of his cage."

"Oh, no," Carly said in dreaded anticipation. "Don't tell me. You rolled over on the poor little thing while you were sleeping and crushed him."

"No." Jesse shook her head and let out a little laugh. "I woke up the next morning and found the 'poor little thing' nibbling my hair. Turned out he'd had quite a feast." Jesse tugged on her curls. "All I had left were little tufts of hair standing out around the big patches he'd gnawed off. My mom gave him to a neighbor kid that day. The day after that, after I took a scissors to Lauren's hair while she was asleep, we got new bunk beds."

Jesse didn't think the story was all that funny. Certainly, at the time, it was a serious matter, but Carly was bent over with laughter. "And you blamed the entire fiasco on the computer at the petting zoo?" she asked wiping her eyes.

"Damn right," Jesse said indignantly. "If it would have suggested a cockatoo or a rabbit or something, I wouldn't have had to walk around with bad hair for five months."

The story was over, and Jesse abruptly turned around again to work on her car. She knew Carly was staring at her. She could feel it. She didn't say a word, but stood there for what must have been ten minutes, just watching her replace the starter.

Not long after her client had left her, she slammed the hood, wiped her hands on her pants, and slid in behind the wheel of her Fiat. "Please, God, let it start."

She turned the key and said a quiet thank you when it rumbled to life. Finally, she thought, I can get back to working on this investigation full time. Needless to say, so far it was not going at all as she had planned or would have liked.

Harley came charging at the car from the stable when Jesse

backed out of the garage. It amazed her how much he looked forward to going for rides, especially since the two of them had spent so much time on the road. She had always felt bad for him, this big, hundred and twenty pound dog crammed into that tiny passenger space. He must have been miserable. But he never once complained. From the moment they left Lauren's house in California until they settled into an apartment in Atlanta two years later, he was always happy and upbeat.

Nobody could ever convince Jesse that dogs don't know what humans are saying and thinking. The first time she set eyes on him, she *knew* that he understood what she'd been through, and that he understood her need to get as far away from California as possible. He was - and continued to be - her rock.

Jesse cut the engine to the Fiat and grabbed her jacket from behind her seat as she got out. "You big goofy mook," she said, rubbing his big head as he jumped up on her. "Do you honestly think I'd leave without you?"

His black fur came off in clumps in her hand, and it occurred to her at that moment that she'd been neglecting him. They hadn't spent any quality time together since she began working on this case, so she grabbed his tennis ball from under her seat and took him down to the water's edge.

While playing with him and teasing him and exercising him, she thought back to the hot July day when he first came into her life. She and Lauren were in Lauren's Volvo. Being a psychologist, Lauren worked closely with her doctor while Jesse was confined. She had just been discharged, and Lauren was bringing Jesse to her house, because she no longer had a house to return to. Joan and Lauren had packed everything and moved it while she was still in the hospital.

The air conditioner wasn't working in her car so they had the windows down. Jesse just stared straight ahead.

While she was well enough to come home, she wasn't so sure that she was ready to face life without Abby. Even though she was still hurt and angry, she missed her desperately. And she knew that visiting her was out of the question as it would only result in a return trip to the nut house.

"Tomorrow we'll go shopping for some new clothes," Lauren told her, keeping an eye on her as if she expected her to go crazy and fling herself out onto the freeway. "You've got to have something nice for the trial, and you've lost so much weight, I don't think anything you have will fit you anymore."

Jesse felt like a zombie, more dead than alive. Nothing mattered to her.

Until they got to Lauren's house. Joan was sitting on the front porch holding this little roly poly puppy. She jumped to her feet, grinning from ear to ear when she saw them pull up.

"Look who's here!" she said excitedly to the puppy, letting him run free to greet them. "Mama's home!"

Jesse looked at her twin. "You guys got a dog?"

"God, no!" Lauren exclaimed. "He's all yours. And you'd better train him fast, because I don't want our house smelling like dog crap."

Jesse didn't realize it at the time - in fact, it didn't occur to her until this very moment - what a Godsend Harley was. And she owed it all to Joan and Lauren. They knew that had she not had the responsibility of a pet, had she not had someone by her side to love, someone who loved her unconditionally, she would most likely have died young. And they were right. All the way home in the car that day, Jesse was planning to take off on her motorcycle, get a case of beer, a carton of cigarettes, and disappear into the mountains with her gun, where she would pray for the courage to kill herself. But the following morning, after that little guy chewed up her only pair of shoes and then smiled up at her, she knew she was hooked.

It was no accident that God made puppies so damn cute and irresistible; how else could we forgive them their misdeeds and continue to love them so much? Jesse knew he'd be counting on her, and she wasn't about to let him down.

When she tossed the ball again and watched her now full-grown shepherd fly down the water's edge to retrieve it, she wondered where the time went. This coming April would be four years without Abby, and the pain was as real today as it was the day they parted. Would it ever change? She doubted it.

When Harley came back with the ball, he looked up at the house and barked, and when Jesse glanced up to see what had caught his attention, she saw the drapes move in the library window.

Hovering, she griped to herself, lighting a cigarette. She found a big rock to sit on, and before she even finished her cigarette, her client strolled down the path from the driveway to join her.

"My security team just called," she told Jesse as she approached and handed her a note. "They found it."

"Who's Karen Romanesco?" Jesse asked, reading the message.

Carly leaned on one leg, looking out into the water. "I don't know. I've never heard of her."

"How much has she taken so far?"

"At least six and a half million from my company, another eight hundred and forty-five thousand from my personal accounts. She's breaking through the security in our mainframe - which is very tight, by the way. Our top analysts were able to follow her trail, but they're still trying to figure out how she was able to breach the system. She's diverting money to one of my personal accounts, then transferring it to her account. From there it goes to an off-shore account in the Cayman Islands. After that, we lost the trail."

"You're sure she never worked for you?"

"I'm positive. I've interviewed and hired every single person who works for me, and I've never hired anyone by that name." She gestured toward the note. "I don't know if that's her real address. I tried calling the number for her, but it's been disconnected."

Slowly, Jesse turned her head to look at Carly. She was smirking. "What would you have done if she'd answered?" She held her hand up to the side of her head as if speaking on a phone. "Hi, this is Carly McCray; I'm calling to find out why you're stealing money from me and if you're the person who's trying to kill me?" Carly smiled wearily at that, and Jesse glanced back at the note. "She lives in Chicago," she muttered to herself. "Looks like I'm going to Chicago."

"Do you think she's the one who…?"

"Killed Susan and is trying to kill you?" Jesse finished her question. "Well, let me put it this way: it'd be a pretty strong coincidence for this all to be happening at about the same time. Usually, if someone's being threatened, the smartest thing to do is to follow the money trail."

"You don't seriously believe that you'll find her in Chicago, do you?"

"No, but it's a good place to start. I might find someone who knows her, someone who might know how she's connected to all of this, and who - if anyone - she's working with." Jesse didn't wear a watch, but she guessed it was somewhere between four or five o'clock. "If I drive down tonight, I'll have all day tomorrow to…."

"Why don't you wait until tomorrow to drive down? It's only a few hours' drive. Or if you prefer I can arrange for Chris to fly you there. That way, you'll be able to catch up on your sleep tonight and still have a full day in Chicago. And I'll be at the office all day, so there won't be much chance of my running into this Karen character."

Shit, that's right, Jesse thought. "But it might take me longer than one day," she said in a worried voice. "Maybe we should find someplace for you to stay for a while, someplace safe…"

"That's out of the question. I need to be at the office tomorrow. I'll be fine."

"Are you sure? I mean, I don't want you to be a sitting duck, but, you know, I can't just sit back, either, and wait for things to happen."

"I'll be fine," Carly repeated. She had that insistent gleam in her eye that Jesse knew not to challenge. "As I said, I'll be at the office all day. Hopefully, you'll be back by the time I get home. And I think Doug will be home tomorrow. I'll have to check his schedule."

"Okay. But this Karen obviously has access to *your* schedule, so I want you to leave earlier than you normally would and take a different route home tomorrow. And don't put any of your appointments, anything, on the computer."

Carly nodded her understanding, her eyes never moving from the Lake. "Do you swim?"

"Huh?"

"I was planning to do a few laps in the pool before dinner to work off some of this stress. You're welcome to join me."

Frankly, it sounded like a good idea to Jesse. A little distraction might be just what the doctor ordered. "Well, okay, sure, but unless you have a spare suit, I'm gonna have to go in this," she responded, gesturing toward her trousers and t-shirt.

"I have plenty of extras." Carly gave her a warm smile and chatted nervously all the way back to the house.

Ferns and huge green tropical plants were tastefully situated amongst the patio furniture along the tiled deck. Next to the large rectangular pool was a whirlpool with its jets running, creating a foam of bubbles that danced on the surface.

The room glowed from the lights on the sides of the pool. The chlorine smell burned the inside of Jesse's nostrils, and her sneeze echoed over the quiet hum of the whirlpool.

"Bless you." Carly hit a button on the near wall and the room filled with music. Not classical stuff, but a soft jazz. She opened the door to the changing room and came back with her arms full of bathing suits, some plain, some with wild and exotic colors and designs. "Do you prefer a one-piece or two?" she asked, holding them out for her.

Jesse grabbed a plain turquoise Speedo one-piece and followed Carly to the changing rooms, which were like department store dressing room, each with partitions separating one from the next. A mirrored vanity took up the entire back wall, and along the counter were combs, brushes, hair dryers - all of the necessary equipment to restore one's 'natural' beauty.

Jesse closed the door to her cubicle and took a seat on the padded bench. While leaning to pull off her cowboy boots, she happened to glance beneath the partial wall that separated her booth from Carly's and saw Carly's navy slacks gather around her ankles. She looked away in prudish embarrassment when the white lace panties followed.

"Thank you for agreeing to go with me Saturday night," Carly said through the wall. "I wouldn't bother going at all, but Senator Garvey will be there - he and his wife will be modeling - and he's the main reason we were chosen for a very lucrative pharmaceutical contract. And if that works out well, we might be in line for a Defense Department contract at the beginning of next year."

Jesse heard Carly's door open and reflexively checked the handle on her own door to be certain that she'd locked it.

"I'll be right out." She slid into the bathing suit and turned to look in the mirror. "Oh, shit," she muttered. The suit hung on her in a most unflattering manner. It was far too long. The material that was supposed to cover her crotch was down around the middle of her thighs, and her breasts were standing out over the top, completely exposed.

Carly was setting out some towels for them on one of the tables near the whirlpool and looked up when Jesse finally stepped out of the changing area. Jesse knew that she wanted to laugh out loud, but - to her credit - she didn't. Her face was as perfectly composed as it was when she first turned to see her.

In an effort to customize the suit to her body, Jesse had to tie the two shoulder straps in a knot. Her curls hid most of it, but Jesse was sure that Carly could plainly see the bulge of material under her hair.

Carly watched Jesse walk to the shallow end of the pool, staring at the dark bruises that blemished just about every part of her body. Patting Harley on the head once, she walked to the deep end, dipped her foot to test the water, and dove in head-first. She broke for air and swam vigorously to the other end, performing a perfect flip and starting back when she reached the edge.

Jesse waded in slowly, taking her time to let her body adjust to the tepid water. It felt so good. It was the perfect temperature. She leaned back and floated around for a while, staring at the ceiling, thinking.

Carly was a serious swimmer. Her pace was swift, her strokes strong and sure. She finished five or six laps before she slowed. Even at this reduced speed, there was no way Jesse would be able to keep up with her. Not even if her body was completely intact. But she did her best.

Flipping onto her front, Jesse joined Carly in her laps, trying to match her quick pace. After a while, when Carly finally stopped to rest, she shook the excess water from her hair and watched Jesse, who touched the wall a short distance from her, did a quick turn, and headed to the other end. She did this three more times, each time moving farther and farther away from where Carly was stationed in the deep end.

Jesse came to rest at a spot about ten feet from her. Holding the edge of the pool, she submerged herself completely and as she came up for air, she threw her head back to keep her wet curls from sticking to her face. She was breathing hard, wheezing and coughing. To her surprise, Carly was right beside her when she opened her eyes.

"Are you okay?"

Jesse saw her expression change as she watched the perfectly shaped water beads fall from Jesse's curls to her chest and drip from the tips of Jesse's tiny breasts. Her glance moved to intercept Jesse's, which was narrowly focused on her voyeuristic behavior. Jesse felt heat rise to her face. Carly's eyes smoldered with desire, and although Jesse should have expected this, she was totally unprepared for it.

"No," she said, having forgotten that Carly had asked her a question. It was more in response to what she knew Carly was thinking.

Carly's eyebrows rose. "You're not okay?"

"I mean, yeah. Yeah, I'm okay." Jesse's voice broke with nervousness. Her foot accidentally touched Carly's foot under the water and they simultaneously looked down at it, then at each other.

Taking a deep breath, Carly moved still closer to Jesse and reached to caress her hand. All Jesse could do was stare at it, slim and elegant, as it gently moved up to her elbow, then slowly back to her fingers.

Jesse cleared her throat. "Carly," she rasped softly, withdrawing her hand. "I don't think we should...ah..." Her mouth ceased functioning as Carly put her arms around Jesse and sandwiched her between her body and the edge of the pool. She shivered at the sensation of Carly kissing her neck ever so delicately and slowly tracing a line up to her ear.

Carly's bare legs brushing lightly against Jesse's bare legs excited Jesse to no end. But a little voice in the back of Jesse's mind told her to put a stop to this. Fast. "Carly, wait," she whispered her impassioned plea. "This isn't...."

Jesse made a quiet noise as Carly tightened her grip, as her mouth found Jesse's mouth. Their lips met once, briefly, lightly, and Jesse pulled back and opened her eyes. Carly was leaning closer with her lips parted slightly, eyes shut, moving in for more.

Carly tentatively outlined Jesse's lips with her own, and then gently tugged Jesse's lower lip into her wonderfully warm and enveloping mouth.

Jesse's heart pounded madly in her ears as Carly's experienced hands prowled her naked back. Her nipples hardened. Submitting, Jesse pulled her closer, feeling the length of their bodies make contact, kissing her client with a sequence of soft, gentle kisses.

Jesse's participation seemed to be exactly what Carly wanted. Moaning, her breath warmed the skin on Jesse's cheek. Carly's hands moved down Jesse's body and came to rest on the curve of her hips. Her kissing intensified, bringing another quiet noise from Jesse as her tongue explored the innermost regions of Jesse's mouth.

Turning her head, she kissed Jesse's cheek, made her way to the side of Jesse's head, where she kissed Jesse's neck, her warm breath in Jesse's ear bringing a small tremor from the detective.

Abby's words echoed from somewhere in the chaos of Jesse's mind. "Jess, I love you. I want you to be happy. Don't let what happened to us sour you on other relationships. Let her in."

At the same time, between kisses, Carly breathed Jesse's name, and like a molecule of air as it breaks the water's surface, the voice snapped the spell and brought Jesse back to full and alert consciousness.

"No!" she gasped, backing away as if Carly was some sort of frightening demon. "Oh, God."

Carly's alarm was evident by her stricken expression. "What is it, sweetheart?" She reached to touch Jesse's hand, but Jesse pulled back. "What's the matter?"

"I'm sorry, Carly," Jesse said quietly, her eyes downcast. "I...God, I'm sorry," she repeated lamely. "I didn't mean to...I mean, I can't..."

"But...." Obviously stunned and bewildered by this turn of events, she searched Jesse's face. "I don't understand. I thought you..."

Jesse put her head down and mumbled helplessly, "I'm really sorry. It's...I can't. I can't do this."

"Is there someone else?" Desperately seeking an explanation, she moved a little closer, holding the edge of the pool. "If there is, I apologize. I just assumed..."

Refusing to look at her, Jesse did not respond. Her intense discomfort was contagious.

"Is it me?" Carly asked. The realization hit her like a cold slap in the face when Jesse looked up. "That's it, isn't it?" she concluded dismally. "It's me."

"No. Well, partly..." Jesse said, offering no other details. "I...aside from the fact that you're my client, I'm...I'm not interested in casual sex or a one-night stand. If I was looking for a relationship -

215

which I'm not - it'd have to be long-term. As in forever."

Trying unsuccessfully to conceal the intensity of her disappointment, Carly said at last, "I see." Her voice barely escaped her contracted throat. She swallowed what little pride remained. "And you don't think I could offer you any kind of commitment, is that it?"

In Jesse's mind, that question had already been answered. Without responding, she lifted herself out of the pool, wrapped a towel around her waist, and walked out with Harley close behind.

Upstairs in her room, she grabbed a tissue from the box on the night table and blew her nose. She changed her clothes and clicked on the bedside lamp before climbing into bed where she sat with her back against the headboard. Harley jumped up beside her and rested his head on her lap. She let out a deep breath while scratching his neck.

"What're we going to do, boy?" She looked at him. "Why does this always happen? I don't think I've done anything to bring this on. It's not like I've been flirting with her." Her hand played with his pointy ears as she stared off into the distance. "This is exactly what happened in Atlanta, remember?" she asked her dog. "Remember Clara?"

Harley raised his head and thumped his tail on the bed at the mention of the name.

"Yeah." She smiled sadly at her canine companion. "You really liked her, didn't you?" She sighed and shook her head. Her eyes narrowed. "Lauren says she's still calling, looking for us."

"Are you okay in there?" a voice called from the bathroom. Karen appeared in the doorway. "I was collecting your clothes for the laundry and I couldn't help but overhear."

"I bet you couldn't," Jesse griped under her breath, wiping her nose with the tissue.

Karen stepped into the room. "I don't know what happened between the two of you, but Carly's simply miserable." She glared at Jesse. "I've known her since the day she was born, and this is the first time I've seen her like this. When Shawn, her father, died, she poured herself into her work. You couldn't tear her away from her desk. That was how she dealt with it. But this..." She shook her head. "She's downstairs right now, just staring at her computer screen." She kept a watchful eye on Harley as she took a step closer to the bed. "And look at you. You're not any better off than she is."

"Just leave me alone, will you? This doesn't concern you."

"The hell it doesn't," she snapped back. "Look, I like you." Incredibly, she smiled kindly. "You seem like a decent young lady. You're considerate, responsible, and attractive. I can see why Carly likes you. I don't know if you've put it together yet, but that young woman down there is like a daughter to me. I don't work here because I have to. And I'll tell you this: You're the first person I've seen who's affected her so profoundly. I've seen that woman talk to Presidents, Senators, CEOs, movie stars, some very famous and important people. I've seen her seduce dozens of women, and not

217

once did she show her nervousness. But when you walk into a room, she…she changes."

"Look," Jesse told her. "There's nothing you can do. This is between Carly and me."

"Fine. Then you won't mind if I send her up here to talk to you, so you can work out whatever problems you're having." With that, she turned and left the room.

A few minutes later there was a faint tapping on Jesse's door. "Jesse?"

"Come in."

Harley's tail thumped on the bed as Carly cautiously approached them. She was wearing jeans and a sweatshirt. Her hair was still wet and dangled down past her shoulders.

"Karen said that you wanted to see me?" She took a seat beside her on the edge of the bed. "First, let me apologize. I…I'm so sorry for the way I acted in the pool. I had no right to…to do what I did."

Jesse slowly wiped her arm across her eyes. Her reddened gaze looked not unkindly upon her. "You didn't do anything wrong."

Carly considered her for a moment with her head tipped to one side. "I didn't mean to pressure you into anything. I should have stopped when you asked me to. It's…I care about you Jesse. It was so nice being close to you." She brushed aside a fallen lock of hair from Jesse's face. "You're not upset with me, are you?"

Jesse rubbed her bloodshot eyes and laughed a pathetic little laugh. She shook her head. "If anyone should be mad, it should be you. I was there, too. I could have stopped it, but I didn't. I let it happen."

"And was that wrong?" Carly asked gently.

"I don't do one-night stands."

Carly stared at her for a few moments. "What if I told you that I'd want much more than that with you?"

Jesse sighed in exasperation. "Carly, I don't want to hurt you. I'm flattered that you, you know, that you're interested in me in that way, but I'm not looking for any kind of relationship. It's not you. I swear this has nothing to do with you. I'm just not ready to get involved with anyone. I don't know if I'll ever be ready. I'm sorry." She ventured a peek in Carly's direction and saw the warmth and sadness and confusion behind her pale eyes. "You know the woman...in the picture with me? At my cabin?"

Carly nodded, and Jesse continued. "Her name was Abby Cohen. She was the only person I've ever been with. We were together for seven years." A tear slid out of the corner of Jesse's eye as she quietly added, "Until she died." Before Carly had time to react to this bombshell, Jesse continued because she wanted to explain, not elicit sympathy. "Lauren and Joan think I have a fear of abandonment. They're both psychologists and they think they've got it all figured out. But that's not it," she insisted.

"You think if you start a relationship with someone else you'd be unfaithful to Abby?" Carly asked quietly, thinking of why it was her father had never remarried after her mother's death.

"Yeah, but that's not all. I don't know how to explain it. I, uh, Abby and I were so close. I loved her so much, I...feel like....like there's nothing left for anyone else."

"Oh, Jesse," Carly said with such compassion that it brought more tears from Jesse's eyes. "How can you say that? You have so much to give." She reached to take Jesse's hand and squeezed it tight, holding it for a long while. "I'd settle down with the first woman who gave me half as much as you've given me."

Jesse wiped her eyes with her forearm and peeked over it at Carly, who was looking at her with such love in her pale gray eyes. "I don't know, Carly. I really do care about you. I do. I just...I don't know where to go from here," she confessed at last.

The kindness never left Carly's expression as she stood up and grabbed the blankets. "You're tired. You've had a long day," she said as she encouraged Jesse to get under the covers. She turned off the light on the nightstand and crawled in beside her to hold her. Jesse sniffled as she rested her head on Carly's shoulder. She felt a gentle kiss on top of her head just before falling asleep.

- Friday -

Jesse woke at four-thirty and found herself alone in bed with Harley. She quickly showered, dressed and got herself ready to leave for Chicago for the day. When she opened the bedroom door, Harley took off down the dark hallway to the foyer below where he scratched and cried to be let out. Jesse looked at Carly's bedroom door, which was closed tightly. She sighed. Using the handrail to guide herself through the darkness, she quickly descended the staircase and opened the front door for him. She stepped out onto the porch to have a cigarette while she waited for him to return.

"Hurry up." She watched him slip into the blackness that surrounded the estate. Thunder rattled the ground; lightning illuminated the skies as the rain poured down around her. "Har-ley!" She waited for the bark of her faithful companion, and as her eyes scanned the blackness, she thought she detected a motion in the distance.

Thunder rolled across the sky. It was such a loud, deep rumbling that even if Harley had replied, Jesse would not have heard it. A long jagged lightning bolt ran from the heavens down into the surrounding woods, and the moment the light reached her, Jesse saw a dark figure. It wasn't canine, but human in form. And it was now directly in front of her, about ten feet away.

Without thought, Jesse hurled her body off the porch like a

mountain lion pouncing on its prey. The intruder gave way to her assault, and her momentum carried them together a good five yards in the cold soppy grass.

Jesse pulled her gun from her holster and stuck it under the chin that protruded slightly from the hooded rain poncho. She pushed the cold steel end of the barrel into her victim's neck. "One move and I'll blow your fucking head off!"

"Jesse," said the choked voice. "It's me."

Jesse tore the gun away from her and released the hammer. "Jesus! I could have killed you!" She was breathing fast. "What are you doing out here?" She asked in an unnerved whisper as she crawled off her client and offered her a hand up. "Christ, I could have killed you! You scared the shit out of me!"

"I scared you?" Carly's laugh was the tight nervous type that always accompanies a brush with disaster. She pulled herself up with Jesse's assistance. She had serious difficulties breathing and speaking as a result of her shock, and the blow to her throat when they landed.

Undaunted by the rain, Harley came slapping up in the water, splashing them both.

"I'm really sorry. I thought…Are you okay?"

Jesse offered her arm for support and as they approached the porch, Carly turned back to the site and stuttered, "M-m-my shoes."

Jesse looked down to see her nyloned feet sunk deep in the mire of the flower bed. Turning, she saw the pumps planted in the yard where she had dislodged Carly from them. "I'll get them later. Let's get you out of the rain."

Once inside, Jesse took inventory of her client. Her business suit beneath the raincoat was soaking wet, soiled from top to bottom. The toes of her mud-covered nylons stretched a good three inches beyond her toes, making them look like shriveled elf slippers.

Jesse hoped to find something positive to tell her. "At least your face isn't…" She pushed Carly's hood down to reveal a mud-stained forehead, dirty cheeks, and mud-caked hair. "Oh," she said quietly. "Sorry." She guided Carly up the stairs, through her bedroom to her bathroom, apologizing the whole time.

Carly was not unaffected by the incident, but she thought that Jesse was more shaken by it than she was. "It's okay, Jesse. I'm fine. You didn't know. It's okay." Foundering for a moment as her wet feet slipped on the tiled floor, she caught herself on the counter. "I heard you call my name and assumed that you knew it was me out there."

"I said 'Harley', not 'Carly'." Jesse watched her lean on the counter for support, tug off her nylons, and throw them into the nearby waste basket. "What were you doing out there?"

Carly looked at her in the mirror as she calmly twisted out of her blazer. "I was feeding the horses before I left for work. I didn't turn on the outside light because it's right below your bedroom window and I didn't want to wake you." While sliding out of her dirty silk blouse, she turned to the mirror and burst out laughing.

The cups of her sheer bra, which, in parts, were still a brilliant white, were now full of sludge, stained a dingy brown.

Once Jesse noticed, she joined Carly briefly in her laughter, then backed out of the bathroom slowly.

* * * *

There was no time for breakfast. Carly was in her library, sorting papers, packing her briefcase for the day when Jesse walked in with a fresh cup of coffee in one hand, her duffel bag in the other. Carly glanced up at her. "Do you have everything you need?"

"Yeah."

"Are you sure you don't want Chris to fly you down?"

"I'm sure."

"You're taking the Lexus?"

"Nah, I'll take my car."

"I wish you'd take the Lexus instead. I'd hate for you to be stranded. Karen filled it for you last night."

"Okay."

"Will you be home tonight?"

"I don't know. It depends."

"If you need to spend the night there, go to the Four Seasons Hotel on Lake Shore Drive. We have a corporate discount there." She plucked an American Express Corporate Gold Card from her briefcase and pushed it across the desk. "Use this. And take this, too, please." Digging in her briefcase, she pulled out a cell phone and slid that across the desk. "I'll be tied up in meetings most of the day, but I should be able to steal a few moments here and there to check my voice mail. Or you can press nine and talk to Charlene."

With that, Jesse was dismissed, apparently, as Carly returned to her previous activity. She adjusted the strap over her shoulder and turned to leave.

"Jesse." She turned back to see Carly's warm smile. "Drive safely."

* * * *

It was growing light by the time Jesse took the exit for I-43 South in Green Bay. She took a sip of her coffee and thought of Carly when she passed the 172 interchange. She was certain that that was the route Carly took to get to her office.

She reflected on their exchange earlier, how Carly had made her feel like she was a kid getting final instructions from a parent before being shuffled off to summer camp.

"Jess," a voice broke in. "Don't shut her out."

"Abby?" she whispered. This was not just another one of her dreams or memories. Nor was it her imagination. At least she didn't think it was.

"It's time to stop running, honey. I know how you feel about me, but you've got to move on. I want you to be happy, my love. I want you to settle down. You're not Moses. You don't need to wander."

Jesse didn't understand this - or any of Abby's other recent visits.

"Abby, I don't know what you want. Why are you doing this?"

"Haven't you figured it out yet?" Abby teased. "I don't mean to be cruel, Jess, but sometimes you can be so slow. The investigation isn't why you were sent here, hon. *She* is. You were sent here for her."

And with that, Abby was gone, leaving Jesse alone in the car with her thoughts for the rest of the drive to Chicago.

* * * *

"Sure, I know Karen."

"Have you heard from her recently?" Jesse asked the woman.

"Just once since she quit last month."

"Do you know where she is?" The woman shook her head, and reading the suspicion in her eyes, Jesse lied and said, "I'm a claims representative with National Insurance. It's important that I speak with her about an accident she was involved in."

The woman's eyes widened. "She was in an accident? Is she okay?"

"I don't know. I haven't been able to contact her." Jesse opened her notepad and pretended to read from it. "She was driving a red Ford Excursion."

"Yeah. She rented it. I picked it up for her the day before she left," the woman said. "Her car couldn't pull the trailer."

"She had a trailer?"

"Yeah. She sold most of her stuff before she left and took the rest of it in the trailer."

"Do you know where she went? It's important that I find her."

"I don't know where she is. Like I said, she quit last month and the last I heard from her, she was staying in some motel in Wisconsin."

"Where in Wisconsin?"

"Something Bay. I have it written down somewhere. Come on in."

Jesse quizzed her while following her into the lounge. "Ellison Bay? Green Bay? Sturgeon Bay? Sister Bay?"

"Yeah. That's the place," the woman told her from behind the counter. "Sister Bay." She was paging through a phone book. "I know I wrote the name of the motel in here. It probably won't do you much good anymore, though. When I tried calling there two weeks ago, they told me that she'd checked out a while back."

"Did they tell you when?"

"Yeah, but I don't remember. I wrote it down, so once I find it…." She kept flipping the pages. "I always doodle when I'm on the phone," she said absently.

Jesse took out a pen. "Why did she move to Wisconsin, did she tell you?"

"All I know is that one of her clients from here offered her a job. She said she couldn't pass up the money. I guess she got like a fifteen thousand dollar advance."

"Do you know the client's name?"

She shook her head and turned the page, her eyes skimming up and down.

"Did you ever hear her say it?" She shrugged, and Jesse tapped her pen on her notepad. "Tell me if any of these names sound familiar: Chris Masters." Jesse looked up to see the woman pause to think, then shake her head. "Chelsea Johnson." Again with the head shake. "Donna Meyer." The same reaction. "Stephanie Hughes, Doug Heller, Jack Walthrop."

"Sorry," she told Jesse, returning to the phone book. "All I know is that it was a woman, not a man. She kept saying 'she' when she referred to her."

"Did she ever mention the name Carly McCray?"

"I really don't know. Some of those names kind of ring a bell, but I don't know if it's because of Karen or if they were my clients."

"How long did you work with her?"

"Not long. She just started working here in like April or May."

"Does the hotel keep records of your clients?"

"Yeah, but they aren't cross-referenced, they just show the room number and the date and time. If you want to know who was staying in the room at the time, you'd have to go through the registration records."

"Think you'd be able to get me those records?"

"I don't know."

The woman glanced up from the phone book to look over at her, and Jesse affected her most sincere look. "It'd really help a lot. I'm sure she'd like her settlement from the accident, and going through those records might make it easier for me to find her."

The woman took a moment to think it over. "Management frowns on any kind of breach of confidentiality."

"What if I made it worth your while?" Jesse reached into her trouser pocket, pulled out two crisp hundred dollar bills, and held them out to her between her index and middle fingers. "What do you say?"

Glancing nervously around the room, the woman took the money and quickly slipped it into the front pocket of her slacks. "My shift ends at three. Meet me here." Turning the page of her phone book again, she glanced down. "OOOH! Here it is! She was staying at the Seagate Hotel in Sister Bay. Checked out on the twenty-seventh."

The day after Susan died, Jesse recalled. "Do you happen to know if she has family or other friends who might know where she is now?"

"I doubt it. Her family's scattered all across the country. And besides me, she didn't have any friends around here. She's kind of a loner, really. Kept to herself all the time, really shy."

* * * *

Like a phantom, Carly's spirit hung over Jesse all day. No matter how hard she tried, no matter what she was doing, whether interviewing people who knew Karen Romanesco, lunching at a Kosher Deli, or driving back to Moonlight Bay, Jesse simply could not put Carly out of her mind. She wondered, pushing the button to open the gate at the end of her drive, if she was in her thoughts the way she seemed to consume Jesse's.

Everything was so vivid with Carly. Even during their bickering, Jesse felt it, the phenomenon, that strange vibration in the air. How was it that Jesse knew, and why was it so important to know, that every time she puts her reading glasses on, she sets them low on her nose and then slides them up? Or that she's normally right handed, but she always holds a pen in her left hand?

Everything about Carly, her facial expressions, her voice, all of it stuck with Jesse like a scene from a movie that she couldn't get out of her head.

It had been a busy, productive day, and although Jesse could have easily justified spending the night in Chicago, she didn't.

She pulled into Carly's garage well after midnight and breathed a sigh of relief when she saw Carly's Jeep parked in the next stall. Doug's black Hummer was gone.

Quietly, she retrieved her duffel bag from the back seat and went into the house. The control panel near the back door told her that the alarm system was not turned on. The house was quiet. It felt eerie. There were no signs of life from Karen's quarters as she passed them. The hall was pitch black, but Jesse managed to find the back stairs without having to disturb anyone by turning on a light. With the exception of a small beam of light from Carly's room, the upstairs was dark as well.

It was odd that she hadn't seen nor heard Harley. Normally he was right up in her face to greet her the moment she walked through the door. But tonight, he was nowhere to be found. Jesse got to her bedroom door and glanced across the hallway into Carly's room. The door was ajar, which was unusual, and the beam of light didn't seem to be coming from any of the fixtures, but rather from some other source.

"Carly?" Jesse pushed the door open further, and when it met with unexpected resistance, her blood went cold. She reached into her blazer for her gun. "Carly?"

On the floor at her feet was a flashlight with what looked like a male hand next to it. Jesse flipped on the overhead light.

It was Victor. He was on his stomach, and Jesse couldn't tell how badly he had been hurt. There was very little blood, a few small drops on the white carpet.

A fireplace tool had been used on him. It was right there beside him on the floor. His skin color seemed normal. And Jesse could hear him breathing. Her eyes scanned everything in the room as she stepped over him. The comforter was messed, a crystal lamp knocked off the night table, shattered on the floor. The closet door stood ajar.

"Carly?" Breaking into a cold sweat, a shiver running up and down her spine, she brought her gun up and cautiously made her way through the changing room to the bathroom. She said a silent prayer and turned the handle, pushing the door open as she remained in the changing room. A second later, she peeked her head into the bathroom. It was empty, nothing upset.

In a matter of minutes she had every light on the second floor lit, growing more concerned and more desperate with each room she checked.

"Carly!"

Downstairs, she investigated the housekeeper's quarters first. They hadn't been disturbed, but Karen was gone, too. The dining room was next and untouched.

Jesse dashed into the library. A few drawers had been pulled out of the desk, some papers scattered behind it, but there was no sign of her client. "Carly!" she screamed. Taking the spiral staircase two steps at a time all the way to the spire, Jesse looked out the windows into the dark woods and the Lake, down to the boathouse, toward the stable, but saw nothing in the blackness. She took the stairs from the spire back down to the second floor and went back to Carly's room.

Victor was gone.

"What the fuck?" She heard water running in the bathroom and slowly approached it, her gun out in front of her. Victor was bent over the sink splashing water in his face and he spun around when he saw Jesse's reflection in the mirror.

"What happened, Victor? Where's, uh, donde esta Carly?"

He seemed confused, frightened, dazed. He rambled in Spanish, pausing at times to moan and rub the back of his head. Jesse didn't understand a single word he was saying. She briefly considered calling Lauren to have her translate, but then Victor grumbled something about "Senorita Chris."

"Shit!"

The rain didn't slow her one bit. Cruising at eighty-five, she slowed the Lexus only occasionally for sharp curves on the way to Bailey's Harbor. The house was dark with the exception of the light from the television, which could be seen through the crack in the drapes over the living room window. A Ford Ranger was parked in the driveway, and turning out her headlights, Jesse came to a stop across the street. With her gun drawn, she ran to the front door.

It was unlocked. She turned the handle slowly. Inside, the shrill yelp of Chris' Chihuahua had given her away. The element of surprise was gone. But Jesse burst in anyway, prepared for anything.

The first thing she noticed was that Harley was curled up on the couch with a blanket and the Chihuahua.

Donned in sweat pants and a t-shirt, Chris was in a recliner, watching television. She sprang to her feet the moment she saw Jesse. "What the hell?"

"Where is she?"

Right at that moment, Carly came out of the kitchen with a bowl of popcorn. She was wearing blue and white striped flannel pajamas and matching slippers and was about to put a piece of popcorn in her mouth, but stopped when she saw Jesse. A mix of emotions crossed her face, but mostly she seemed shocked and concerned. "What are you doing here? What's the matter?"

"Have you been here all night?" Jesse asked, taking a quick glance around the house. She wiped the rain from her face.

"Yes. Well, since about eleven-thirty. It was getting late and I didn't think you'd be back tonight. Doug and Stephanie went out, and I didn't feel like staying home alone so when Chris showed up..."

"Where's Chelsea?"

"She's at work," Chris told her, keeping her distance from Jesse. She stooped to pick up the Chihuahua, who was hopping on her hind legs in front of her. She looked foolish dressed in the sweater that Jacey had given her.

"Where's Karen?" Jesse asked Carly.

With increasing concern, Carly questioned her with her gaze. "She went to see her sister-in-law. Why?"

After replacing her gun, Jesse lifted a trembling hand to her face and wiped her forehead. "Did you set the alarm at the house before you left tonight?"

"Yes. Why?"

"Did Victor know the code?"

"Of course not," Carly replied. "What's the matter?" She looked at her friend. "Get her something to drink, will you? Some water." She waited for Chris to leave the room, then invited Jesse to join her on the couch beside Harley, who seemed very glad to see Jesse. "What's wrong? Tell me what happened."

"Someone clobbered Victor," Jesse told her, calming herself. "I don't know what the hell he was doing there. I got home - to your house - and I found him out cold on your bedroom floor."

"My God! Is he okay?"

"He's got a big knob on the back of his head, but I'm sure he's fine." Jesse turned her eyes to her client. "It wasn't a burglary, Carly. Whoever was there, they were there for you. And they knew the code for the alarm system." Pulling a cigarette out, Jesse searched her pockets for a lighter. Her hands were still shaking. "It's a damn good thing you weren't there." Peering out toward the kitchen, Jesse asked, "Does Chelsea know the code to your alarm system?" Carly nodded uncomfortably. "Did she know you were here?"

Carly shook her head.

"Did she know that I'd be gone all day, that I might have been spending the night in Chicago?"

"I don't know. I told Chris. She might have mentioned...." Carly cut herself off when Chris returned with a can of Diet Coke and a glass of ice cubes.

Jesse watched her stretch her long legs out in front of her as she lowered herself into the recliner with her dog. She said to her client, "Do me a favor and call Victor and make sure he's okay. I'm guessing he's still at your house. See if he knows who attacked him. I couldn't understand him."

Once Jesse heard Carly on the phone in the other room, she turned her attention to Chris. "Do you know Karen Romanesco?"

Without hesitation, she replied, "Nope," as she scratched the underside of her dog's chin.

"The name doesn't sound familiar to you at all?"

"No. Well, Carly talked about her tonight, about the money and stuff, but no; I don't know her."

"Are you sure? I think you do. Up until the middle of last month, she was the masseuse at the Four Seasons Hotel in Chicago." Chris responded with an impassive shrug, and Jesse added, "According to the hotel records, she visited your room seven times this past summer."

"So?" Her brows came together as she grew to understand the implication of Jesse's questions. "What are you saying, that this masseuse and I are working together?"

"Are you?"

"God, you're crazy." Chris laughed and shook her head. She adjusted her glasses and gave Jesse a severe look. "Why the hell would I want to kill my best friend?"

Jesse calmly ticked off the items on her fingers: "Maybe because she's stinking rich and considers you a part of her family. Maybe because as of July, you don't have a cent to your name. Maybe because you're over two months behind on your mortgage payment and your second mortgage and all your other bills. Maybe..."

"You little bitch!" It took Chris less than a second to cross the room, and with the fabric from the front of Jesse's t-shirt clenched in her fist, she lifted Jesse up off the couch.

Right away Harley moved in on her, but caught in Chris' steel grip, Jesse told him to leave it. She looked from her dog to the other woman. "I can handle this."

The Chihuahua, Mickey, had chased Chris' feet and was dodging at them brainlessly. Chris was so close that Jesse could smell onion on her breath. With that one hand on her shirt, she nearly lifted Jesse off her feet. "I swear to God, if you ever tell Carly, I'll…"

"She's gonna find out sooner or later, about the money, about Chelsea's bogus nursing seminar…"

That must have been the final straw. In the next moment, Jesse found herself being sent backwards into the oak entertainment center across the room. Harley rushed in to protect her while Mickey let out high-pitched yaps.

While recovering, gasping for breath, before she saw it coming, Chris tackled her hard to the floor. Jesse used her legs to kick and buck her off, but Chris was relentless in her pursuit. She again managed to sit on Jesse, her big hands at Jesse's throat, gripping hard. Mickey nipped at Jesse's shoulders, while Harley growled, using his nose to butt the small dog away from her.

"What are you doing?" Carly flew in from the kitchen to break them up. Chris' elbow caught her on the side of the head and cast her to the floor on her back. "Stop it!"

But Chris didn't ease off one bit as she continued to strangle Jesse. Her eyes took on a dark, damning glow. Jesse was completely defenseless beneath her, choking and making ghastly gasping noises.

Carly got to her knees and tugged on her friend's shirt. "Chris!

Get off of her! Stop it! Let her go!"

"Stay out of this, Carly!" Chris shoved her away again, sending her into the cocktail table.

Angry now, Carly pushed this time instead of pulling. She threw all of her body at her friend to move her off of Jesse, who quickly curled into a tight ball and rolled from under their flailing limbs.

"Chris," Carly wheezed, holding her friend back from charging Jesse again. "Stop. Please stop."

Chris finally relented, and the moment Jesse was able to, she rolled over to get the rest of Chris' weight off of her. Climbing to her feet, she got a glimpse of herself in the mirror over the couch and saw the prominent imprints, in the exact shape of Chris' hand, on her throat, and the thin stream of blood that trickled down from the wound above her eye. Coughing, taking deep breaths, Jesse rubbed her neck and swiveled her head to make sure everything still worked.

"Would somebody mind telling me what that was all about?" A button had been severed from Carly's pajama top, revealing a significant portion of her chest. She seemed not to notice. She was sitting on her heels on the floor beside the cocktail table and brushed the hair from her forehead, looking at Jesse. Jesse returned her glance without flinching. Still waiting for an explanation, Carly shifted her icy stare to Chris. "What did she do?"

Chris was reluctant to reply, so Carly turned once more to Jesse. "What did you do? Did you attack her?"

"What?" Jesse was a little confused by the allegation but didn't make an effort to defend herself against the charge. She just stared at Chris and waited for her to build up enough courage to speak up.

"She didn't attack me," Chris said after a few moments. "I attacked her."

In astonishment, Carly looked at her friend, who let out a deep sigh and shook her head. "I knew this would happen! I knew it! Shit! Shit! Shit!" Slamming her fist against her muscular thigh, she threw herself back in the recliner. "The minute you told me she was a detective, I knew this would happen!" Through her glasses, her dark eyes pierced the thick air and found Jesse. "You had no right! You had no right to intrude into our personal lives! You're like a human wrecking ball!" She put her head down for a long moment and when she looked up again at Carly, a tear slipped down her cheek. She took off her glasses to wipe her eyes. "I'm sorry, Carly. We...I didn't want you to find out. Oh, God. Oh, Jesus."

Carly didn't understand. She looked like she was anticipating that Chris would give her a big confident smile and a hug and tell her that there's nothing to worry about, that everything would be fine. Instead, Chris sat there, her head in her hands, looking like she'd just lost her best friend. And in a voice that conveyed a fear of that same sentiment, Carly said quietly, "Find out about what?"

"You're going to hate me. I know you are. You'll never speak to me again."

"Chris," Carly said, frightened, seemingly bracing herself for an admission of cataclysmic proportions. "Whatever it is, I could never hate you."

Taking a deep sniffling breath, Chris kept her head down and said, "Chelsea wasn't at a nursing seminar this past May. She was inpatient at Park Ridge in Minneapolis." She started talking faster, perhaps thinking that would make it less painful, like when you rip off a bandage. "She was withdrawing from amphetamines. I didn't even know she'd had a problem until I found her in the shower one morning having a seizure. I found out later that she'd been addicted to them for over a year." Chris took a quick glance to gauge Carly's reaction.

In a reflective daze, Carly was watching the smoke rise from the cigarette that Jesse had just lit.

"I, um, we paid the bill in cash because we were afraid that St. E's would find out about it from her health insurance, or that it might show up somewhere and she'd lose her job. And probably her nursing license, too."

"So you lied to me." Carly's voice was remote and frigid now. "You've been lying to me for the past five months."

Chris nodded, keeping her head down, and Carly struggled to absorb all of this, tried to understand what it was that made her normally mild-mannered friend resort to violence. "And Jesse found out, didn't she? She confronted you with your lie and that's why you attacked her."

Chris glared at Jesse. "It wasn't just that. She implied that Chelsea or I might be involved with Karen in some plot to kill you."

"Karen Romanesco? You know her?" Chris shrugged and nodded at the same time, and Carly took another long moment to assimilate all of this. Her eyes suddenly grew wide. "Susan knew about Chelsea's drug problem, didn't she? She kept commenting about how much weight Chelsea had lost, how high-strung she was all the time. She knew and so....what? Was she blackmailing her? Is that why Chelsea had her killed?"

Jesse finally found her voice. "Wait a minute, Carly. You're jumping to conclus..."

Chris breathed out a sigh of annoyance. "Chelsea didn't kill Susan, Carly. God! We were the first ones there to comfort you after it happened, remember?"

"Yes, and I also remember how determined you were to convince me that it was an accident."

"Carly, I..."

"And you were the one who asked Sheriff Richmond to hurry the investigation along. Why'd you do that? Were you afraid they might find something to implicate Chelsea?"

"I did it for you! Christ, Carly! Don't you remember what you were like when your dad died?" Carly's eyes flared at the mention of her father's death. "It was like you were driven by your grief!"

"Don't you dare bring Fath..."

"I couldn't bear to see you like that again. Don't you remember how bad it was? You worked all day every day, even when you had pneumonia, when you were so sick you could hardly stand. You never slept; you never ate. You were so depressed you pushed everyone away - Donna, Karen, Doug, even me!"

"Let's calm down," Jesse suggested. She got up off of the couch to physically place herself between Chris and Carly. "First of all, Carly, I don't think you should assume that Chelsea went from being a drug user to a killer just like that." She snapped her finger and peripherally saw Harley look up at her, study her for a moment, then put his head down on the arm of the couch again.

"She's not *just* a drug user. She's a thief. She probably stole the drugs from the hospital. Am I right?" Carly and Jesse both turned to Chris, who looked at Carly, then bowed her head again. "Just as I suspected. And she's a liar. She not only lied to me, she lied to Chris, abusing amphetamines for over a year without her own lover even knowing!"

"Oooh! Do I smell popcorn?" came a voice from the back door.

Talk about bad timing, Jesse thought.

Still in her nurse whites, Chelsea walked into the climate of the overcast room smiling, but it was a short-lived grin. Chris was near tears, Jesse's expression was grave as she puffed on her cigarette, and Carly denounced her with her glare. "What's wrong?"

"Did you and Karen arrange to have Susan killed?" Carly asked Chelsea.

"Carly," Jesse warned. "You're jumping to conclusions. Chelsea's not the only one who knows Karen. Stephanie knows her, Doug knows her, Donna Meyer knows her..."

242

"And so do you, Carly," Chris added. "You and Susan were always getting massages after horse shows and golfing and stuff, any time we stayed in Chicago."

"Yes, but it's not likely that I'd conspire with her to kill myself, now is it?" Carly snapped back. She looked at Chelsea again. "Did you?"

"What are you talking about? Who's Karen? Are you talking about your housekeeper?" Chelsea asked, suddenly feeling like she was on trial for her life.

"Karen Romanesco," Carly growled.

"Who is Karen Romanesco? I've never...."

"See? She doesn't even know who you're talking about, Carly! Hell, I didn't recognize the name until Barney Fife here told me that Karen worked at the Four Seasons." She waved an angry hand in Jesse's direction. "I'm telling you we're not involved."

"How do you know Chelsea's not involved?" Carly asked with a quick gesture toward the nurse. "How could you possibly know? She's been deceiving us all for over a year. Everything she says, everything she does is suspect now. I don't see how you can even stand to be with her!" She sat back on her heels, her arms folded across her chest.

Chris threw her hands up in despair. "I knew you'd react this way and that's exactly why I didn't tell you. I knew you'd make all kinds of judgments about her, that you'd try to convince me that we shouldn't be together. Well I'm not like you, Carly. I can't throw away an entire relationship because of one mistake, the way you did with your sister."

Every vein in Carly's neck bulged below the skin. Color actually appeared on her face. And as she spoke, she brought out her arsenal of gestures. "What happened between Anne and me is ancient history and has nothing to do with this!"

"It has everything to do with this! Why do you think we kept it from you? Do you think I enjoyed making up stories about the nursing seminar, about why Chelsea and I were arguing so much, why we couldn't afford to take time off to go to California with you and Susan? Christ, Carly, I felt so guilty I thought I was going to burst. But I knew - **I knew** - how you'd react if I'd told you. I knew you'd do the same thing with Chelsea and me that you did with Anne when you found out about her problem. And I couldn't bear losing you."

Carly related her confusion and shock with a distant look. Her tone became quiet and calm. "The problems Anne and I had went much deeper than her drug use, Chris. You know that. But you and Chelsea...I ...Had you told me, I never would have..."

"Yes you would have, Carly," Chris said gently. "I know you. Once you found out that Chelsea had a problem, you'd be suspicious of everything she did and said, just like you are now. And eventually things would get to the point where I'd have to choose between the two of you, and I didn't tell you about it because I didn't want to have to make that choice."

"It seems to me that you made that choice when you decided to lie to me."

"I did what I thought was best under the circumstances. I didn't mean to hurt you. And I can't believe after everything we've been through together that you'd actually think that Chelsea or I would ever - ever - consider hurting either you or Susan." Chris took off her glasses to wipe her eyes again. "It hurts me to think that there's even a small doubt in your mind."

"I'm really sorry, Carly," Chelsea said in quiet dejection. She had moved to sit on the arm of the recliner that Chris was occupying, and Chris put her arm around her.

Carly looked like she was about to say something, then censored herself.

"Chris and I are still trying to deal with everything. Not just the drug thing, but the fact that I hid it from her for so long. But I'm telling you, neither of us are involved in any kind of plan to hurt you."

That seemed to shake Carly from her trance. "You're an addict, a thief, and a liar. How can I possibly believe anything you have to say to me?"

Without saying a word, Chris marched into the kitchen and returned with Carly's overcoat and briefcase. She held them out to her friend. "Looks like you've made your own choice. I love you dearly, Carly, you know that. And I know it hasn't been easy dealing with everything you've been through lately, but I won't have you talking like that to Chelsea. I want you to leave now. And until you can treat Chelsea with the same respect that you've shown to me for the past twenty-seven years, I don't want you to come back." She sounded numb. Both she and Carly appeared deeply wounded as they stared at one another.

On their way to the Lexus, which was parked across the street, Jesse asked Carly what Victor had to say about the attack, why he was at her house.

"He came back to tell me he'd gotten another job and to give me his forwarding address. He said that he saw the red Excursion in the driveway and the front door was standing wide open, so he went in to check it out. That was the last thing he remembered."

Jesse opened the back door for Harley and cringed when she heard his nails on the leather seats. Slipping behind the wheel, she waited for Carly to situate herself before starting the car.

There was a tremor in her voice as she added, "I told him that he could stay in his quarters tonight, until he was feeling well enough to drive."

From the light of the dash in the car, Jesse saw her client's bottom lip quivering, saw her entire body shiver. "Are you cold?" she asked, turning up the heat, but Carly shook her head.

She pulled a tissue loose from the box in the glove compartment and blew her nose. Harley rested his head on her shoulder and she tipped her head to rest on his.

Jesse reached over to hold Carly's hand. It was ice-cold. "Do you want to talk?" she asked quietly.

Carly said nothing so neither of them spoke again until Jesse pulled the Lexus into the garage for the second time that night. "Change the code on the alarm system before you go to bed. Don't tell anyone what it is. Not a soul."

* * * *

Harley trotted a path from the door to the bed and back again. He whined, and Jesse rolled over. Having fallen asleep just a few minutes earlier, she groaned. "No, Harley. It's bedtime."

He scratched the door and whined again, this time throwing in a quick bark, and concerned by his drastic need to get out of the room, Jesse threw back the covers.

The hallway was dark, but Jesse could see that Carly's bedroom door was closed. She had heard her in there earlier, tidying up and taking inventory after checking on Victor. Right now, though, everything was quiet and still.

It wasn't until Harley led her to the bottom of the back stairs when she heard the noise, like someone coughing or retching. "Carly?"

"Please don't turn on any lights," she said from the bathroom off the laundry room. She sounded different, weak, nasal, miserable.

Jesse heard her vomit and rushed to her side in the darkness. "What's wrong?"

"It's nothing." Carly leaned back against the wall, her head down. "It's one of my migraines." Pulling herself to the counter, she ran some water and then leaned way over and threw up in the sink, gasping between heaves. "Oh, God," she groaned. Even without the light, Jesse saw the reflexes at work as her back drew up again. This time nothing came out.

"Take a deep breath," Jesse suggested, matching her tone to a near whisper. To calm her, Jesse placed her hand on Carly's low back. The dampness had soaked through her pajama top, and Jesse couldn't help but be reminded of Abby. "Relax and take a few deep breaths. Try to swallow." She waited for Carly to rinse her mouth. "Are they always this severe? Do you want me to call someone? A doctor?"

"No. I just need to...." Her frail voice trailed off altogether, and Jesse helped prop her up.

"Okay. You're okay. I've got you." Half dragging her, half carrying her, Jesse led her out of the room. It was awkward because Carly was so much taller. They weren't going to make it up the stairs like that. Carly was simply too weak, so Jesse guided her to the darkened library and lowered her onto the couch, urging her to recline fully. She took a throw from the back of the couch and covered her with it. Moving to the end of the sofa, then, she leaned to rub her client's head.

Carly reached up to grab her hand. "Please don't. I can't stand to have anyone touch me when I..."

"It's okay. I know what I'm doing," Jesse said softly, massaging the temples. "I used to do this for Abby. It was the only way I could get her to stop crying and fall asleep."

"I never sleep," Carly murmured.

Eight minutes later, according to the clock on the desk, her hand dropped to her side. Jesse stroked her hair a while longer until she knew for sure that she was asleep. She kissed her forehead and took a seat on the other side of the sectional, where she kept a silent vigil for her.

- Saturday -

Carly wore an eloquent black dress; its plunging neckline spoke volumes. A diamond and gold necklace rested on her chest. Her ebony hair was drawn back tightly into a French braid. The braid was pulled up in the back and secured by a gold comb, giving her a classic look of elegance. Her matching gold earrings, which dangled to the middle of her neck, shimmered brilliantly in the light from the hall.

The impact of her beauty hit Jesse like a speeding locomotive, and she couldn't prevent her jaw from dropping. "You look...." As her mind searched for the precise adjective, she thought of words like gorgeous, awesome, sensational, stunning, sexy, magnificent. The word "wow" even popped up, but even that would have been an extreme understatement. In the end, all she managed was an awkward "nice".

Looking down, Carly smiled sedately.

"I'm sorry I'm running so late. I'll be ready in a little bit."

Carly nodded. "I'll wait in the library."

They hadn't had a chance to talk at all during the day. Carly didn't wake up until after eleven and had to leave right away to have her hair done, and while she still looked a bit peaked, she appeared as beautiful as ever. Jesse wasn't comfortable having Doug chauffeur his aunt around, but she didn't have much choice. She spent much of the day in Sister Bay, a small town Northwest of Bailey's Harbor, and barely had enough time to run her errands before returning to Carly's house to get ready for the fund-raiser.

In her line of work, a case of the nerves was no stranger to her, but it almost never presented itself when she was getting dressed. She wore her new black linen suit that looked almost like a tuxedo with its shiny strips down the legs. Matching material boarded the thin lapels of her blazer, under which she wore no shirt. The pants were nothing like the shapeless trousers that she was accustomed to wearing. These pants weren't nearly as comfortable, either.

Taking a final inspection in the mirror, she fussed with her hair a bit longer, made sure that her stitches were covered, released a deep breath and went downstairs.

Carly was standing behind her desk, skimming through a stack of papers that she'd taken from her fax machine. She fumbled to take off her reading glasses while rearranging her documents. She seemed very edgy. "We should leave," she said tightly. She put a book on top of the thick pile of papers.

Jesse pulled her gun from her pocket and handed it to her. "Can you put this in your purse or something? I don't have any place to keep it."

Carly took it from her, keeping it a good distance from her body, holding it and looking at it as if it were a foul-smelling diaper. "Do you really need it? Can't we leave it home tonight?"

"I'd rather not," Jesse told her. "But if you're not comfortable...."

They took the Lexus and as if by some tacit agreement, Jesse drove. It was a clear night for a change, the traffic steady but light.

"Your uncle Alvin says 'hi'," Jesse said as they pulled onto the highway.

"Alvin Pinkett? You saw him today?"

"Saw him? I couldn't get rid of him!"

Carly chuckled. "He's not really my uncle. He worked for Father at the factory. I haven't seen him for years, since he and his wife bought the Seagate. How is he?"

"Fine, I guess. He's quite a yacker." She glanced at Carly. "He sure had a lot to say about you." Carly's face melted into a shy smile as she looked out the window, apparently reflecting on those times.

"He had to tell me about your performances at your dad's Christmas parties for his workers, how you'd get all dressed up and sing and dance for everyone. I didn't have much time to look through the trailer that Karen left behind. I was afraid he'd come back and start talking again, so once I got the trailer opened, I just, you know, there was a desk in there, so I emptied a box and dumped the drawers into it. I'll have to check it out later, see if there's anything in there that'll help me track her down."

"Did you have a chance to stop back at your cabin?"

"Yeah. Susan's birth certificate finally came in the mail. I didn't have time to look at that, either. It's in the box of stuff I have to go through." They both grew quiet again, but this was an easy silence that neither of them seemed to mind.

In the foyer of the Carlton, in the middle of a small but growing crowd, Carly took Jesse's elbow as they made their way toward the hall. "Look at this place, will you? It's exquisite! Look, they've restored the stage. Oh, and the lights, the curtain, the fixtures. Everything is perfect, don't you think?" Turning backwards, she looked up into the balcony. Her big excited smile reminded Jesse of a child's face on Christmas morning. Carly started to walk with her and suddenly stopped flat. One of the pictures, a daguerreotype, on the wall had caught her eye.

She steered Jesse over to it. "Look. Look. Oh, I've always loved this print. It's a depiction of Green Bay shortly after the turn of the century. Here's where our corporate headquarter are," she said, pointing to what was an empty space on the very edge of the diagram. Jesse's gaze followed her finger as it traveled into the heart of Green Bay to a small brick building. "And here's where Mother grew up."

"In that house?"

"Mm-hmm. Actually, it was a bakery. Mother's family owned it and lived in the apartment above it. That's where my parents met - in the bakery. Father lived in Sturgeon Bay and had an appointment at the bank. He was getting a loan for the factory he was planning to build. His car broke down right here," Carly told her, pointing to a spot on the street in front of the bakery. She smiled. "He'd tried to fix it himself and gotten oil all over his one good suit, his hands, and his face, how he had finally given up and gone into the bakery to use the phone. Mother was in the back, up to her elbows in dough.

Father said that when he first laid eyes on her, he thought there was a halo over her head. Turned out it was just flour in her hair." Carly smiled and made her voice affectionately deeper. "'Don't ever let anyone convince you that there's no such thing as love at first sight', he used to tell me." She sighed. "I used to make him tell me that story every night before I went to bed. I thought that was so romantic."

Through the reflection of the glass covering the print, Jesse was blindsided when she caught the tender and loving and vulnerable expression on Carly's face.

"Shall we go in?" Carly asked without noticing Jesse's reaction.

"Huh?" Jesse's voice shook. She cleared her throat. "Oh, yeah."

They were almost in the banquet hall when someone grabbed Carly's arm. "Carly! There you are! I've been looking all over for you."

Carly turned to the voice, smiling her warm, disarming smile. "Hello, Nina. I love what you've done with the place!" she exclaimed with a grand sweeping motion of her arm.

Taking great care not to wrinkle her dark blue dress, the woman returned Carly's hug and added a quick peck on her cheek. "You do, truly?"

"Yes. It turned out beautifully. I love it."

"Tony'll be so happy to hear that. He was petrified that we wouldn't have it all done by tonight. Late this afternoon we found out that there was a problem with the new curtain." Carly, Nina and Jesse

254

all looked to the front of the room to the stage. "Tony and six of his men had to climb up on the old catwalks back stage to rig something up for tonight so we could get it up and down." She laughed quickly. "Poor Tony. He's been going through the Tums this week like you wouldn't believe. He so wants everything to be perfect."

A nervous woman, she talked really fast. She was probably a few years older than Carly, but seemed to have the energy of a six-year-old. "Why don't you come with me and I'll show you where your table is. And then I'll show you how to get backstage." Taking Carly by the arm, she whisked her away. Jesse followed at a distance.

"We were going to seat you with the Senator, but since there were so many in your party, we decided to give you your own table. Here we go. Right here."

Before Carly could say anything, Nina swept her off to the side of the banquet hall. "We've given you the green room tonight. We don't have enough dressing rooms for a show like this so Tony set up a bunch of temporary booths on the other side of the stage. There's absolutely no room back there to get around. And since Tony didn't have time to finish the stairs, we thought it would be best if you came through this door and down this hallway. Take a left and...Oh, what is this?" She kicked some thick wire cables out of the way. "I'm sorry about the mess. Tony was so concerned about getting everything set up for the models, I guess he forgot to clean this area up for you. I wish he would have at least finished with the lights."

As patient and gracious as always, Carly followed her through mounds of snaking cables, ducked under the metal framework for the lighting and waited for Nina to open the door to the green room.

"You can check your make-up in here before you go on," Nina told her as she opened the door to a private lavatory and flicked on the light. "I want you on at eight-thirty sharp, so you'll want to come back a few minutes earlier. There are some notes on the table there by the couch in case you want to run through the models and the outfits and such. If Tony timed this right, the show should run about an hour. And you can help yourself to whatever's in the fridge over there. And if you want to leave right afterwards, if you're not staying for the dance, that door over there leads right outside."

Jesse walked over to the exterior door, peeked outside, then closed and locked it, double-checking it before hurrying to catch up to Nina and Carly backstage.

"Ooop! I see the Senator's finally arrived. You'll find your way back, I'm sure." And in a flash of midnight blue, Nina was gone.

"Jesse?" Revolving on her heel, Carly pushed aside a nylon cord and walked deeper into the backstage area. "Jesse?"

"Over here," Jesse told her, shining her penlight on her. "I don't like this. This whole area is unsecured. The door from the parking lot to the green room was left open. Anyone could've gotten in. And I don't like the fact that you have to walk down that hall. Did you see how dark it was?"

"There will be over five hundred people here tonight. I'm sure I'll be safe."

"Well I'm not." Jesse shone her penlight up to the ceiling, along the catwalks, into the lighting fixtures, everywhere, searching for signs of trouble. "I don't like this. Look, there's easy access everywhere back here. And those people way back there in the kitchen aren't going to hear anything. I don't want you walking around back here alone. I'll come with you."

"That won't be necessary, Jesse," Carly said kindly. "I appreciate your concern. I do, but all I have to do is walk down that hall to the stage, host the show, and go back to our table. I'll be on stage the majority of the time. Nothing is going happen. Only a fool would try something tonight with all of these people here." She started for the hallway.

Jesse followed. "Well let's face it, we're not exactly dealing with the sharpest tool in the shed. Or the most original. I mean, come on, running your car off the road, a rag in your tailpipe, poisoning your crab salad?" Jesse scoffed. "And only an idiot would need four or five attempts to kill someone. If you're gonna do it, you have to do it right and do it once. Stop trying to make it look like an accident and just *do* it."

Jesse stepped out into the growing crowd of the banquet hall with her. "But she's gotta know that she can only have so many of these unsuccessful accidents before people - a lot of people - start getting suspicious. Look how many people already know about the Mercedes and your accident on the bridge. And if she tries something tonight, it'll probably be something big. Maybe one of those giant

257

lights conveniently falls on you while you're on stage...or the apparatus holding the curtain collapses or a bomb or something."

"You've been watching too many old movies. Don't you think you're being a little melodramatic?"

"Think about it, Carly," Jesse retorted. "The place blows sky-high. With the Senator and all these highfalutin people here, you think they're gonna say, '*geez, I bet whoever did that was trying to kill that McCray woman*'?" She stopped her before they reached the table. "You know, we could probably neutralize her, at least for a little while, if we went public. I know who she is; I know what she's driving. If we went public and turned this matter over to the pol..."

"It's out of the question, Jesse. I told you that from the beginning."

"Dammit Carly!" Jesse said a little too loudly, drawing the attention of a few people nearby. Carly led them to a quiet corner near the stage, and Jesse lowered her voice. "You're tying my hands. Quit thinking of your reputation for once, will you? What good's your reputation if you're dead? This is your life we're talking about."

"It's not just my life, Jesse," Carly snapped back quietly. "I have over thirty-eight hundred people working for me. Do you have any idea what a huge responsibility that is? They all count on me for their livelihood, and I won't allow something that's happening in my personal life to jeopardize their jobs. And believe me, I know what would happen if word were to get out that someone is breaking into our mainframe and stealing money from the company, that they're trying to kill me..." She waited a moment, smiling at the group of people walking past them. Then, getting closer, she continued in a whisper. "First of all, it wouldn't be a very good endorsement for my company, would it? Having a hacker break into a company whose business is security software. And whether it's something I can control or not, business would take a nose-dive, I wouldn't be able to put any capital into development so we'd lose our technological edge, I'd have to lay off - possibly fire - a good portion of my workforce. These are talented, dedicated people we're talking about. They're a part of my family." She shook her head with determined vigor. "I won't let that happen. My business is my life, Jesse."

"Could very well be," Jesse responded simply.

"You don't understand." Carly frowned and checked her gold watch.

"Yes, I do. I know how loyal you are to your employees. I think it's great, but that's the one thing this Karen has on you. She knows your weakness and she's using it against you. She knows that she can try to kill you as many times as it takes because you're not going to do a damn thing about it because you're afraid of how it will affect your business."

"Look. Ultimately, I am responsible for everything that happens. I'm responsible for the missing money. I'm responsible for the security breaches. And so long as I'm the one who's accountable, I must insist that we do this my way and not involve the authorities or the media until it's absolutely necessary. You agreed to that, Jesse.

You agreed to that at our very first meeting in Beth's office."

"Yeah, but now I'm telling you that it's necessary to involve them."

"Not yet."

"But Carly, I didn't count on this. I'm close. I'm so close now. I don't have all the pieces, yet, but I've got some *really* strong leads. Another day or two and I'll have it all pieced together. All I'm asking is that you let me tell the cops what's going on - at least let me do that. I can have them working on finding the Excursion and finding Karen."

But Carly shook her head. She smiled and waved to someone across the room.

"I can't stay with...I can't protect you twenty-four hours a day, seven days a week. What's gonna happen to those people who count on you for their livelihoods when she finally succeeds? Who's gonna take over when you're gone? You think your nephew's gonna be able to run things half as well as you do? You think he gives a shit about any of those people?"

"Stop," Carly warned, her expression turning quite harsh. "I won't have you talking that way about Doug."

"Why? Because he's *family*? You think just because he's related to you...."

"Jacey's here," Carly announced quietly. Her eyes shifted from the red-head in the doorway to Jesse. The understanding calm behind her gaze extinguished Jesse's temper. "Let's just get through tonight, okay? We'll talk about bringing the police in on this. Tomorrow. I promise."

They met up with Jacey and her husband, Benjamin, at the table, and as Carly introduced him to Jesse, Jesse saw the vague gaze of recognition on Mr. Elder's face. Jacey saw it, too, and leaned in to whisper to him how they knew her.

"Of course," he said, nodding. "Of course."

Glancing around the room while Carly and Jacey and Benjamin chatted, Jesse spotted Donna Meyer. She was accompanied by three young Robert Palmer-type women and her husband, a skeleton of an old man who looked ridiculous in this setting with his tuxedo drooping on his infirmed body. Donna had just finished dancing with one of the young women and was returning to her table. She caught Jesse's eye and made an obscene gesture with her tongue.

Carly's conversation with Jacey lulled at that moment and she looked up just in time to see it.

"Look how low-cut her breast is," Jesse whispered to her.

Carly made a strange face, looked over at Donna and started to laugh. "Do you realize what you just said?" she asked. "You said, 'look how low-cut her *breast* is."

"No I didn't." Jesse shook her head. "I said *blouse*," she insisted, her face flushing. In the next moment, while smiling at Carly's laughter, she said a little less certainly, "Didn't I?" Swept up in Carly's outburst, Jesse gestured in Donna's direction. "Well, Christ! Look at her! She looks like she should be a guest on Jerry

Springer."

That's when Carly lost it. On the verge of incontinence, she bent in half, laughing her silent laugh under the curious stares of Jacey and her husband.

Just at that moment, a man stepped up to the podium on the stage and gave the restless crowd a preview of the evening. When he announced Carly's name, Jesse glanced at her and was impressed all over again by her self-assurance, and by how quickly she had composed herself. Nothing ruffles this woman.

"I'll be right back," Carly said, excusing herself as she rose from the table. She motioned for Jacey to go with her, and Jesse watched them walk over to the Senator's table. When Carly touched him on the arm, he looked up at her and smiled. Jacey was beside her, but Carly was doing all the talking. It was quite a thing to watch her in her element.

Doug and Stephanie didn't arrive until after the dinner portion of the evening. Carly had left the table to retrieve another club soda for each of them before beginning with the fashion show.

"Nice going, *detective!*" Doug growled in Jesse's ear as he and Stephanie neared the table. After seating his fiancé, he pulled out the chair beside Jesse and turned it to face her. "You're quite the trouble-maker, aren't you?"

"Lower your voice," Carly warned him. She had returned with the drinks, putting a hand on each of Jesse's shoulders as she leaned in closer. Jesse inhaled the scent of her tangy herbal perfume. "What are you talking about?"

"Chris is gone, thanks to her." Doug jerked his thumb toward Jesse. "She's supposed to fly me to New York tonight for the Giants game tomorrow, but when I called her to find out what time we were leaving, Jake told me that she wasn't there. He told me that she and Chelsea had a huge blow-up last night and that she'd taken off this morning. Didn't file a flight plan, didn't tell anyone where she was going or when she'd be back, just left."

"How is this Jesse's fault?" Carly asked her nephew.

"She's the one who stuck her nose where it doesn't belong."

Drawing a finger, Carly took aim at him. "Jesse was doing her job. Chris could have easily avoided the confrontation had she been honest with me from the start."

"Yeah, but if she needed answers, she should have confronted Chris and Chelsea alone - without you there." Carly simply shook her head and looked away, but he drew her attention back by saying, "Aunt Carly, she doesn't know what she's doing. It's obvious. And it's obvious that this is just another accessory for you to wear on your arm and take to bed."

Carly leaned in closer, and Jesse could feel the pressure of her breasts against her back. "This is neither the time nor the place for this. I don't want to hear another word about this. Do I make myself clear?" Doug looked like he was about to protest, but Carly cut him off. "And you're not going to New York. I cancelled your trip. I'll need your help with the horses tomorrow."

She kept her hands on Jesse's shoulders as she straightened up. "Time for the show to start." Giving Jesse's shoulders a slight squeeze, she said, "Wish me luck."

Jesse stood to follow her, and Carly hesitated briefly until Jesse gave her a resolute grin and motioned for her to go ahead.

Silently, they walked together through the doorway, down the dark hall to the stage, where Jesse stood in the wings to watch.

Carly confidently took swift strides into the eye of the spotlight to the podium with growing applause from the audience.

"Good evening ladies and gentlemen and welcome and thank you for coming to the Service League's tenth annual Fashion Show. I'm Carly McCray and I'm honored to be tonight's emcee and the League's Chairperson. To begin, I have good news and bad news for you: the good news is that we have three starters for the Packers here tonight to model for us - Joe Doogins, wide receiver; Harlan Banks, offensive tackle, and Orlando Rivera, linebacker." Waiting only a moment for the applause to die down, she said, "The bad news is that those three are here tonight because they're injured and won't be playing against the Giants tomorrow."

The audience groaned, and Jesse watched Carly in awe as all the right words flowed from her mouth so easily and so smoothly. She was a natural at public speaking, so poised, so articulate. Once the preliminaries were out of the way and the show began in earnest, Carly had cue cards for describing the various ensembles that were being modeled and cheat sheets on the models themselves, but she rarely used them. Most of her descriptions were ad-libbed and probably much better than anything written on the cards.

Jesse relaxed after a half hour. She assumed from the indirect nature of the previous incidents that Karen wouldn't try something in front of all these people. If she did, it would have to be at a time when she could catch Carly alone, and that wasn't likely so long as she was there to walk her back to her seat. As long as she was on stage, Jesse figured, she'd be okay.

"Senator Garvey is running for re-election this year, and won't he look smart strolling around Capitol Hill in this classic suit from Armani? Incidentally, Mr. Garvey's opponent was expected to join us this evening, but he's been temporarily detained on assault charges stemming from an ugly incident at Chuck E. Cheese. It seems he had been stealing tokens from some of the young children there and when the mouse confronted him, well, let's just say a mouse's tail doesn't belong there."

The audience burst into laughter, and Carly discreetly tossed a quick wink at Jesse. The Senator strutted onto the stage, and Jesse pretended to watch him. But really, she was staring beyond him at Carly. The Senator was nothing but an annoying screen that occasionally blocked Jesse's view of her. She was so deep in her reverie of Carly that she almost didn't hear it, the squeaking noise above her. Almost. It was faint, but definitely there, and Jesse took a step back and looked up into the catwalks. With every sense tuned in, she spotted something moving about in the metal framing.

She wondered if it was someone involved in the show, a lighting technician, maybe. She backed up another step and tilted her head way back to search for it again, to try to identify it, but it was gone.

She almost decided to ignore it, attributing it to her paranoia, but when she saw Carly glance upward in that direction and then look at her, she changed her mind fast.

Getting up to the catwalks was no easy feat. The rise in the old metal steps was really steep, not exactly suited to a short woman in close-fitting pants. When Jesse climbed to the landing, she took her shoes off so as not to be a distraction. She was concealed from the audience by the valence from the stage curtain as she walked slowly to a spot directly above Carly.

From up there, twenty feet from the stage, she could tell that Carly was alarmed. Jesse saw her glance over to where she had been standing, then discreetly look around for her. Not once did she falter in her hosting duties. But Jesse didn't have the time to stand there and admire her because she'd just seen it again, that dark prowling figure of a woman.

She was on a scaffolding that ran parallel to the one Jesse was on, but ten feet lower and three feet upstage from her, and Jesse kept her eyes glued on the woman. From the lights below, she could make out her facial characteristics easily. She was a young woman, maybe twenty, very thin, dressed in black. Her dark hair, parted in the middle, hung symmetrically on either side of her head and down just past her shoulders. She had a dark birthmark or blemish above her right eyebrow.

Jesse would have moved a little faster to get to her, but the metal wobbled and swayed and creaked with every step she took. In the outside edge of her senses, she heard Carly wrapping up the show.

The woman Jesse was after reached over and began untying a mass of thick rope that was knotted around a metal beam. The other end of the rope ran up into the darkness of the rafters, and Jesse couldn't see what it was attached to.

Directly below, Carly was thanking the audience again and inviting everyone to stay for the dance that followed.

Jesse's concept of time ceased to exist. In order to get to this woman in time, she would simply have to jump. She quickened her pace when the applause started. She couldn't remember when she took her last breath. Her eyes were glued to this figure, and she was absolutely intent on getting to her before she got this rope untangled. As the applause began to fade below, Jesse looked in horror as the woman got the rope untied from the beam.

Without thinking, she leaped over the railing and dove for the rope before the woman let go. Her pants tore on the metal as she slammed down on the woman while reaching for the rope at the same time.

But she was too late.

Carly waved to the crowd as she began to walk off stage. She heard the commotion and looked up.

At the same time, the rope slid up into the rafters, and helpless,

Jesse looked down to see what was about to happen to Carly.

The woman stood up beside her. "What are you doing?" she asked, brushing herself off.

The curtain lowered smoothly to the floor, and once Jesse realized that her client had been in no real danger, she turned to the woman with a sheepish grin. "I didn't hurt you, did I?"

"No, but…"

"Sorry," she said over her shoulder as she quickly made her way across the catwalk and down the stairs to get to Carly.

Backstage, Jesse found her shoes and saw Carly in the middle of a crowd of the models from the show. She was thanking them all for their participation, and Jesse craned her neck to watch her. Carly gave her a beautiful smile and slowly and methodically began to work her way out of the crowd.

"What happened?" she asked, gesturing upward, as she approached the detective.

Jesse chuckled, embarrassed. "I found out how Tony rigged the curtain." They started their walk back to the main floor, being careful not to get in the way of the people who were preparing things for the band. In the meantime, a slow romantic ballad was being played over the p.a...

"I'm telling you, you've seen too many reruns of *Murder, She Wrote*."

"How would you know to make that reference unless you've seen them, too?" Jesse quickly replied, bringing a chuckle from Carly.

"Touché." Carly nudged her with her elbow as if to say, "good one".

As she ducked under a wire, Carly asked Jesse if she wanted to stay for the dance. "I would," Jesse said, " but..." Turning, she showed Carly the tear in her pants. It was on her left rear hip and extended nine inches down her thigh.

Carly glanced at it quickly and just smiled. "Let me stop in here for a minute. I've had to go for the past half hour."

They stepped into the green room together, and Carly reached her arm around into the bathroom to turn the light on. She turned back to see Jesse in front of the mirror twisting around to check the damage to her pants. "But I will take a rain check on that dance," she added with a smile before disappearing behind the closed door.

On their way out the front door, Jesse said, "I'll get the car. You stay here."

"Don't be ridiculous," Carly replied. She linked her arm through Jesse's and gazed up at the clear sky. Countless stars gleamed back at her. "It's a beautiful night, isn't it?"

"Huh?" Jesse looked up. She was enormously distracted by her client's closeness. "Oh. Yeah."

She missed the quiet hum of the approaching SUV. It was a red Excursion with its headlights off. Its driver wore all black, including a black ski mask. She pulled up just behind the couple, who seemed completely oblivious to her presence. She reached to the passenger seat and picked up the shiny knife. Her eyes never left the taller woman in front of her.

Jesse turned around at the sound of a car door closing right behind her. She saw the gleam just as it made contact with her client.

"Oh!" Carly gasped.

Jesse shoved Carly hard in the space between two cars to get her out of the way. It looked like something you would see on roller derby. With one swift motion, she hit the woman's arm at the wrist, causing the knife to clatter to the ground. The woman started to struggle with the detective, but thought better of it after Jesse hit her hard in the face a couple of times. She smacked Jesse back – three punches to the head, - and made a hasty retreat to the Excursion. By the time Jesse got her bearings, the SUV was gone. She turned back to her client, who was leaning up against a BMW.

"Are you okay?" she asked, crouching down beside Carly.

Carly had her right hand clamped around her left arm. She wasn't moving.

"Carly," Jesse said, hoping to snap her out of it. "Are you okay?" She put her hand around Carly's shoulder and tried to help her to her feet. That's when she felt it. She felt the warm liquidy substance through the fabric of Carly's dress.

"Jesus," she murmured breathlessly, "you've been stabbed."

"I'm okay," Carly said as if trying to convince herself of just that.

"You're not okay. You're bleeding. We've got to get you to a hospital."

"I'm not going to a hospital. It's just a scrape." Carly was struggling to stand, but as Jesse slipped her arm around her to help her up, she let out another quiet whimper and slid back to the ground.

"God," Jesse whispered, shocked by the blood. "Hold still," she said quietly. She stepped over her client and crouched down to inspect the wound more closely. From the dim light of the parking lot, she found that the expensive fabric of her dress had been sliced from her elbow to the middle of her bicep.

Jesse put pressure on it. "Let's get it elevated." She put her arm around Carly and felt something on her back. Something wet and sticky. "Hang on a minute." Jesse guided her forward and separated the material between Carly's shoulder blades.

Carly whined and twisted away quickly, but Jesse held her tighter. "Hold still, honey. I want to see how deep it is." Her voice was as shaky as her hands.

"I...ow..." Carly squirmed away again as Jesse bent in to look at the wound. "I didn't even feel it."

Jesse stared in utter shock as the red blood trickled out of her client. . "It doesn't look that deep. I want to stop the bleeding, though, so I can get a better look." Her troubled eyes met Carly's. "I've got to get you to the hospital. They can stitch you up and give you a Tetanus shot."

"I had a booster after I broke my arm." Carly smiled but it wasn't a happy smile. "I don't suppose you know first aid."

"You hate hospitals, too, huh?" Jesse frowned and evaluated the wounds again. "I guess we could stop at a pharmacy. I might be able

271

to patch you up." She helped Carly to her feet.

At Carly's suggestion, after Jesse ran into a nearby Walgreen's, they went to Carly's house in Ashwaubenon, a suburb of Green Bay. It was a big ranch, nicely appointed, but certainly not like her home in Moonlight Bay. When they entered, Carly explained to Jesse that she hadn't been to this particular house in over a year, and that she only stayed there when the weather absolutely prohibited her from driving back to Moonlight Bay.

"Doug spends a lot of time here." She turned on the light in the foyer. "And I see that he's not cleaning up after himself."

Jesse followed her through the kitchen, which was a real mess, even worse than the living room. Dishes overflowed the sink and onto the counter, dirty pans were left on the stove top, newspapers and empty pizza boxes peppered the table. The mess spread to all areas of the house, including Carly's bedroom.

She looked shocked and angry when she turned on the light and found her bed unmade. The empty bottle of champagne on the night table made her even angrier. "I told him this room was off limits," she said through clenched teeth as she crossed to her closet for a change of clothes. "Probably couldn't stand the filth in his own room." Pulling out a t-shirt, she turned to face Jesse. "There should be some scissors in there if you need to cut the gauze."

Jesse followed her gaze into the bathroom, and while searching the cabinets, she spotted a crystal bottle on the counter. Picking it up, she brought it to her nose and nearly gagged.

"Phew!" She muttered. "Smells like bug spray."

"Jesse?"

"Yeah?" Jesse poked her head out. Carly was on her stomach on the bed. She had taken the French braid out of her hair; it now fell in a rippling mound on the pillow. She had changed into a pair of jeans but her top half was bare to give Jesse access to her wounds.

"I...think...Is my back still bleeding? It feels like..."

"I'll bring a towel," Jesse told her after noting the amount of blood that had accumulated. Returning to the bed with all of her supplies and the bag from Walgreen's, she knelt down beside Carly on the bed and gingerly set the warm damp towel on her wound. Carly jumped a little as she pressed to slow the flow, but she didn't cry out at all. "Tell me if it hurts." She waited a few minutes before lifting the towel to see if the stream had slowed at all. It did a little, but not enough to be attended to. "I'll take care of the other one while we're waiting."

Cringing, she wiped the slice in Carly's arm with a warm soapy cloth, cleaning the dried blood as well as she could. After letting it air-dry, she broke open the Benzion Tincture and used the sterile applicator, spreading it all around the wound. "Okay so far?"

Carly's head was turned away from her on the pillow. She nodded.

The skin needed to be pinched together a little bit in order to get the steri-strips to stick, but all in all, Jesse thought she did a decent job. "You're probably going to have a long hideous scar," she said, dabbing at the steri strips with her finger.

"Oh, damn!" Carly said. Her voice was muffled a little by the pillow. "There goes my arm-modeling career."

Jesse smiled. "Yeah. Too bad. Guess you'll just have to find some other way to support yourself."

After a few minutes, Jesse pulled back the towel from the other wound, which, she thought, was much more serious than the one on her arm. She dabbed the blood that led away from it. Fresh blood was still seeping from the two raw edges of skin, but it looked like it was sufficiently under control.

Carly rested her head on her forearms while Jesse cleaned and bandaged it as she had done with the arm wound. Jesse could feel her staring at her, watching her work. "Looks like your days of wearing backless gowns are over, too," she told her while finishing up. Placing the final steri-strip across the slice, Jesse tossed the left-over supplies in the bag at the foot of the bed. "Do they hurt? I've got some Dermaplast. That'll numb it for a little while."

"No, no. They're fine."

While gathering up her provisions and the towels, Jesse met her client's eyes. "I'm so sorry...I didn't even hear..."

"It wasn't your fault, Jesse," Carly assured her. "She...she just appeared out of the blue."

"Yeah, but I...I was supposed to be protecting you," Jesse said quietly.

"And you did," Carly insisted as she watched Jesse walk into the bathroom. "If you hadn't shoved me into that car, I'm sure my injuries would have been much worse. That was very quick thinking on your part." Carly lifted herself off the mattress and carefully reached for the t-shirt she'd gotten for herself.

"I never should have let her get that close," Jesse scolded herself. She returned from the bathroom after putting everything away and hurried over to her client when she noticed how Carly was struggling to get into her t-shirt.

* * * *

"Do they hurt?" Jesse asked, reaching over to take Carly's hand. They were on their way back to Carly's house in Moonlight Bay because Carly had refused to spend another minute in the filth of the house in Ashwaubenon.

"No," she replied bravely. "They're fine." By her tone, Jesse guessed that she was being truthful and wondered how she could have gotten over the attack so quickly, how Carly seemed less affected by it than she was.

After parking the car in the garage, Jesse headed for her Fiat. She swung the driver's door open and was reaching for something on the passenger's seat.

"What are you doing?" Carly asked.

Jesse looked over her shoulder. "I'm getting the box that I got from the trailer this afternoon so I can go through it."

"Can't that wait until tomorrow?" Carly asked with a sweet pout, leaving no doubt about her intentions.

Jesse quickly abandoned all other plans and slammed the door.

Harley was waiting for them inside the back door when they arrived home. He jumped up on Carly and licked her furiously the second she entered.

"Hey!" Jesse snapped her fingers and he dropped to the floor. "He didn't hurt you, did he?"

"Not at all." She was busy punching numbers into the panel for the security system. That done, she smiled as she bent to scratch Harley's side. "You're just happy to see me, aren't you, Mister Harley?" She spoke to him in baby-talk, and Jesse watched, amazed, as Carly hit a sweet spot that set Harley's hind leg to tapping on the hardwood floor. Jesse herself had never been able to elicit that reaction from him.

A short while later, freshly showered and wearing sweat pants and a t-shirt, Jesse appeared in the library. Carly was already there. She was sitting on the sectional in a fresh pair of jeans and a new, crisp white t-shirt. She had a fire lit in the fireplace, soft music playing, and the lights low.

Jesse smiled. "How are you?" she asked, gesturing toward Carly's cuts.

"I'm fine. I really am. Thank you for asking."

Jesse stood there for a few moments, staring at her. "Can I get you anything? Do you want something to drink?"

"No. Thank you."

"I think I saw some cheesecake in the refrigerator. Do you want a piece?"

"No. Thank you."

Jesse paused for a moment, then asked: "Uh, do you mind if I have some?"

Carly smiled warmly. "Of course not. Help yourself."

"Thanks." She started walking toward the kitchen, but turned back. "Are you sure I can't get you anything?"

"I'm sure. Thank you." She watched Jesse walk away and called out to her: "You can eat your cheesecake in here if you like."

"Okay," Jesse replied over her shoulder. "I'll be right back." She returned a few minutes later, kicked off her slippers, and sank down beside Carly on the couch.

Carly watched her take a bite of cheesecake.

"Oh my God, Carly. This is the best cheesecake I've ever had. Raspberry. Have you had any of this?"

Carly smiled and shook her head.

"You've got to try it. It's delicious!" She put some on her fork and offered it to Carly.

"No thank you, Jesse," Carly said, backing away a little.

"C'mon. Just a bite. You won't regret it." She moved the fork closer to Carly's mouth, to tease her, but Carly pursed her lips shut and shook her head, causing Jesse to laugh. Not to be outdone, Jesse kept moving the fork closer until she got the cheesecake to touch

Carly's mouth. "Try it," she encouraged in a menacing tone.

Carly smiled, but kept her mouth closed.

"Try it," Jesse warned.

Carly shook her head. She laughed, and at the moment her mouth opened, Jesse tried to forcibly feed it to her, but Carly shook her head again and the cheesecake smeared across her cheek.

Jesse laughed and set her plate on the coffee table. She leaned over and used her index finger to wipe the mess from Carly's face.

Turning quite serious, Carly grabbed Jesse by the wrist and drew Jesse's hand to her mouth. While staring into Jesse's emerald green eyes, she very slowly wrapped her lips around Jesse's finger and cleaned off the cheesecake.

"Mmmm," she said quietly, still looking deeply into Jesse's eyes. "You're right. It is delicious." They stared at one another for a long moment. Carly was still holding Jesse's hand in both of hers. She looked at it again and brought it to her mouth again, this time sucking on her finger, letting her tongue roll around it a little.

"Carly," Jesse whispered. Her voice was so quiet.

Carly stopped. She withdrew Jesse's finger from her mouth and opened her eyes. "I'm sorry." She released Jesse's hand from hers. "I'm so sorry, Jesse. I..."

Jesse's expression cut her off. The detective's eyes blazed with bold anticipation as she took her time considering her client. At last, Jesse leaned forward and planted a kiss right on Carly's lips.

The kiss went on without pause until it morphed into a slow

licking and gentle sucking on Carly's neck. Carly gasped and moved a little closer to the detective. Jesse pushed Carly against the back of the couch, and began wildly licking and kissing up and down both sides of her neck. Carly was thrilled by the hot, quickening breath in her ear.

With her lips never leaving Carly's skin, Jesse slid down off the couch and knelt on the floor between her knees. She reached for the button on Carly's jeans and looked up into the burning gaze of her pale gray eyes.

She opened Carly's zipper tooth by tooth. By the time she grasped Carly's hips and slid the jeans over them, Carly's eyes had closed; her head had tilted back against the couch. She lifted Carly's legs over her shoulders and ran her hot tongue down every inch of the inside of her long, beautiful thighs. The higher Jesse reached, the louder and higher pitched Carly's gasps became. Jesse guided Carly to the floor where she crawled on top of her. She moaned loudly when she felt Carly's desire straining back against her pelvis. She leaned forward over Carly's face and began to tease the outside of her mouth with her eager tongue. Carly responded by grabbing the back of Jesse's head and coaxing her to enter her mouth completely. When she did, Carly found it hard to control herself. Her hands ravaged Jesse's long mane of curls pulling her closer and deeper into her mouth.

Jesse was so aroused that she had to touch more of Carly. She pushed her t-shirt over Carly's head and marveled at the perfection of

Carly's breasts. She had to have more of her, so she took one of Carly's hard pink nipples into her mouth and began tugging at it, then alternating, moving from one breast to the other. Carly arched her back and sighed when she felt the insistent pulling and the warm breath in a rhythmic cadence against her erect nipples.

Jesse sat upright on Carly and looked deeply into her eyes as she feverishly pulled her own t-shirt over her head and shed her own pants. Carly was eagerly taking in the view of this beautiful woman straddling her. When she felt Jesse pressing her pelvis into hers, she quivered and let out a cry. Carly couldn't stand it anymore; she had to have all of Jesse. Now. She pushed Jesse back on rug and kissed her wildly, moving closer to the place they both wanted her to be. The closer Carly got, the louder Jesse's cries of desire became. Jesse slipped under Carly, where she was delighted by the full weight of Carly's warm soft, flesh on her.

Jesse couldn't contain herself. Her tongue immediately sought out the source of wetness between Carly's legs. Carly cried out as the sucking became more intense, and with her passion unleashed, she responded in kind to Jesse. As the time drew near for both of them, they increased the flurry of the licking and sucking and kissing and probing.

They ran their damp fingers over each others' bodies, trying to touch every inch of the other. As the climax approached they frantically pushed and undulated until they both reached the point at the same time. They reached for each other's hands, clasped fingers, and used the other for strength as they collapsed in each others' arms.

Glazed in sweat, Jesse moved to take Carly in her arms and kissed her gently while brushing her hair back. Neither of them spoke for a long while. Carly just kept sighing contentedly. In a kind of wonder, she stared into Jesse's barely-opened eyes.

"I have a question for you," Jesse said quietly at last. She tapped on Carly's nose with her index finger. Carly's smile widened in anticipation, her eyebrows rose. "Why's there a tattoo of Mickey Mouse on your hip?"

Carly laughed out loud. She kissed Jesse's forehead, and they both looked down at her small tattoo. "Don't you like it?"

"Yeah," Jesse told her. "I like it a lot. It just kinda surprised me when I was...I mean, you don't strike me as the type to have a tattoo." Jesse leaned over to get a closer look and traced the tattoo's outline with her finger. "Why Mickey Mouse?"

"When we were much younger, Chris used to call me Mickey instead of McCray. The summer after we graduated from High School, we were in San Francisco, and Chris dared me to get a tattoo. At the time, Mickey Mouse seemed the obvious choice. Father was furious with me when I told him about it."

"I can imagine." Jesse smiled, her intent look moving from the tattoo to Carly.

Now they took more time with each other to explore and experiment, and while their lovemaking was incredibly intense, they both enjoyed almost equally the way they talked afterwards, the way they both finally let down some of their strongly fortified defenses.

At times they grew silly and playful together only to become quiet and serious in the next moment. It was an evening neither would ever forget.

- Sunday -

At seven o'clock exactly, Jesse rolled over and opened her eyes. She had heard Harley upstairs in the bedroom for the past few moments, scratching on the door, whining to be let out.

She realized, while glancing around the room, that the previous night was not a dream. It really happened, and while reaching with her free arm for her clothes, she struggled with the emotional onslaught that accompanied that reality.

They had fallen asleep after dawn. The last thing she remembered was Carly's quiet confession that it had never been like that with anyone she'd ever been with as she covered them both with an afghan from the couch and snuggled in close.

Jesse looked at her and was touched by her tranquil expression. Her hand was resting on her abdomen. Her long, elegant fingers, which had given her so much pleasure not that much earlier, twitched a little, as if she was typing something or playing the piano.

Harley's yelp snapped her out of her trance. Careful not to disturb Carly, she slowly disentangled herself from her and was about to stand up to put her pants on.

"Come back here," Carly purred, her eyes still closed. She pulled Jesse down to the floor again, moaning as her hand slid up Jesse's bare thigh. Opening her eyes, she smiled at Jesse. It was such a warm and beautiful beam, Jesse felt as though she would die if Carly ever asked her to leave. And the next words from Carly told Jesse that she felt the very same way. "Don't go," Carly whispered.

"I'll be right back," Jesse promised her, kissing her on the forehead. "I've gotta put Harley out before he busts down the door."

Carly stretched languorously, happily groaned, and reluctantly released her. "Hurry back."

Jesse felt Carly's gaze on her as she got dressed, loving the way those gray eyes canvassed her body. When she stopped at the desk for her cigarettes, her eye caught something, and she moved a book off of the stack of papers. She picked up the first couple of pages, browsed over them, then looked at Carly.

"What's this?"

Carly looked stricken as she sat up. "What's what?"

Jesse's internal alarms sounded. She paged through the pile of papers, and then tossed them in Carly's direction. "Where'd you get this?" she demanded. A mix of confusion, excruciating pain, and anger surged through her. "It's from your attorn...It's from Beth! It's the transcript from my trial." She stopped for a moment to go through more of the papers. "Christ, you've got my medical records, too?" She glared at Carly. "Why did she send this to you?"

"I didn't...I never asked..." Carly was desperate. "Last night when..."

"You had me investigated?" Jesse asked incredulously, clearly feeling violated. When Carly responded by looking away, Jesse screamed, "I don't fucking believe this! You had me investigated?"

"It's not like that, Jesse. Beth just…"

"She had a list of my references, wasn't that good enough for her? Wasn't it good enough for you?" Her voice trembled with the anguish of betrayal. "You've known the whole time, haven't you?"

"No! It's not like that. If you'll let me explain…" Apparently feeling vulnerable on the floor, naked, she reached for her shirt and scrambled to her feet. "God, Jesse, if you'd just let me…"

Jesse gave Carly a look that could split atoms. "You had no right! Christ, what was I thinking? How could I have….Jesus H. Christ! *I trusted you!* And you….you…." Too livid to think clearly, Jesse picked up a heavy gold paperweight from the desk and hurled it across the room, smashing the glass on a barrister bookcase into a million shattered pieces. Jesse hurried to the staircase.

"Jesse, please!" Carly tried to catch up to her. "What are you doing?"

"What the hell does it look like I'm doing? I'm leaving!"

Carly intercepted her on the landing upstairs. "You can't leave!"

"Let go of me, bitch!" she screamed as she stormed to the bedroom to pack her things, slamming the door behind her. Her former client seized upon her in the back hall as she was on her way out with all of her possessions, Harley in tow.

Her voice cracked in desperation. "Please, Jesse, stay! We'll talk!"

"Talk? What's there to talk about? It's all in the file you got from your attorney! Or wasn't that enough?"

"Jesse, I've been trying to tell you, I didn't read any of that. I just got it last night!"

Jesse grunted a snort of disbelief. She dropped her duffle bag beside Harley. "Well, then, let me fill you in! Where do you want me to start? Want me to start with how I killed the only person I've ever been with? How I went crazy after she died and ended up in a fucking loony bin? How I put the gun inside my mouth but couldn't pull the trigger?" Like a provoked animal, Jesse's voice had a deep rumbling quality to it that sent chills down the length of Carly's spine. "Wanna hear about the sick bastards at the nut house who tried touching me?"

"Jesse, please stop. Please."

But Jesse couldn't stop. Anger had taken over, and it wasn't about to give way to other more complicated and difficult emotions. She shoved Carly up against the wall, causing Harley to bark. "Wanna know what it's like when the woman you love more than anything has a malignant brain tumor? Wanna know what it's like watching her live with the pain, crying every night, praying to die, knowing there's not a fucking thing anybody can do about it?" Her hands were trembling uncontrollably as she stepped back and tried to light a cigarette. Her entire physiology had changed. Her eyes were wild, her nostrils flared, and when she spoke, spit flew from her mouth. "Wanna hear how I did it? How I killed her?" Jesse strained, making a global gesture with her arms. "Wanna hear what happens when someone gets too much morphine?"

"That's enough!" Carly cried out at last. "I'm sorry, Jesse!"

"Sorry for what?" Jesse asked viciously, her voice hoarse and ragged with emotion. "You wanted to know more about me, didn't you? That's why you had me investigated, right?" She inhaled deeply on her cigarette. "Anything else you want to know?"

Near tears now, Carly was unable to respond. But Jesse wasn't quite through. She wanted to make Carly pay for making her relive the darkest period in her life. "Why don't you go cry on someone else's shoulder? You've got a whole lot of people who call themselves your friend. Only problem is, they can't tell you what they really think of you because their lips are surgically attached to your ass!"

She saw that Carly was deeply stunned, but she was on a roll. Her face twisted into a bitter sneer as she took another drag from her Marlboro. "The only thing you care about besides your goddamn company is a good fuck! It's your whole life! You don't give a shit who you're with so long as she gets you off! You're worse than Donna Meyer! At least she's up front about her motive," she spat, putting her half-smoked cigarette out on the floor at Carly's feet. Reaching into her pocket, she pulled out a roll of cash and threw it at her, hitting her squarely on the mouth. "Go fuck yourself, you pompous slut." She knew by the look on Carly's face that she'd landed the knock-out punch - for whatever that was worth.

* * * *

Carly spent a positively miserable morning. She had gone to Jesse's cabin to talk to her, to work things out, but Jesse wasn't there. Neither was Harley. The place was absolutely deserted. The resort owner hadn't heard from her; his son had ferried them from the mainland to the island and back again earlier that morning but aside from that, they hadn't heard from her. She was gone.

Not knowing what to do with herself, Carly went home and wandered aimlessly around her empty house a good portion of the time before coming to the door of the room that Jesse had occupied. Her eyes filling with tears, she turned the knob and walked in. Outside, under the dark clouds, the wind picked up, bringing the rain with it. In the absolute stillness inside, she walked over to the bed and sat down. Her hand delicately brushed across the pillow where Jesse's head once rested. A strange psychological urge to add to her misery made her pull the pillow tight to her chest, to inhale the lingering scent of Jesse on it. She sat there, clutching the pillow, rocking, wishing that Jesse would have picked up the phone just once out of the thousands of times she'd tried calling her at her cabin or on the cell phone that Carly had given to her.

Carly reached for the phone again, this time dialing a different number. She cleared her throat, and the woman on the other end picked up. "Hi, Lauren? This is Carly McCray. I don't know if you remember me, I ..."

Lauren's raspy voice, very similar to Jesse's, further broke Carly's heart when she heard her say happily, heartily, "Hi, Carly! How are you?"

"I'm...um, have you heard from Jesse at all today?"

Apparently picking up on the desperation in Carly's voice, Lauren's tone changed. "What's wrong?"

Carly hesitated, not wanting to get too specific. "I, ah, she left this morning and I can't seem to find her or... get in touch with her. I....I was wondering if maybe you had heard from her."

"Oh, God, Carly," Lauren said so sympathetically that it brought a flood of tears to Carly's eyes. "What happened?"

Without revealing too many fine points, Carly briefly relayed to her what it was that set Jesse off. "I didn't even ask Beth for it, Lauren. She just had it faxed to my house. Jesse was wild when she saw it. She...she wouldn't let me explain."

Lauren kindheartedly responded that this pretty much followed Jesse's protocol, that this wasn't the first time Jesse found an excuse to leave abruptly, unexpectedly, and permanently when things started getting uncomfortable for her.

"I thought," Carly said, wiping her eyes, "that after last night, I... thought she..."

"What happened last night?'

"We...Jesse and I made love and we..."

"She slept with you?" Lauren interrupted, incredulous.

"Yes," Carly replied. "And when we got up this morning, that's when she found the papers on my desk."

"She slept with you," Lauren stated quietly, more to herself. After a moment, she said thoughtfully, "well this changes things."

That gave Carly a little hope. "What do you mean?"

"Well, Jesse's never...since Abby died, there've been a lot of women who were interested in Jesse, but she's never slept with any of them. She's usually long gone before it comes to that. She got close to a woman in Atlanta a few years ago, but she took off when things started to get a little serious. She left the woman heartbroken. I don't know how she got our number, but we still hear from her."

"Do you think...?" Carly sniffed involuntarily. "Do you think she'll come back, Lauren? Do you think that it's different this time because we made love last night?"

"I don't know, Carly. I mean, I know Jesse doesn't...she takes being intimate with someone very seriously. She wouldn't have slept with you if she didn't really care about you." All hope was dashed, however, when Lauren added, "I would guess it's more the guilt she's feeling." She sighed again. "I don't know what to tell you, Carly."

* * * *

The floodlights in front of the house barely cut through the dense fog that had engulfed Carly's estate in an eerie shroud. Bundled in a heavy outback duster with the collar turned up, she waved good-bye to her nephew from the front porch as he left in his Hummer. She

290

watched the headlights retreat into the darkness, then ran to the stable with her head down to protect her face from the stinging breeze and driving rain. The bare branches of the maples and oaks that graced the land danced violently above her head while the rain landed in loud chaotic splats at her feet.

After her phone call with Lauren, she was more despondent than ever. Doug showed up just after noon to help her clean out the stalls. He was attentive and soothing, giving her encouragement as they worked together. He even offered to stay home with her that evening, but Carly knew that he and Stephanie had made plans to meet friends in Green Bay, so she insisted that he go.

When she entered the stable to feed the horses, the excited whinnies that greeted her did not have their usual affect on her. Not even they could lift her depression.

She stacked bales of hay on the wooden cart and dragged it behind her as she trudged down the aisle, stopping at each stall along the way. The wind howled outside, and as she opened Damien's stall, she realized that she had forgotten the oats and supplements.

On her way down the hall to prepare and retrieve them, the door at the front of the stable slammed open with a loud bang, causing some of the horses to fuss loudly in their stalls. The wind and rain came crashing in, and Carly hurried to close the door again.

She was half-way there and stopped dead, looking like a deer caught in the headlights of an oncoming Peterbilt. Her eyes grew huge. "Susan?"

Without bothering to close the door, Susan drew a gun from her jacket pocket and pointed it at Carly. Her stare was as frigid and icy and determined as the wind outside.

"I thought you….What are you doing?"

Her frightening laugh made Carly back up a step. She shivered. "How typical of you, Carly. Right to the very end. *What are you doing?"* She said, mocking Carly.

No longer able to recognize this woman, Carly took a step back. "I don't understand. You're dead!" Her knees were barely able to support her, she was shaking so violently.

"Very good, honey. Did you have a nice time at my funeral?" She laughed. "Isn't it funny how once you're dead, people don't suspect you of trying to kill someone?" She motioned with her gun. "Let's go. You know how I hate long good-byes." She directed her to Damien's stall. "This time I'm going to make sure it gets done properly." Carly watched her open the stall door. "Was the detective a good fuck?" she asked, taunting Carly. "Pity she had to leave. At least it made my job a lot easier." She started to shove Carly into the stall. "You're about to have your final accident," she said with exaggerated and phony sympathy. "It'll be most unfortunate. Your remains will be found in there. You see, that latch never did work properly, and, well, lets' face it, Victor's a lazy wet-back and never did get around to fixing it." She shook her head, again with phony sympathy. "And how many times have you asked him not to leave all that hay near the space heater? Doesn't he know that's a fire hazard?"

Carly's face was tight with contemplation and panic. She pulled her arm from Susan's grip and turned to face her.

"Get in there!" Susan ground the barrel of the gun into her side.

But Carly shook her head, stalling, trying to find a way out of this deadly predicament. "I'm not taking another step," she said, trying to sound courageous. "If you're so intent on killing me, you're going to have to look me in the eye when you do it, and I don't believe for a moment that you'll be able to bring yourself to do that."

The diabolical look in Susan's eyes left no doubt about what she was capable of. Without blinking, she raised the gun to Carly's head. "You have no idea how long I've wanted to do this."

Everything happened all at once, but it was so vivid that it seemed to be happening in slow motion with a dream-like quality.

Susan pulled the hammer back on the gun.

Carly closed her eyes tightly, waiting in terror for the bullet.

Like Sigourney Weaver in an *Alien* movie, Jesse dropped from the rafters and landed directly on top of Susan.

Harley's huge black body charged them with a frightful growl. His upper lip was raised in anger, causing his long slender nose to wrinkle as he exposed his vicious cuspids.

A shot rang out in the stable as Susan crumpled under Jesse.

The horses went wild with fear in their stalls. Time was suspended.

The shrill sound of a dog's cry carried over the noise of the horses and the wind and the other chaos in the stable. Still on top of

Susan, who was struggling beneath her, Jesse momentarily looked over her shoulder. Harley was ten feet away, flat on the ground, with a river of bright red blood coming from his right side.

"No-o-o-o!" she screamed, realizing he'd been hit. Acting on instinct, she turned back to Susan, grabbed her by the hair, and pounded her head against the red brick floor over and over. The fact that she'd lost consciousness didn't stop her. It only seemed to make her angrier, knowing that she couldn't feel the pain of her skull cracking open.

Carly was already at Harley's side. "Jesse." The sound of her voice seemed to snap Jesse out of her fury. "Get the cart!" she yelled, pointing to the wooden cart with the hay on it. "Bring it over here!"

With her booted foot, Jesse kicked the gun out of Susan's reach and right away turned her attention to Harley and Carly. Carly was saying something to her, but all she could do was stare at her dog. He wasn't moving. He wasn't even blinking. His eyes, which usually had such an animated gleam to them just stared straight ahead. He was panting. The river of blood that flowed through his thick fur formed a growing puddle beside him.

"Oh, God, Harley," she groaned hoarsely, scrambling along the bricks to get to him. "Please be okay. Please. Oh, God." She lifted his head and held him tight against her chest. "You're gonna be okay, buddy. Hang on. Hang on." With her head against his, she rocked back and forth with him and whispered reassurances. Her hand was warm and wet with his blood as she held it over his wound. His breathing was labored. So was hers.

Amid all of the confusion, Carly ran into the office for the phone. When she returned to Jesse and Harley in the aisle, she crouched down to gently pet Harley's head. "The police are on their way, Jesse. And I've called my vet. Her clinic is attached to her house, so she'll be waiting for you. I'll stay here until the police arrive." Putting her trembling hand on Jesse's shoulder, she tried to reassure her. "He's going to be fine, Jess. He's going to be fine. I'm going to get the car." She stood and paused only for a moment. "Jesse? Did you hear me?"

Turning her vacant eyes to her, Jesse said in a barely audible, emotionally charged voice, "Hurry."

With the speed of an Olympic sprinter, Carly took off. A moment later the Lexus came to a grinding stop just inches from the stable door. Carly pushed the wooden cart up to Harley. "Come on, Jesse. Take his front. On three."

Harley whined and groaned as they gingerly lifted him onto the cart, and Jesse was so intent on him, she didn't notice that Susan had regained consciousness. She didn't notice that her hand was inching toward the gun.

Carly, her back to Susan, didn't notice, either.

It wasn't until they started pushing the cart toward the door that Jesse saw Susan's upper body lift off the bricks. The gun was already in her hand. She was in the process of lifting it to take aim at Carly, and Jesse knew that she didn't have time to reach into her blazer, get her own gun free, and finish her off. So, instead, she screamed to distract them both.

That got Carly's attention. Right away, she turned just in time to see what was about to happen. Turning, she saw Jesse reach for the pitchfork that was leaning up against the wall. In the next moment, she watched Jesse plunged the steel tines into Susan's back, hearing the bones crack, watching Susan sink to the ground once more. She knew it was over.

Jesse let go of the pitchfork, which was driven in so deep, it remained in its place. She stared down at her. Susan made a gurgling sound. Her head dropped to the bricks. Her hand released the gun. There was nothing but the blank stare of death behind her open eyes. Blood oozed from the holes in her body where the pitchfork entered.

Jesse looked at Carly, who was staring down at the body in utter disbelief. Carly then looked at Jesse with that same expression.

Without saying a word, Jesse picked up Susan's gun and helped Carly push the cart containing Harley past Susan's body to the door.

"You take him," she ordered once he was safely situated in the back seat. "I'll stay."

"But Jesse…."

"Don't argue, Dammit! You know where it is! Just go! I'll meet you there later."

"Dr. Dobson's house is north of here on Clipper road. It's the last house on the left."

In the pouring rain, Jesse said a silent prayer for her dog as she closed the car door and watched Carly speed away with him.

* * * *

The headlights of the squad car shone through the window as it turned into the drive. Inside, Jesse could see Carly looking out at her. It had taken her over an hour to lay out her evidence and explain the events to the police. It was her suggestion, in fact, to have them send someone to get Carly's statement while she was giving hers, and when it came time to leave, Jesse got behind the wheel of her Fiat only to find that it would not start.

"How is he?" she asked hopefully, pulling the door closed as she looked beyond Carly to the rear of the clinic. One of the police officers had loaned Jesse the bulky blue bomber jacket she was wearing, and it was way too big on her, hanging down to her mid-thigh. She looked like a child playing dress-up.

Carly jumped up to hug her and help her off with the coat. "Still in surgery," she replied quietly while hanging the coat on the wooden peg near the door.

Jesse pushed the wet hair from her forehead and took the orange vinyl chair beside her. "Did Sheriff Richmond talk to you? He said he was gonna..."

"He was here."

Carly's face was totally void of expression, and Jesse put her hand on her leg. "Are you okay?"

She shrugged and shook her head at the same time, shifting her mystified glance to Jesse's hand. "I don't understand! I...I identified her body!"

"No you didn't. You identified Karen Romanesco's body." She reached into her trouser pocket and pulled out a small plastic card and handed it to Carly. "It's Karen's ID from the Four Seasons. I found it among the stuff she left in the trailer at the Seagate. I was watching that video of your interview with Victor earlier. He said something about the woman in the red Excursion looking like Susan's sister and that got me thinking." Jesse leaned over and pointed to the woman's mouth in the picture. "See? She's got all sound natural teeth. Susan had fillings and that one silver tooth, so she had to chip those out before she sent her on the boat because you'd have known that it wasn't her. She pretty much thought of everything. Too bad she didn't know about the trailer."

"You knew that Susan was still alive?"

Jesse nodded. "And this pretty much told me her motive." She handed a folded document to her client and watched her unfold it.

"Susan's birth certificate?" Carly asked, squinting to read it. Jesse's finger directed her to the name of Susan's father, and Carly read it out loud. "Jack Walthrop."

"I didn't put everything together until I saw that."

"I never..." Carly looked at her in amazement. "So you aren't...you didn't move away? What did you do, follow me?"

Jesse nodded a little. "More like kept you under surveillance."

Carly paused for a moment. "So you know that I...that I went to find you at your cabin?"

Jesse nodded again.

"I thought you'd left forever. Your cabin....it looked like everything was gone."

Still Jesse said nothing.

Carly waited a long while before saying quietly, "I called Lauren to see if she'd heard from you." Jesse nodded her head as if she'd already known that, but she remained quiet. "She...I didn't think you were ever coming back."

Jesse's eyes were on the dried blood on her hands. When she did speak, her voice shook a little. "I left him in the car. I locked him in, but he must have known that... that..." She shook her head. "God, I was there the whole time. I wasn't going to let her hurt you. He *knew* that! Why? Why'd he go rushing in like that?" In the next moment Carly's hand came to rest on top of hers and, needing the added comfort of human contact, Jesse leaned into her.

Jesse felt Carly's head turn to look toward the rear of the clinic. "He'll be fine, Jesse. He couldn't be in better hands. Pam's the best."

Jesse pulled her hand from Carly's and stood to pace. "Why's it taking so long? He's been in there for hours." Swiveling on her foot as the door opened, she looked at the tall woman in green scrubs. "Are you the Vet?" she demanded. "How's Harley? Is he okay? Can I see him?"

Exhaling a deep breath, the woman pulled off her green cap and ran a hand through her dark blonde hair to reestablish its order. "He's quite a trooper," she said. "The bullet didn't hit any organs; that's the good news. It lodged in his right shoulder. I put a tube in there for the fluid to drain." She leaned on the counter and looked from Jesse to Carly. "But he's lost an awful lot of blood; that's the bad news. He was shocky when he got here and I had to stabilize him before I could operate. The damage isn't all that extensive, but he'll be limping around for quite a while until he rebuilds that tissue."

"You mean he's gonna live? He's gonna be okay?"

Dr. Dobson smiled cautiously at Jesse's relief. "I'll keep an eye on him tonight. I've started him on antibiotics and I'll send some home with him, too. He's young, he's strong; barring any unforeseen circumstances…"

Jesse was bouncing with relieved excitement, trying to look past the Vet and into the kennel area. "Can I see him?"

Carly reached for her hand as they followed Dr. Dobson. She opened the door to the large, brightly lit room, and the sterile smell mixed with the subtle aroma of Carly's perfume. The disturbance woke a few of the other animals, causing them to skitter and yelp in their wire cages.

Jesse spotted Harley dozing in a cage in the far corner. He was lying on his left side. His right shoulder was shaved, leaving a large patch of dark gray skin around the seven-inch long row of stitches. Jesse released Carly's hand and walked over to him, never taking her eyes from him.

She opened the cage door and was careful not to touch the IV apparatus as she reached in to touch his head. "Hi, boy." His ears perked up a bit but his glazed eyes did not seem to register her presence. "What you did tonight was really brave, Harley, but I told you to stay put. I had everything under control." Harley moaned, and Jesse stroked his head, inspecting him, inspecting his wound, confirming in her heart that he would be fine. "I'll be back tomorrow, okay? Bright and early." Leaning her upper body into the cage, she kissed the soft fur on his forehead. His eyes closed, and she kept petting him. "Sleep well, buddy. I love you."

"He'll be fine." Carly had come up behind her to see him. "Pam has my cell number."

Jesse just nodded, staring at him a moment longer. "Is there a hotel around here? I wanna stay close."

Carly didn't know what to make of that last comment. Obviously they had unfinished business, many things to work out, but why wouldn't Jesse just assume that she was welcome to return to her house with her? "The Latham Lodge isn't far away - about twenty minutes."

"Didn't I see a place on the way here? Just up the road?"

"The All Niter?" Carly asked, wrinkling her nose. "Jess, why don't you just..."

"Yeah. The All Niter."

Silence clung to them in the car, and Carly didn't know what to make of Jesse's state when she pulled into a spot at the far end of the deserted parking lot. The space was obscured by overgrown shrubbery. Not knowing what to do, Carly kept the car running.

Jesse opened her door and got out. The headlights shone brightly on her as she walked toward the office. Carly put the car in reverse but kept her foot on the brake when she saw Jesse turn back.

Jesse poked her head in as Carly rolled down the window. "Did Susan know a lot about computers?"

"What?"

"Never mind." She sighed and contemplated Carly for a moment. "Do you want to come in for a....."

That was all Carly needed to hear. She closed the window while throwing the car in park. She was stepping out before Jesse even had a chance to finish her sentence.

Once they were safely locked in the hotel room, Jesse took off the too-big jacket and tossed it onto the bed. She went into the bathroom area to wash her hands. "Are you hungry?"

Carly set her keys on the vinyl card table in the eating area, then stood in the middle of the room, the bed on one side, the "kitchenette" on the other side. She didn't know how to respond, and she looked over as Jesse walked back into the room, drying her hands on a towel.

"I was thinking I could run and get us something for dinner," Jesse said.

"Oh. Yes. Sure."

Without a word, Jesse picked up the room key and the car keys from the table and started to leave. She turned back and confused

Carly even more with her look, and then left.

When she returned with a few bags, Jesse locked the deadbolt on the door and set the packages on the table. They looked at each other once, briefly, and Jesse noticed that Carly had washed up while she was gone. She still wore the same clothes, but the blood was gone from her hands and arms.

"I'm gonna shower," she told Carly. "I got paper plates if you want to..." she made a gesture as if instructing Carly to set the table and put the groceries away. She reached in the bag and pulled out a t-shirt with a big bear on it. Written beneath it were simply the words: "Door County, Wisconsin". She tucked it under her arm. "I'll be right back."

Jesse came out of the bathroom in her new t-shirt -- which hung down past her knees--just as Carly put her cell phone down, pulled out a chair and sat down. She watched Jesse dry her hair with a towel before approaching the table.

"Who were you just talking to?" she asked.

"I had to let Doug know where I was. He...."

Jesse sat down next to her. "I wish you hadn't done that," was all she said.

Silence again gathered around them until Carly finally said, "I want you to know that I didn't ask for - and I didn't read - any of the material that Beth sent me." In the process of unwrapping her sub sandwich, Jesse looked at her. "I'm sorry, Jesse, truly sorry for what happened, for what happened to Abby. And to you. I can't imagine what you've been through. It must have been...."

"I don't want to talk about it," Jesse told her resolutely, taking a bite of her sandwich. She took a few more bites, thinking, and then said quietly, "I'm sorry for the things I said to you this morning. I...I..." She shook her head and bit into her sandwich again.

In the long silence that followed, Jesse felt Carly's stare on her. She set her sandwich down. "You want a soda?"

"Yes, please."

Jesse pulled two plastic bottles of Mountain Dew from the eight-pack on the table and handed one to Carly. She twisted the cap off and took a big gulp, noting that Carly was just sitting there, staring at her bottle. "What? You want a glass with ice?"

Carly looked from the bottle to Jesse and quickly reached for it. "No. No, this is fine."

"You haven't touched your sandwich. Don't you like pastrami?"

"No. I mean yes. I...."

"I know these aren't the five-star accommodations you're used to, but the least you can do is..."

"That's not it, Jesse."

"Well then why the hell are you just sitting there staring at me like that?"

After everything that had happened today, their fight, what happened in the stable, her relief at Jesse's return, Carly had no idea what to expect from Jesse. How - at this moment - could she possibly tell Jesse everything she was feeling? How she loved watching Jesse devour her food, loved the way her jaw tightened and relaxed as she chewed, loved the way she retrieved the occasional bits of corned beef or string of onion hanging from her mouth.

Jesse looked like she was in her own world and didn't seem to be expecting a reply. After finishing up her sandwich, she got up, retrieved two peaches from the refrigerator, and threw her leg over the back of the chair, setting the fruit in front of them.

Carly moved her glance to the peaches and turned a quizzical expression in her direction.

Jesse looked at the peaches, then into Carly's dove gray eyes. "Dessert." She picked one up and wiped it on her shirt. "Here."

Carly looked down at the enormous peach in her hand and looked over Jesse's shoulder into the kitchenette area. "Is there a knife? I could..."

Jesse just shook her head. "A knife? What, pray tell, do you want with a knife, Ms. McCray?" She extended her pinkie to feign her manners.

"I need to slice it."

"And if I gave you a little cognac, would you make us some peaches flambé?"

"No, but if you have some powdered sugar, I could..."

"Does it look like I got any goddamn powdered sugar? Christ, just eat the damn thing!" She picked up her own peach and took a bite. "See?" she said with her mouth full. "It's simple!"

Upset by Jesse's shortness with her, she took a massive bite of the peach and immediately turned to Jesse for some sign of approval, and when Jesse saw those pale, innocent eyes of hers, she tempered herself. "I'm sorry. I didn't mean to yell. I...I forget that we grew up in two totally different worlds."

Carly nipped off another piece of the peach. "They're really very good like this." A stream of juice ran down from her mouth, and Jesse jumped to lick the nectar from her chin. Her tongue continued down to the underside of her jaw and came to rest at the point where her neck meets her shoulders.

As she sucked gently, her muttering was muffled by the warm flesh surrounding her mouth. "Next time you want to know something about me, just ask, will you? Don't call your attorney, don't call my sister..." Before Carly could respond, Jesse bit the base of her neck. She could tell by the intensity of Carly's gleaming eyes that she didn't know if she should be frightened or aroused.

To her surprise, Carly pulled her to her chest and kissed her savagely. Her tongue delved deeply into Jesse's mouth, which seemed to be expecting her.

During their frantic exchange, Carly asked, "Do you really think I'm a pompous slut?" Then she plunged her teeth sharply into Jesse's bottom lip.

Jesse winced in pain but didn't struggle to free herself. Giving one final twisting tug, Carly relented. Opening her eyes, she watched Jesse drop to her knees in front of her.

In one swift move, Jesse grabbed her shirt and ripped it open, tearing the buttons from their moorings. She watched her firm, pale breasts rise and recede in her silk lace bra. As she heard the spontaneous release of air from Carly, her head, cupped in Carly's hand, was snapped back. Their eyes met.

"Well? Am I a pompous slut? Do I have a silver spoon lodged up my ass?"

With a sly little smile, Jesse ran her fingers from Carly's shoulder to her wrist, gently guiding the straps of her bra down her arms in the process. When she reached her hand, she delicately brushed each of her fingers with her own, running her hand over the half-eaten peach that she still, remarkably, had perched in her hand.

Jesse slid her juice-covered hand from the V at the base of Carly's throat to her navel and began to lick at the sticky substance as her hand covered Carly's hard nipples with the same sweetness. A small, desperate sound escaped Carly as her head lolled back. The half-eaten peach dropped to the linoleum.

While Jesse hungrily sucked the syrupy liquid off Carly's nipples, Carly wound her long legs around her, pulling Jesse's pelvis to her own. "Please, Jesse," she uttered in a dry whisper.

Jesse didn't hesitate. She slid Carly out of the rest of her clothes and moved her mouth to where her lover wanted it. Her tongue darted in and out of her flesh, and her moaning matched Carly's when she felt the awakening in her own body.

Running her fingers through Jesse's tousled mane, Carly moved in the same rhythmic motion that Jesse prompted. Jesse urged her hips even closer when she sensed that the moment was near, and Carly made a low whimpering sound as she climaxed. Her legs tightened around Jesse like a vice. In the next moment, she leaned forward and guided Jesse's face to hers, kissing her deeply as the wetness from her mouth combined with her own moisture fresh on Jesse's lips.

Without delay, Carly pressed Jesse's shoulders to encourage her to lie back. She straddled Jesse's body on the floor, and Jesse's hips slid against her in eager anticipation. In her haste to get Jesse out of her clothes, she ripped her new shirt, but Jesse barely noticed. And she certainly didn't care.

Sliding down Jesse's trembling body, Carly moved her warm mouth to the key of Jesse's pleasure, and her tongue glided through the hot moistness there. Jesse lifted her hips from the floor to meet Carly's avid tongue, letting out a low moan each time she brushed past Carly's mouth.

As if she knew it was time, Carly slipped her long slender finger inside and answered the fevered motion of Jesse's hips with her hand. Jesse rocked hard against her, and as her release began, she moaned a low, rapturous moan.

Carly crawled up her body, still feeling Jesse's pulsing contractions on her enveloped fingers. She grazed Jesse's lips with her own, and Jesse smiled, but her eyes remained closed.

"That made my toes cramp," she said, chuckling.

They moved over to the bed to settle in for the evening. Jesse reached for the ashtray on the nightstand and put out her cigarette while Carly fit her naked body to Jesse's. Lying back, the sharp edge of a spring poked painfully into Jesse's side, and she moved closer to Carly to avoid it.

On her back, with Carly's head nestled on her chest, Jesse lay motionless, staring wide-eyed at the ceiling, listening to her lover's soft breath. She envied Carly's ability to sleep so soundly after all that had happened.

The charred images of the case still occupied Jesse's every thought. As she listened to the rhythmic dripping of the sink, she wondered if she should have informed the police of her theory that Susan hadn't acted alone. She wondered if she should have given them the name of the co-conspirator.

Thoughts were temporarily forced out of her mind when Carly stirred beside her. She kissed the top of her head and stroked her hair to lull her back to sleep. The soft breath against her chest encouraged Jesse to close her eyes and at least toy with the thought of sleep. She closed everything down and faded out as the sound of Carly's breathing and water dripping swirled in her head.

Wait a minute? Her eyes flung open. What was that? Had she heard a new noise in the symphony, or was she dreaming? Suddenly totally awake again, she strained to hear. The low humming from the parking lot made her whole body tense. Slipping away from Carly, she threw on her t-shirt and trousers and crept to the window.

With one finger, she opened the heavy curtains. The razor sharp beam of light startled her. She blinked to focus on the dark pick-up parked directly across from the building and stared intently as the truck's door opened. The dome light shone brightly on the face of Chris Masters.

Jesse was shocked. How could this be? Wasn't she supposed to have been out of town indefinitely? How could she have misjudged her so badly? How could she have been so wrong? Jesse had been positive that Chris' relationship with Carly was exactly as it appeared. She was so positive, in fact, that she'd left a gift of atonement in their mailbox earlier.

Jesse ran to the bed and shook Carly by the shoulder. "Get up." She tossed her her clothes while keeping an eye on the door. "Come on, honey, you've got to get up."

Carly lifted her head. She was groggy. "What is it?"

"We've got company." Jesse looked over her shoulder to see Carly, standing upright, slipping on her pants. She grabbed her and jerked her roughly to the floor. "Stay down!" Hustling to pick the lock to the adjoining room, Jesse shoved her into it. "Stay in there and don't make a peep and don't turn on any lights, understand?" Jesse knew she was terrified by the look in her eyes.

"But, Jess…"

Jesse tried calming her by running her fingertips down her cheek. "Lock yourself in. No matter what happens…just…just stay in there, okay?" With an attempted reassuring smile, Jesse added. "It'll be okay." She emphasized her point by pushing Carly deeper into the vacant room. When she heard the door lock click into place, she moved with reckless abandon to find her gun and to position herself offensively for the impending attack.

The banging of her heart became deafening. Nothing came. No footsteps, no fumbling with the doorknob, nothing. Jesse crept back to the window. Chris was standing just on the other side of the glass. It looked like she was debating with herself as to what she should do. She looked nervous. She took something out of her jacket pocket. Jesse couldn't see what it was, but Chris looked at it for a moment and then replaced it. Jesse saw her take a deep breath. In the next moment, she heard the woman's knock at the door.

"Carly?" More knocking, a desperate pounding. "Carly, I've got to talk to you!"

Jesse tucked her gun into the back of her trousers at the small of her back and opened the door. "Carly's not here."

Chris didn't look like she believed her. "Where is she? Is she okay?"

Was this genuine concern for a friend or an Oscar-caliber performance on Chris' part? Jesse couldn't tell. She stared at her with a blank face, waiting for her to tip her hand somehow.

"Look," she said, shifting the weight on her feet. "I know she's here. Just let me see her, will you?"

She put her hand in her pocket, and when she did that, Jesse drew her gun. "Don't move!"

Chris' hands flew into the air. "Hey! Take it easy, okay?"

311

"What's in your pocket? Take it out. Slowly."

Terror shone in her eyes. She was breathing fast. "Okay, just don't shoot me! Christ! It's...All I've got is this." She carefully withdrew her hand and held out her palm to show Jesse the thick roll of money, all neatly bound together with a rubber band. Jesse recognized it immediately. "I wanted to make sure Carly was okay and I...I wanted to give this back to her. She must've left it in my mailbox and I..."

"What made you think to look for her here?" Jesse demanded, relaxing only slightly.

Chris stared at the gun with huge eyes. She kept her hands raised, talking fast. "I...I called Doug. I heard what happened at her house tonight - it was all over the news - and I thought...I don't know. I tried calling her earlier and she didn't answer so I called Doug. He...He told me she was here." She hesitated. "Look," she said, her eyes still on the gun. "If she's not here, will you just tell her...just tell her to call me?"

"Chris?"

Jesse turned to see Carly standing in the middle of the room. "Dammit, Carly! I told you to..."

Chris interrupted Jesse by brushing past her on her way to her friend. The two of them hugged for a long while, whispering to each other, apologizing. Chris was crying. When they finally separated, Chris handed the wad of money to her friend, and Carly looked at it in bewilderment.

"What's this?"

"We can't accept it. Chelsea and I appreciate the gesture, but..."

"I didn't give this to you, Chris," Carly told her, looking just as confused as Chris as she gave the money back.

"Well if you didn't, who did?" Chris demanded. "Nobody else knew that we were in trouble, that we needed it. And nobody else I know has that kind of money to throw around."

Jesse was still at the door with her gun in her hand, and Carly cast a suspicious glance in her direction. "How much is there?" she asked her friend while staring at Jesse.

Chris replied with a shrug. "I don't know. I didn't count it all, but it's gotta be at least ten thousand dollars."

Jesse wore her best poker face, but she knew that Carly saw right through it. She turned her glance to Chris. "Maybe Donna gave it to you," she said, causing both Chris and Jesse to huff out a small laugh.

Carly walked her friend to the door, and Chris hesitated and turned back to her, her dark eyes intent. "I've missed you, Mickey. But Chelsea and I..."

"I know," Carly assured her. "We'll all get together soon, okay?"

Standing just inside, Jesse waited for Chris to cross the threshold before closing the door. She was just about to secure the deadbolt and the chain lock when she heard a noise outside. It was a short-lived disturbance, and before Jesse could open the door to check on it, the sound of ripping and splintering wood filled the air.

An agonizing burning hit Jesse and sent her to the floor.

Instinctively, she groped for her aching left shoulder as she fell. Through her fingers the warm wetness drizzled from the wound, and Jesse knew she'd been shot. The bullet had gone clean through her shoulder.

On her back, she groaned and kicked out toward Carly. "Go!" she commanded in a pained whisper. She scarcely had enough time to bring her gun up with her right hand when the door exploded open in front of her. It hit her and sent her gun skidding across the floor. She tried to follow the sound of metal rushing against the linoleum, but someone grabbed her hair and yanked her to her feet.

Jesse could smell the booze on his breath as he pressed his lips to her ear. "Hello detective," Doug growled. "Where's my lovely aunt?"

Jesse looked back at the door and saw the unmoving tennis-shoe-clad feet of Chris Masters on the sidewalk and assumed that Doug's attack had taken her by complete surprise, too. She took a quick look around the darkness of the room to see if Carly had indeed left. "She's not here. After I killed Susan, she went to her house in Ashwaubenon to look for you. That's where the two of you were staying, isn't it? Wasn't that her perfume, that shit that smells like bug spray, in Carly's bathroom?"

Apparently Doug wasn't in the mood to buy into anything Jesse had to say. He jerked her head back. "Don't fuck with me. Where is she?"

"All right, all right. She's over there." Jesse motioned in an arc to the other side of the room, and Doug's absent-minded glance gave Jesse a window. She took one step forward and landed an elbow soundly in his solar plexus.

As Doug reeled from the blow, Jesse turned and smacked the heel of her palm into his nose. The bones snapped like kindling. Off balance, he stumbled backward, and Jesse hurled her body against his chest. He blew back against the picture window, pulling the draperies with him as he plunged through the glass and onto the sidewalk beside Chris.

Holding her shoulder, Jesse stuck her head through the gaping hole. Doug appeared to have lost his gun in the commotion. He lay in semi-consciousness on the scattered glass on his back, blood oozing from his nose.

Jesse crawled along the floor, feeling in the darkness for her gun. From the periphery of her senses, she thought she heard a noise in the room next door. Stay there, Carly, she thought desperately. Please, just stay there.

Doug's body cast a dark shadow over her. In the next moment, a huge weight fell upon Jesse's back and sent her sliding against the rough grain of the floor. The wind puffed out of her, and she couldn't breathe. He was sitting squarely on Jesse's back, flattening her chest.

Jesse lifted her head a little and turned it to the left. There it was. Her gun. Despite her scorching shoulder wound, she made a move for it, but Doug must have spotted it at the exact moment she did, because he snatched it up before her hand even came close.

"Nice try." He pulled Jesse to her feet again and pressed the cold muzzle of Jesse's own gun against her jawbone. "Real tough, aren't you?" He forced the gun against Jesse so hard, it made her gasp. He laughed heartily. "Not tough enough, though." He wrapped his arm around Jesse's neck and urged her forward. In a child-like voice he chimed, "Aunt Carly..." He paused. "Listen, bitch, if you don't come out here, your little girlfriend is going to get it!"

He cranked Jesse's injured arm, but Jesse didn't give him the pleasure of crying out. Instead, she wheezed, "I told you she's not here, you stupid asshole!"

"Shut up, bitch!" Doug struck her temple with the butt of the pistol, causing a starburst of white light to explode in Jesse's head. She was fighting a losing battle to stay conscious. He cocked the gun and placed it against Jesse's badly bruised head. His finger tensed on the trigger as he waited. "I'll do it, Carly! I swear to God I'll blow her brains out!"

"Let her go, Doug."

Supporting all of Jesse's weight in his free arm, he turned his head toward the voice to see Carly standing in the doorway. Somehow, among all the debris and glass on the sidewalk, she had managed to find his gun, which she was now aiming at him.

"Let her go right now." Carly's voice was hard and deadly serious. She briefly took her eyes from him to get a look at Jesse, who was slouched over his arm. Blood was pouring down the front of her shirt. "Drop the gun."

Jerking Jesse up to use her as a human shield, Doug smiled. He, no doubt, saw how violently the gun shook in his aunt's hand. "Drop the gun? Why? What are you going to do if I don't? Are you going to shoot me?" He laughed. "I'm *family*, Carly," he said with a perverse kind of sympathy. "You'd never kill your own flesh and blood, would you?"

"It's over, Doug. Susan's dead. The police are on their way."

"Susan," Doug growled. "Don't you get it? *I* was the one behind this, not Susan! I planned everything, the boat explosion, everything! But you wouldn't die! Not even tonight in the stable!"

Maybe it was Divine Intervention, or maybe it was because of the tears rolling down Carly's face that kept Jesse conscious through all of this. There was nothing she could have done to save Abby, but she'd be damned if she was going to let this son-of-a-bitch take Carly from her.

Doug underestimated Jesse's determination - and Carly's - because he continued taunting his aunt, pushing her to make a life-altering decision. "And let me tell you something, it wasn't hard to get her to go along with my plan. And she was a pretty good fuck, wouldn't you say?"

"You stupid bastard!" Jesse hissed through a hacking laugh. She was still slumped over his arm, barely able to lift her head. "You don't even know, do you? You don't have a fucking clue!"

"Shut up, cunt! Nobody's talking to you!" He slammed her in the head again, and Carly gasped. But Jesse laughed. She kept laughing, and the more she laughed, the more worried Carly appeared. Obviously, she was beginning to realize that she was pretty much on her own here because Jesse was in no condition to help. Jesse only hoped to buy Carly enough time - time for the police to arrive - or time to come to grips with what she needed to do. Jesse hoped even more that when the time came, she'd be able to pull it off. She opened her eyes at the growing puddle of blood at her bare feet and knew she didn't have a whole lot of time left.

"You weren't using Susan, Einstein! She was using **you!**" Jesse's neck couldn't support her head any longer. It just kind of hung there limply as she kept laughing that weak, hoarse laugh. When she spoke again, it scared the hell out of Carly to see the blood that sprayed out of her mouth. "She was gonna kill you once the estate was settled, you stupid fucker! She was gonna take it all!"

"You'll never get away with this, Doug," Carly said reasonably. Her voice was steady, and Jesse couldn't see it, but she hoped that the same could be said of the gun in her hand. "If it's money you want, you can have what's left of the trust that Father set up for you. That's all. I won't tell the authorities a thing, but I never want to hear from or see you again. It's over. Do you understand?"

"Oh, I understand," he replied wickedly. "I understand that I *will* get away with it. See, right now, I'm in Green Bay, sound asleep. Imagine how devastated I'll be tomorrow morning when the phone rings and I find out that my dear aunt and her private detective have been killed in an unfortunate rampage brought on by your friend out

318

there." He adjusted Jesse in his arms, lifting her up a little. "Chris shot you, shot the detective, and somehow, the heroic detective here managed to shoot her as she tried to get away." He clucked his tongue and said, "So tragic. And with her financial problems, it'll be easy to convince everyone that she was in collusion with Susan." He laughed an ugly laugh.

In her last moment of consciousness, Jesse heard the sirens somewhere off in the distance. She felt Doug's grip tighten on her. She used all of her might, all of her will to lift her head. She opened her eyes. She saw the tears spill down Carly's cheeks. She saw Carly pull the hammer back on the gun in her hand. She saw the way the weapon shook in her grip. Before she could anticipate it, before she could open her mouth or say a word or make a move, a bright orange flash briefly illuminated Carly's face in the darkness as she squeezed the trigger and released a round.

Carly screamed in horror when she saw what she had done. Her Nephew and Jesse lay crumpled on the floor at her feet. She dropped the gun.

Epilogue

Condolence calls, sympathy cards, and flower arrangements from all across the state continued to pour in at a heavy and steady pace. Chris and Chelsea had taken care of everything for Carly; the media, the funeral arrangements, the disposition of personal effects, the lawyers.

Jacey Elder and Charlene made frequent visits to the house to keep Carly informed of everything going on at McCray Technology because not once in the three weeks that followed did Carly make an appearance at her office. Jacey managed it alone.

During one of her visits, shortly after it happened, Jacey brought the Rabbi from her Synagogue, Rabbi Levine, who spent hours with Carly to console her and help soothe her conscience.

But things had clearly taken their toll on her. She was not the same person she was three weeks ago. Things were different now; her priorities, her perspective on life. She began spending more time with Harley, which was where she was now, down on the beach behind her house, walking, with him at her side.

The early evening November sky was overcast and bitterly cold. A vapor cloud puffed out of her mouth as she released a deep sigh. She'd been on the phone most of the day with Lauren. The two of them had been in constant contact since everything happened, and

Carly quickly grew to appreciate Lauren, both as a close friend and a psychologist. Sinking her hands into her jacket pockets, she glanced up at her mansion, looking pensive and forlorn.

A small piece of driftwood lay at her feet. She picked it up and threw it to the water's edge as if expecting Harley to go limping off after it. When he didn't, she crouched to pet him. "What's the matter, sweetie?" she asked in her warm maternal voice.

Tiny stubbles of dark hair had already begun to grow over his shaved area, and she was careful not to touch his wound, which was healing nicely. "Do you miss her? Hmmm? Me, too. Is your shoulder bothering you?" She pet him and hugged him tight and let him lick her face. "How about if I take you out for ice cream tonight? Would you like that?"

"He's never going to get better if you don't stop babying him like that," Jesse called from the driveway above.

Carly looked up at Jesse as she limped her way toward them, and putting her arms on her hips, Carly playfully scolded Jesse with her look. "I thought I told you to stay in bed."

Grinning as she neared, Jesse put her hand over her wounded shoulder. "I'm never going to get better, either, if you don't stop babying me."

"I can't help it," Carly protested. With gentle insistence, she wrapped both arms around Jesse and pulled her close. She tucked her hands in the back pockets of Jesse's trousers and, looking dauntlessly into her eyes, she said the three small words: "I love you."

Jesse hugged her with all her might and with her mouth scarcely touching Carly's ear, whispered her reply.

Printed in the United States
123511LV00004B/262/P